T0267522

JOINED
AT THE
JOINTS

JOINED

AT THE

JOINTS

MARISSA ELLER

HOLIDAY HOUSE • NEW YORK

HOLIDAY HOUSE is registered in the U.S. Patent and Trademark Office.
Printed and bound in May 2024 at Sheridan, Chelsea, MI, USA.
First Edition
1 3 5 7 9 10 8 6 4 2
www.holidayhouse.com

Library of Congress Cataloging-in-Publication Data is available.

ISBN: 978-0-8234-5621-5 (hardcover)

For Mom, Dad, and Grayson—
my family that's somehow better than fiction

CHAPTER ONE

• —— • ——

MON, AUG 3, 5:51 P.M.

Dad: Are you yelling? I hear yelling.

Ivy: just watching TV.

Dad: Food network?

Ivy: yep.

She's going for the ice cream machine. That's a rookie mistake. I'm surprised she even made it to the dessert round. She was my pick to win, but she clearly doesn't know how to play the game.

"Iggy?" I hear my little brother call. It's my dad's nickname for me, and Ethan only calls me that when he wants something.

"In here," I yell back. I'm on the couch, extremely comfortable under the electric blanket, and I am so not moving unless it's an emergency. I'm talking life or death. I took my weekly handful of chemo meds yesterday, so I'm in the purgatory between last week's meds wearing off and yesterday's meds kicking in. The heat calms my raging joints just the slightest bit.

Ethan comes stomping into the room, and I mean literally stomping. He has his baseball cleats on, for some reason. His footsteps are so booming, they have to be damaging the hardwood.

Even if they're not, they're impairing my ability to hear what this chef is doing with the Bartlett pears he received in his ingredient basket for the dessert round. My grandmother had this amazing recipe for a mixed-berry fruit tart. That's probably what I'd make.

Since his competitor decided to use the ice-cream machine, he's my new pick to win.

"Look," Ethan says, throwing a foot over my lap. "I got new cleats."

"That's wonderful." I shove his foot away, because despite them being brand-new shoes, they still somehow already smell. Ethan's thirteen. I should never doubt his ability to stink. Nausea is a side effect of this immunosuppressant purgatory, and his stench is not helping.

Onscreen, my former favorite drops a spoon in the ice cream machine. "Oh my God, no way," I groan. It clunks around like change in a dryer. I knew making ice cream was a mistake. Making ice cream is always a mistake.

"What are you watching?" Ethan asks. He sits next to me, putting his new cleats up on the coffee table. They're neon green and seriously obnoxious. I see why he loves them so much.

"*Chopped*. It's a special season where Alton Brown makes the baskets, so they're all horrible. It's awesome."

"You're really weird," Ethan says. The show goes to commercial, and I actually look at him. He has dirt all over his face, for some reason. The cleats are spotless, but he's a giant mess. I haven't seen him much today, which probably explains it. If my sister or I don't keep an eye on him during summer days like this when our parents are at work, he gets into trouble.

"Did Mom take you shopping for cleats with dirt all over you like that?" I ask, because I know she didn't. My fingers itch to wipe crumbles of dirt off the throw pillow behind him.

"No, we went shopping then went to meet my new coaches. One of them is—"

"Shh. The show's back on."

Ethan shuts up, because he knows what's good for him.

"What's so horrible about these baskets?" he asks eventually, because talking about the show is really the closest thing to shutting up that he's capable of doing, long-term.

I laugh. "The terrible thing in this one is livermush. It was submitted by a fan from North Carolina."

"Oh, gross." Ethan makes a horrified face.

I don't make a habit of considering anything about regional cuisines disgusting, but since livermush is a part of *my* regional cuisine, I'm just going to say it: it's disgusting. The thought of it actually makes me queasy (or maybe that's the meds again). These unlucky people have to put liver, and who knows what else, in their desserts. That's why it's so ridiculous that she chose to make ice cream. I'm still upset about it. I was rooting for her.

The show goes to commercial again, and I turn back to Ethan.

"Okay, what about the coaches?" I don't enjoy social situations, but both my siblings are innately social creatures, and I do enjoy hearing about their unique brands of chaos.

"One of them is your age. He's, like, a really good baseball player or something. He's so cool."

"Why is someone my age coaching baseball?"

"I don't know. He didn't say. I didn't ask. But he said he liked my new cleats and my Braves shirt, and he taught us how to slide—"

"Taught you how to slide? Is that how you got dirt on your face?"

Ethan nods.

"What did Mom say about this?" Mom, the only other person on the side of calm in this hectic household.

"Nothing. The other coach was talking to the parents while we were on the field. When she asked how I got dirty, I told her I fell."

"On your face?"

He shrugs. It's not so unbelievable, actually, the idea that he could fall on his face.

"This guy sounds like a bad influence."

"He said bad words, too."

I roll my eyes. I'm about to ask him which ones, but the show comes back on. They tell Ice Cream Lady that her dessert tastes like metal because she dropped a spoon in the machine, and her ice cream base wasn't that good to begin with. (She put her liver-mush in the ice cream, so I could've told them that.) She gets chopped.

"Is that why you came in here, to tell me about baseball?" I ask

Ethan as I stretch out my locked-up joints. I try to stand, but my left hip and knee decide they've taken the day off from being a hip and knee, so I sit back down.

"No. I was going to ask you to make lemon chicken for dinner."

Lemon would smell a lot better than he does right now. I could probably handle cooking at this level of queasiness.

"Fine, but you have to do the dishes."

"Deal."

CHAPTER TWO

·

TUES, AUG 4, 4:32 P.M.

Caroline: Can you chill, pls? I can't hear myself think over here.

Ivy: Let me live.

Caroline: What are you making?

Ivy: Grandma's marinara sauce.

Caroline: Never mind. Carry on.

I'm in the kitchen, like always. The rest of my family is rustling randomly around the house. Someone will be drifting in soon to ask what I'm making for dinner. It'll be Mom, probably. I'd say it's her watching TV in the living room right now: the news is on, and I hear something about a backup on I-85. In Charlotte, there's always a backup on I-85.

I stop chopping for a moment; the blurriness in my eyes is making my precise knife cuts come out all wonky. I rub my eyes against the sleeve of my worn black T-shirt. Everything feels better today. The nausea, my joints, and my general disposition—despite the aromatic tears.

"It smells good in—wait, are you crying?" Mom asks as she

walks into the kitchen. She leans against the island where I'm working, and I notice she still has faint pink marks on her face from the throw pillow on the couch. She hasn't been watching the news, then. She's been sleeping through it.

I hold up the onions I just finished chopping. Dinner really doesn't smell like anything yet; I don't even have these onions cooking. She's probably just smelling the spice jars open in front of me. I always do it that way—open the spices first. I like the barely-there scent of them all mixed together. In my imagination, it's what a Food Network set smells like.

Mom sits down at the dining room table, and I put my finely diced onions into my favorite saucepan with a heavy dose of freshly minced garlic. They're met with sizzling applause, because I have the oil temperature just right. There's nothing better than that noise.

"So how was your day?" Mom asks. I think about how to answer.

"Fine. Pretty typical." It was just another summer day. Sleeping entirely too late, doing entirely too little. Cooking. Watching other people cook on TV. The end. "I started watching an old season of *Worst Cooks in America*. Someone tried to cook a whole rack of lamb in a toaster oven."

"I'm sure you found that personally offensive," Mom remarks.

I did. But it was hilarious. Bad cooking like that is my ultimate comic relief. I chuckle to myself at the memory.

"How was *your* day?" I ask, chopping tomatoes to tip in next.

Mom is in the middle of prepping for a new school year. As a counselor, she's neck-deep in paperwork and placement test scores. I can already see the exhaustion setting in. The tension in her shoulders is visible from here.

"You should see my office. It looks like the kitchen when you're done with it." Mom smiles at me, running her fingers over her forehead as if she can smooth out the lines already forming.

"I don't know what you're talking about! I always clean up my messes." To illustrate my point, I swipe away tomato juice that jumps from the sparkling silver saucepan. I even move my grandmother's recipe cards farther away from the danger zone.

I have them all memorized, but they mean more to me than the words scrawled across the torn, yellowed paper. And I've been trying to do this...challenge, I guess. The goal is to make all of my grandma's recipes gluten-free, and thus safe for consumption in this house. She's been gone a while now, and I've been making gluten-free stuff for years, so I thought it would be easy. Something easy enough to accomplish over a summer. But summer is winding down to an unceremonious close, and there's still a stack of recipe cards left unadapted.

"I wish someone would clean up mine," Mom huffs.

"Why don't you take Caroline with you tomorrow? You know she's an organizational genius."

My older sister is the only reason we can find anything in our home, and the reason my kitchen runs like a navy-ship kitchen.

Or an *Iron Chef* kitchen. I've seen a lot more *Iron Chef* kitchens than I have navy kitchens.

"Speaking of Caroline . . ." Mom starts to say.

Caroline herself appears in the doorway, dressed to go out. Not *go out* go out, just go out somewhere. She went out last night, actually, even though it's not the weekend. I guess all summer days are weekends, in a way. It was a date, I think—she didn't call it that, but she didn't come home until after midnight. Even though I'm happy here, with my baking supplies and my cookbooks, there are parts of Caroline I can't help but wish I could be more like.

I envy her casual style. Her easy confidence. Her distinct lack of anxieties, social or otherwise. Even the headband in her auburn hair seems to sparkle. Everything about Caroline is just *more* than everything about me. Her jeans fit better. She speaks more freely. She actually enjoys going outside? I don't know why, but she does. The idea that we're so closely related is just strange.

They call us Irish twins. Not *us*, specifically, but kids as close in age as we are. Though, with the red hair and the green eyes, we look as much like actual Irish twins as anyone else.

"Yes, speaking of me." Caroline smiles. It's one of those *I'm about to get you in trouble* smiles I've been on the receiving end of for all of my seventeen years. She convinced me to follow her up a tree once, and this was the smile she used to do it.

I turn away, taste my building marinara sauce, and add more oregano. Grandma's recipe doesn't specify how much to use: her philosophy was to make that decision with your soul. I almost grab the cilantro, but Caroline's one of those people who thinks cilantro tastes like soap, so that's a catastrophe narrowly avoided. The cilantro shouldn't be right next to the oregano, anyway. My spices are supposed to be in alphabetical order. I start to reorganize them, but I stop when I realize Mom and Caroline are both still staring at me.

"Listen, Ivy, come sit down." Mom waves me out to the dining room, sits, and pats the seat next to her at our giant wooden table. I'm not in the mood for a sit-down discussion. I'm not particularly in the mood for any kind of discussion, to be honest.

"Spaghetti, cool!" Ethan appears, beelining right for the stove.

"Nope, don't you dare!" I point my wooden spoon at him, knowing he's about to stick a finger in the sauce. He reaches past me, grabs a spoon from the drawer, and steals a taste.

"No fingers, see?" he teases.

"You better put that spoon right back where you found it!" I say, hoping I sound intimidating. He's as tall as me now, so I don't have the advantage I used to. He reaches over me again, like he's *actually* going to toss his spit-covered spoon back in the drawer. "Gross, wash it first!"

"Kids, can we be civil for just one minute, please?" If there's a way to beg with authority, that's what Mom is doing. Ethan drops the spoon in the sink and leaves the room. He's not a fan of common civility.

"Ivy, honey," she begins again, "we need to talk."

God, how I hate those words. I hate when life stops for a minute for everyone to sit down face-to-face. Talking, I can do…but bent over a stove, or with flour-coated hands.

I sit down at the head of the table with a huff, keeping an eye on my simmering sauce. Maybe I can just pretend I'm still standing there stirring it if I try hard enough. Caroline stays standing leaned against the doorway, one ankle crossed over the other, careful not to scuff her pristine white sneakers.

"I went to Dr. Anthony's last week…" As soon as Mom starts speaking, red flags pop up in my head like my brain's infected with a computer virus. Mom's visits to her rheumatologist are standard operating procedure around here. She's had lupus since shortly after Ethan was born, and I don't remember a time before her illness was a part of our lives.

But we barely even talk about doctor's visits like these—especially not over a week after the fact. I feel the hairs on the back of my neck stand up. If we're talking about it, that must mean something bad. Lupus is a giant wrecking ball hanging over our entire house, and it feels poised to drop. Is something wrong? They'd have told me already if something was wrong. Dad would be here for that kind of talk. So would Ethan. I saw her last blood work results myself. They weren't bad—but maybe they were?

"Nothing's wrong; I can see the terror in your face," Caroline says. She relaxes some, and so do I. I hadn't realized how tightly I've been holding my hands closed under the table. Now I can't move them. Oops.

"No, no. Everything's fine. Sorry, I should've led with that."
Mom smiles. "I just . . . I saw a flyer for this support group."

I feel myself brighten, just a little. This is good. Mom doesn't take her illness seriously sometimes. A support group would be good for her. She does too much and doesn't rest enough. Maybe a group could help with that.

"It's for teenagers. Kids like us," Caroline says.

"What do you mean, *like us*?" For a second, I don't put those pieces together. Besides the way we look, there aren't many things Caroline and I have in common. Other than being sisters and almost twins, there isn't much that makes us an *us*. Then, it clicks.

"Kids with chronic illnesses." Mom doesn't whisper it or lower her voice as if she's telling a terrible secret, the way some people speak about chronic illness. I appreciate that, but my spine tightens all on its own.

This was never about Mom, then. It's about us.

I want to tuck and roll out of here. Or find some way to travel back in time and prevent this conversation from happening.

But instead I wait, because I know Caroline will keep talking. She always does. "I thought it would be good for us to talk about this kind of stuff with people who get it."

"Isn't that what we're doing? We have each other. It's not like any of us is alone."

"Come on, please? I don't want to go by myself."

I look up at my sister. There's something genuine in her eyes. I know Caroline's always felt this kind of *otherness* since she was diagnosed with celiac disease as a kid. It makes her different from her cornucopia of friends. I don't feel the same way. At least, I try not to. I've only been diagnosed with rheumatoid arthritis for a little over a year, but I know that sense of awareness of my differences will grow.

I think over everything for a minute. They're silent, knowing I would never just mindlessly agree. I don't know what they want from me, or what part of social anxiety they're not understanding.

I'm going to say no. I don't willingly go out and talk to people for fun—I'm *certainly* not going to go out and talk about being sick.

No way.

Not happening.

"You know I'm not going to talk," I find myself saying.

I don't want to be saying it. I don't remember telling my mouth to form those words, but here we are.

I just can't seem to say no to her. It's her eyes. They're the same eyes I see in the mirror every day, in the same face—but I physically can't make the pouty expression she always uses when she doesn't get her way.

This is our typical compromise, anyway. As long as I don't have to talk, I'll begrudgingly go almost anywhere, just to get Caroline to *stop* talking. So why fight it this time?

"No one will force you to talk," Mom promises.

"I'll do all the talking. I just don't want to walk in alone."

I imagine Caroline walking in alone anywhere. Music blares

from invisible speakers. There's a wind machine. Spotlights appear from the ceiling, hitting the high points of her face. It's a display of the kind of brightness and vividness that everyone sees when they look at her.

In contrast to me. If there's a brightness near me—say, the brightest ray of sunshine North Carolina has ever seen—I'll hide *behind* it, with decaying joints and too many freckles.

I hear a gurgling noise that means my sauce is getting too hot. I jump up, hitting my knee against the solid wood underside of the table. It throbs, but just the slightest bit more than my baseline level of pain.

"When is this?" I ask. I feel myself calming down as I rhythmically stir, even though my hand threatens to lock around the spoon.

"Tonight. We have to leave in half an hour."

I lean my head forward against the solid oak cabinets. This was an ambush, then. They did it this way so I wouldn't agree to go and then back out later.

I'll have to change. I'll have to do something with the rat's nest on top of my head. I'll have to abandon the spaghetti I haven't even put on to boil yet. I turn the burner off, place a lid over the saucepan, and sigh. I point the red-stained spoon at my mother. She's smiling, because she knows she's won.

"Don't let Ethan *touch* this while I'm gone."

CHAPTER THREE

— • —

TUES, AUG 4, 6:03 P.M.

Rory: How's ur summer? Haven't heard from u in a while

Ivy: Okay. How's yours?

Rory: Ok I guess. I'm touring colleges in Raleigh

Ivy: Which ones again?

Rory: All of them. there are so many colleges in Raleigh 😔

Rory: we're at Meredith rn

Ivy: sorry I couldn't make it

"Where is this thing, anyway?" I ask. I took so long deciding what to wear that I end up having to do my hair in the car. I didn't *want* to change out of my marinara-stained pajamas, because they're my favorites, but I can't meet people in blue fuzzy pants with pizza slices all over them.

Why social rules like that exist, I'll never know. My life would be so much easier if they didn't exist. It'd be so much easier if I didn't care about them.

"S&F Fitness, that gym near South Meck."

I pause mid-braid. I was expecting a church, or one of the community centers. "We're going to a *gym*? Kill me now."

Caroline laughs, like I'm not serious. "I know. I don't get it, either. I'm sure there's a story there."

"Why are we really doing this?" I wrap a hair tie around the end of my auburn braid, then pull the visor mirror down again. Just one more look.

My hair's frizzing in the southern humidity. It used to be pin straight, like Caroline's, but that was before I started my meds. No one warned me about that—how much my body would change. At least the color is the same.

There's a stray eyelash under one eye. The dark orange is a stark contrast against my pale skin, offsetting the deep green of my eyes. I swipe it away and decide against making a wish. I don't need to wish for anything, anyway.

Caroline sighs.

"I saw the flyer last time I went to my GI, and Mom saw it again last week. I just thought it would be fun to not be the weird one for once, you know?"

Her words are sobering. I haven't been sick my whole life like Caroline has—I just woke up one day hurting, and I haven't gotten better—but I *have* been the weird one. I've always been the weird one. I didn't know she ever felt that way.

We pull into the gym's parking lot, and Caroline parks her tiny car next to the curb. There's a blooming garden to our right. I can see through the walls of windows. People are walking back and forth between the machines. If I have to spill my guts while frat boys lift weights beside me, I'm out of there. I am not above making a swift exit—an Irish goodbye with my Irish twin left behind.

Caroline opens the door and walks up to the front desk like she owns the place. Even though today is a good day, everything about me is stiff as I follow, and I barely even look at the tall guy working reception or the short girl next to him. He directs us toward the half wall straight in front of us. Suddenly, my Harley Davidson leather ankle boots feel heavy against the floor, like I'm one of those Polly Pocket dolls I used to have, the ones with the magnetic feet that kept them standing up on their mat. These boots were my mom's when she was my age. If there are magnets in them, they must only work here.

As we walk, I try to count how many people there are. I see several small groups talking, but most of them have their backs to us.

One of them turns around, and . . . oh. He's kind of . . . oh.

I don't know what the word is, because when I see him, everything in my mind just kind of stops. It's as if everything around us slows down. The gym is loud and overwhelming, but he naturally draws my focus with his warm, soft glow.

He's very pretty. Beautiful, even. I might say something like *striking* if I were capable of accessing my higher vocabulary.

I don't normally notice that about people, how pretty they are. He's just significantly more good-looking than most. I could even be persuaded to say he's significantly more good-looking than *anyone*.

He turns back around and his face goes away and I'm just

staring at the back of his head. I really must be out of practice with this whole socializing thing. He's still there, though, in my mind. He lingers like the scent of cake batter that stays fragrant long after it's baked.

We end up in a circle of chairs. My heart's doing something funny, and I don't know if it's because of all the people in general, or just the good-looking one. I don't make eye contact with anyone, because I'm not good at that kind of thing—after all, I just spent too long staring at the back of a pretty stranger's head—but I can see a variety of shoes on the floor. I start to tense up at the thought of interacting with all these people, but then I remember my fluorescent light bulb of a sister is beside me. I shouldn't have to interact at all. I'm just here for moral support.

A girl stands up. At least, I think she's a girl. She's wearing dark flared jeans and yellow Converse. As bright as Caroline always is, those yellow shoes are brighter. Lighter.

"Hi, everyone. I'm Lilah." I feel more than see her smile. "I started our original group almost a year ago. There were only five of us back then, but we realized we needed to change: we needed to grow. So welcome to the first meeting of our new and improved support group."

I hear Lilah take a deep breath, and the guy next to her shifts closer.

"I thought we'd go around and introduce ourselves. Share anything you're comfortable with, like your age and diagnosis. Where you go to school. Stuff like that. No pressure, though."

Lilah looks around, and I feel her eyes pass over me. She's so welcoming and warm, it almost puts me at ease. Almost. This feels a little too much like the first day of school, something I'm already dreading. I can tell that Lilah is looking to me right now, so I glance up at her. She has burgundy box braids that rest over one shoulder, and warm umber skin.

"Like I said, I'm Lilah. I'm eighteen, and I have endometriosis." She sits.

Now the guy next to her speaks. "I'm Parker." He's wearing dark ripped jeans and a Carolina Panthers jacket unzipped over a red shirt. His blond curls flop all over his pale face. I kind of want to trim them. "I went to Ardrey Kell with Lilah. I'm eighteen, and I have Ehlers-Danlos syndrome."

I guessed that. It's the way his limbs are arranged in his chair, his legs crossed in an odd way no one with normally functioning joints would be comfortable in. I've spent enough time in pediatric rheumatology waiting rooms to know a zebra when I see one.

Suddenly I realize there aren't any shoes in between Parker's and Caroline's.

I know Caroline's going to speak for me. I practically ordered her to. But I wonder what everyone else in the circle is going to think about my silence. I read an article once that said some people fear public speaking more than death, and that's not *exactly* what this is . . . but for someone like me with social anxiety, that's *exactly* what this is.

"I'm Caroline." She points to me, and I feel the burn of a

circle's worth of eyes. "This is my little sister Ivy, if you couldn't tell by the hair. We go to Providence. I'm finally a senior after I did the whole "sick kid gets held back" thing. She's a junior, and we're eighteen and seventeen. I have celiac disease, and she has JIA."

I fight not to roll my eyes. Caroline knows how much I despise those three letters. It would be like saying Caroline is on a gluten-free diet. It's just not the whole picture.

"Just call it rheumatoid arthritis. The juvenile part is bad, and the idiopathic part is worse," I say softly. I'm too old to be called juvenile, and no one wants to be called idiopathic.

There's a moment of awkward silence, brought on by me, of course.

I take the opportunity to look at Caroline in my peripheral vision. She has this self-satisfied look on her face, and I realize she'd been deliberately trying to bait me into talking. I fell for it in an indignant heartbeat.

Right about now, I *do* fear death less than this moment.

But the introductions pick up again. There are a few more people to my right: a soft-spoken girl with sickle cell anemia, and two boys who high-five because they both have type 1 diabetes. They're so smiley and cheerful. They seem like fun.

Until now, I hadn't realized how close the feet directly across from me are. They're stretched out straight, just like mine. We're forming the hypotenuse of a right triangle with our legs. Their feet are in beaten-up black Vans. I have a pair just like those at home.

"I'm Grant. I'm seventeen, and I have rheumatoid arthritis."

Finally, someone said it right.

Wait. My eyes snap up before I stop them. So much for not having the energy for eye contact.

Oh God. It's the gorgeous one. Of course it is. Of course I look up and see the most startlingly perfect face I've ever seen. Now there's a name to that face, and a diagnosis. *My* diagnosis. It's not that I think I'm the only kid in the world with RA, but I've never been this close to someone else with it before.

I shift uncomfortably in my seat. There's no explanation as to why this feels like such a moment. Everything has changed in the blink of an eye. I feel this quiet connection between us now that he's spoken, lying there like an invisible tether between our out-stretched feet.

Caroline elbows me in the ribs. I wish she'd done it more gently. She gestures in Grant's direction with her wonder-filled eyes. She looks like a kid on Christmas morning, as if the idea of finding someone who could relate to her poor, anxious freak of a sister is exhilarating.

When I look back up, Grant is staring at me. He looks away so quickly that I immediately think I imagined the whole thing.

Now that I've noticed him, I can't seem to stop.

He has warm, barely blushed skin, and dark hair that curls the slightest bit over his ears. He's wearing a red S&F Fitness shirt, the same one that several of the other kids are wearing. It looks different on him, though. Cooler, somehow. More interesting. Like it's more than a shirt. It fits him better than shirts should be allowed to.

I'm already curious about him. I have my legs stretched out because my knees will lock up if I sit with them folded underneath me. I kind of want to know if that's why his legs are stretched out, too. His arms are crossed at his chest—it looks like he's hugging himself too tightly. I know that move: it's the best way to keep hands, wrists, and elbows from harsh, cold air without actually covering them up.

This strange, almost mirrored image I see in him is fascinating. I don't even notice when the group moves on.

We are nearly back where we started. I wonder what happens next, after the introductions are over. I'm already anticipating more awkward silences if I open my mouth, because I always experience that when meeting new people. I hate it.

I look up at the last person in the circle. This girl was standing behind the desk when Caroline and I walked in. She must work here—in fact, her straight, subtly confident posture says she does. She's wearing the same red shirt as Grant, but hers is broken in, the letters starting to peel off. She looks like she means something to this gym, and it means something to her.

"I'm Avery. I'm eighteen, and I have fibromyalgia." Avery looks to her left, and Lilah takes over again.

"So does anyone want to start us off?" Lilah looks around at us all, one by one. She really has the brightest smile. My heart flutters nervously when her eyes land on Caroline, but thankfully, my sister stays quiet.

Across from me, Grant raises his hand. He doesn't wait for

anyone else's acknowledgment before he speaks. "I would like to talk about how my best friends are dating and I'm uncomfortable with it."

I can't help it. I giggle. It's a silly puff of air that sounds like a baby seeing bubbles for the first time. Avery leans her head back against her chair like she wants to bang it against the wall. Parker seems annoyed. Oh, wait. He's probably one of the aforementioned best friends.

Lilah handles it in stride. I've known her for all of twenty minutes, but I expect nothing less.

"Would anyone like to talk about anything that shouldn't be saved for another time?" She doesn't look angry, or even frustrated. She must have expected this from him. Interesting.

"Or never talked about at all," Parker mumbles.

I look around again. Everyone looks like the physical representation of the awkward silence I was expecting.

"I'm just kidding," Grant says, grinning. "I knew it was going to get weird in here, so I thought saying something truly bizarre would help."

I laugh again, for real this time. So does everyone else. As laughter fills the space between us all, the circle seems less formal and rigid, and the air seems less cold.

When the dust settles, I look up, and Grant's eyes meet mine.

There's nothing that could've prepared me for those eyes.

CHAPTER FOUR

— • —

TUES, AUG 4, 7:19 P.M.

Caroline: OH MY GOD there's a hot guy here Ivy's age who has RA too

Mom: !!!!!!!!!!!!

Caroline: I know!!!!!!! I hope they get married.

Mom: Let's not get ahead of ourselves.

Caroline is digging for information. I can tell as soon as she walks into the kitchen after we get back from support group.

"You've been awfully quiet since we got home," she says.

I'm doing the dishes, something she never helps with. For her to even *be* in the kitchen is strange enough. I'm not sure how "quiet" is different from my default setting, anyway—I really didn't think anyone would notice. Of course, if anyone would, it would be her. No one has ever seen right through me the way she does.

"Just tired," I say in response. It's not *not* true. I have an auto-immune disease. I'm always tired.

"So…" Caroline starts, her voice trailing off. "What did you think?"

"What did I think of what, exactly?" I wipe my hands with the dish towel hanging on the oven handle and go to put the leftovers in the fridge.

"Of everything." Her tone is playful and leading.

From behind me, I hear the squeak of chair legs sliding against the tile. I sigh. This isn't going to be the short conversation I want it to be. Caroline has physically put herself between me and the door. I could try to skate past her, but with my level of coordination, I'd just end up on the floor.

I know what Caroline's getting at. But if she isn't going to admit it, I'm not going to play along. "I thought that the gym smelled like someone worked really hard to cover up all the sweat. I thought it was weird that they all had the same shirts on. I thought I didn't put enough garlic in the sauce."

Caroline rolls her eyes. I never put enough garlic in the sauce.

"Ivy."

"Caroline."

We stay in this silent stand-off for several moments, neither one of us willing to break.

"Grant's pretty cute, isn't he?" Caroline smiles this mischievous grin that I always hate to see. At least she acknowledged what she's fishing for.

I don't respond.

"I should've phrased that differently," Caroline says, almost thoughtfully. "I mean, it was cool to meet someone else with RA, right?"

I sigh, again.

"He's just another sick guy I sat across from. I do that in waiting rooms all the time."

That's a lie. A straight-up, bald-faced lie. I know it, but I'm not willing to admit it to Caroline's smug face. He's definitely not just another sick guy. He's not just another anything. He's... something. He's someone I actually noticed, and someone I wouldn't mind... noticing again.

"Yeah, but no one smiles at you like that in a *waiting room*."

"And how exactly did he smile at me?" I ask. Giving in to this line of questioning is almost definitely a bad idea, but I really want to know.

I turn to face her. She doesn't look like she's making fun of me. I kind of thought that's what the point of this conversation was at first.

My hands abandon the dish towel and cut a piece of the lemon blueberry cake I made this morning. If Caroline's going to stick around, she might as well eat. This is the most important recipe to make celiac-safe. It's the one I've been trying to perfect the longest.

I add a fork to the plate and slide it across the island. She leans over it, her elbows bracketing the plate. My forearms rest on the cool granite of the island top, too, waiting for her to say something. She doesn't. She takes a bite of cake instead.

"I love this stuff," she murmurs with her mouth full. She

doesn't need to say it. Lemon is her favorite. The recipe card reads *Caroline's Cake* in Grandma's handwriting. It's probably a good thing Grandma doesn't know she hasn't been able to eat it in years.

"This is it," she murmurs between bites. "I think you've finally done it."

Yes. I want to cheer, or punch the air, or jump up and down, but I don't. I simply move the *Caroline's Cake* recipe card from one small, decorated cardboard box to the other, from IN PROGRESS to COMPLETE.

For a moment, I just run my fingers through the delicate pages. Organized alphabetically, of course. As the cards flip, one to the next, I inhale. They smell like dust and the kitchen and *her*, and it hurts as much as it heals.

"Are you having a moment?" Caroline asks.

"No," I respond, even though I totally am.

I turn back to her, leaning forward on the island, resting my chin on my hands. I know she wants to talk, but I don't want to give her the satisfaction of knowing that I actually want to hear what she has to say. Eventually, she sets her fork down and meets my eyes.

"He smiled at you like he wanted to," she says, as if that makes any sense.

"What does that … mean?" I feel my eyebrows knit up.

"You know what I mean. Sometimes you just smile to be

polite, or because someone smiled at you. This wasn't that. He smiled at you like he really wanted to. I was watching him, the way he was with everyone else. He was nice and all, but the way he looked at *you*, the way he smiled at *you*? There's something there. I'm *telling* you."

She's pointing her fork at me as she speaks, but she doesn't need to. I get the message. I sort of noticed that something was different about Grant, but I didn't think it would be visible to anyone else.

"It freaks me out that you just *know* this kind of stuff."

Caroline smiles and gets up off the stool, leaving her dirty dishes behind on the counter.

"Stick with me, kid," she says on her way out. "You might learn something."

CHAPTER FIVE

•

FRI, AUG 7, 1:21 P.M.

Mom: Don't let your brother buy those expensive pencils.

Ivy: Fine, make me be the bad guy.

I don't really like going places at all, but I absolutely hate going places alone.

There's really no need for me to. That's the benefit of my sister and me being so close in age. Anywhere I go, Caroline goes too, and she always drives. That's the first overwhelming part of leaving the house alone: *driving*. It's a necessary evil, I guess, but I can't stand it.

Yet here I am, doing it. I can't help imagining Bad Outcomes. I'm thinking of getting sideswiped by a car I don't even see. Thinking of hitting a bicyclist on a blind turn. Thinking of a stranger judging me as I awkwardly back the car into a too-small Target parking space.

None of that actually happens, though. I breathe a sigh of relief as I put the car in park.

Summer in the South means that the black steering wheel is so boiling hot I drove with just my fingertips. I rest my wrists at ten and two because the heat kind of helps. It's terrifying that my joints are somehow still hotter than the wheel.

Now I can just sit in the scalding car with my skin melting onto the leather seat until my siblings come to rescue me. I'm in this hell because of them, anyway. Mom insisted we get our school shopping done today, and we were planning to go together after Ethan's baseball practice…but then Mom got called in to the school for some emergency, and Caroline left to pick Ethan up while I was napping. It was nice of her to let me sleep, I guess, but I'm paying for it in the form of solitude, Charlotte traffic, teeny-tiny parking spaces, and crowded shopping centers.

Even the best-laid plans to avoid discomfort crumble in the face of family life.

I enjoy the country music song drifting through the radio speakers for like fifteen seconds. Then my phone vibrates in my pocket. It's Caroline. She wants me to get an iced matcha latte for her and a strawberry Frappuccino for Ethan.

Like that's an easy thing to do, walk in there alone, talk to someone I don't know, awkwardly stand in a corner of the Target Starbucks holding all our coffees, and wait for them. It's ridiculous that people do those things all the time. Sometimes just for fun.

But it's either do all that or argue with my sister about why I don't want to do all that.

So, after hesitating long enough that sweat starts to form at the base of my neck, I step out of the car (double-checking that I've locked it, and triple-checking that I have the keys). It's an overwhelmingly humid morning, and there are people everywhere. Back-to-school shopping is in full swing, and as a kid in an all-out sprint crushes my foot on my way through the first set of whooshing automatic doors, I wish again I weren't alone. I wish Caroline and Ethan were here, desperately. No, I wish we weren't old enough to go back-to-school shopping by ourselves—it would be great to have Mom, too. Letting the three of us run wild in Target alone kind of feels like she's opened the cages at the zoo.

Except we have a budget and a curfew, and apparently there are some expensive pencils I can't let Ethan buy.

The Target Starbucks is right inside, and I pause before the final set of automatic doors. They close and open three times in front of me before I convince myself to go in.

At Starbucks, I wait in an exorbitantly long line, and I can't help but squirm the entire time. This whole thing—being out in public by myself—is like pulling teeth to me, and Caroline's need for an iced matcha latte is just making it worse. When it's my turn, I step forward, questioning whether I stepped up too far or if I'm standing too close to the counter or—

"What can I get you?" the barista asks. I'm not making eye contact, because I don't do that, and now I'm thinking about how they'll definitely know something is wrong with me.

"Um—can I get a strawberry Frappuccino? Grande, please." I order Ethan's first. Hopefully it'll keep him quiet, but he'll probably drink it in like three sips and the sugar will do more harm than good.

There must be an awkward pause because I hear the person behind me clear their throat.

"And a grande matcha latte," I add, slightly too fast. "Please. Iced."

I think they nod. I'm not looking, but after enough years of avoiding eye contact, you learn to assess nods and head shakes by feeling alone.

"Anything else?" they ask.

"No, thanks." I try to smile, doing my best to end this interaction as quickly as I can.

My feet slide along the linoleum floor to the other end of the counter. It's at that moment that I realize I forgot to order my own caramel macchiato. Damn. This is why I shouldn't be left to my own devices in public. I always mess something up.

Oh well. I only have two hands, anyway.

The same barista calls my name, and everyone looks at me as I step forward. I hate when everyone's looking at me. *Don't drop the coffee, don't drop the coffee, don't drop the coffee*, I chant to myself over and over. None of this is actually coffee, though, because I forgot to order my own. I let out a self-deprecating chuckle, making me look even more like the social tragedy that I am.

I lean against the wall that separates the dim, earth-toned Starbucks from the bright red Target. After a minute or two, Caroline glides through the same automatic doors I hesitated behind, the flat heels of her brown sandals smacking against the ground. She's in white bell-bottoms and a skintight tank. Her hair is longer than mine, and still pin-straight like mine used to be. Ethan's behind her, stomping the dirt off the cleats I don't know why he's still wearing. With a roll of my eyes, I hand them each their technicolor drinks.

"Why didn't you get anything?" Caroline asks, taking the frigid matcha from my now locked-up hand.

"Didn't want anything," I lie. "Why didn't you change shoes?" I ask Ethan, who apparently doesn't understand that baseball cleats are for baseball only.

"I told him to, but he doesn't listen to me. He's gonna scratch up their floors." Caroline sniffs.

"I like them." Ethan keeps stomping, slurping his drink at the same time. Wordlessly, we walk forward, deeper into the anxiety hellscape that is a suburban Target. Caroline keeps swirling her latte, making it more and more green, until we reach the section of school supplies. It's full of moms and kids and fallen notebooks and loose-leaf paper. It's a disaster area.

Next to me, Caroline unfolds her handwritten lists. Yes, she has *lists*. Multiple lists. For each of us. She's organized in a way that I will never be. The only lists I have are for ingredients.

"Okay, so I'm going to handle me and him. Can you worry about you?" she asks, still sipping matcha through a straw.

She passes me three pages of lined paper torn out of her old notebook.

There's absolutely no way I need three pages' worth of stuff. For one thing, I am set on shoes for the next year. I cross that off the list. She thinks I need a new lunchbox? I've been carrying the same one since I started packing my own lunch in fourth grade. I'm not getting a new one now. I cross that off the list, too.

I wander. Eventually, I end up in front of the stuff I actually need. I sidestep to keep from getting run over by a mom on the warpath, grab a basket from a stack, and consider.

I have choices.

This is the thing about going back to school: it's a time for reinvention. Right? I can hear Caroline behind me, asking Ethan if he's sure he wants the pencil case that looks like a baseball bat. He says yes, like it's as obvious as the sky is blue. *Of course* Ethan wants the baseball pencil case. Just like *of course* Caroline is going to carry the Michael Kors backpack she got for her birthday, because she's too cool for normal-people backpacks.

Backpacks. There's a disordered rainbow in front of me, backpacks stacked from the floor to literally higher than I can reach. This should be easy, picking one. Even picking a shade range. Narrowing it down to two choices. If I were Caroline or Ethan, I'd be done with this already.

If I were my best friend, Rory, I'd *definitely* be done with this already. She's always thinking of college and her career and the future. She's always an assignment ahead, or thinking about the next test weeks in advance. She probably had this year's backpack picked out this time last year. It's probably pink.

This isn't a difficult choice, I tell myself. It's literally just pieces of fabric sewn together to hold books. This shouldn't be this hard.

I take two steps to my right. That way I'm not in front of the red ones anymore. Red reminds me of those S&F Fitness shirts half the support group was wearing. Red isn't me. I know that much. Now I'm in front of the yellows. They remind me of Lilah and her shoes. Yellow isn't really my thing, either.

I take two more steps. Orange is the color people think my hair is.

Two more steps. Green is the color my eyes are, but Caroline's are greener.

Two more steps. Purple was my grandmother's favorite color.

Two more steps. Pink is what Rory would pick.

Two more steps. Navy reminds me of Grant for some reason. I don't know why. I like it, but Grant isn't me.

Two more steps, and someone taps me on the shoulder. I jump, and my empty basket clatters to the floor. It's Caroline. I didn't even see her coming. Ethan's right behind her, both of them with heavy-looking baskets loading down their arms.

"We're done, and you have"—she looks into my basket that somehow landed right side up on the floor—"nothing. I thought you could handle yourself?"

"Mom said I'm not supposed to let you get those pencils," I tell Ethan, and yeah, okay, I'm trying to deflect.

"Come on, Iggy," he whines. I can't stand whining.

"Fine." I grab the pencils from his basket and put them in mine. "Mom said you can't have them, but she didn't say I can't. I'll sneak them in your backpack later."

Ethan smiles like we're plotting a bank robbery, not a transfer of illicit pencils.

"Why can't you have them, anyway?" I ask, still deflecting.

"Because they're like five dollars each and he either loses them or trades them for the gum he's not supposed to have," Caroline explains.

I roll my eyes.

"Now we need to focus on you." Caroline raises one eyebrow at me, daring me to explain what I've been doing all this time. I can't.

I look around. Right in front of me, not even hanging up, is one lone backpack in a light blue. Like a sky blue, sort of. It's slightly distressed and trimmed in black.

That's . . . something.

"I don't have nothing," I tell Caroline as I reach for it.

CHAPTER SIX

—— • ——

TUES, AUG 11, 12:49 P.M.

Ethan: making brownies anytime soon?

Ivy: Would it kill you to say please?

Ethan: probably.

Ivy: You're a brat. I'll make some tomorrow.

"Are you coming with me tonight?" Caroline asks.

I'd been so absorbed in folding butter into a bowl of half-formed bread dough that I hadn't heard her encroach on my territory. This was the first adapted recipe I perfected. Caroline hated every gluten-free bread money could buy, so I fiddled with Grandma's recipe until it worked. That's how the challenge was born.

"Coming with you where?" I take a break, wiping the flour off my locked-up hands. As they start to throb, I try to move each finger a knuckle at a time. I roll my wrists and hope Caroline can't hear the creaking. It's not supposed to be like this. In the weekly medication cycle, this is supposed to be a good day. Instead, it's like I've passed purgatory and I'm descending into hell.

"Support group. It's Tuesday." Caroline looks at me like this is obvious. As if summer is the time for keeping up with what day of the week it is.

It's easier to let myself be consumed by thoughts of butter and gluten-free flour. I walk to my spice rack, trying to decide what to use in the loaf this week. I go with rosemary and thyme.

"Where are my good measuring spoons?" I ask, fiddling around in the drawer where I keep my baking supplies.

"There's a set of them right there," Caroline says. She points directly in front of me, right at the front of the drawer.

"Those aren't my good ones. Who unloaded the dishwasher last?" I close the drawer, none too gently.

"You did." Caroline crosses her arms. I know she's going to demand an answer soon. I just don't know which one to give her.

I walk back to the counter where my unfinished dough sits. There are my good measuring spoons, right beside the container of my homemade gluten-free flour mixture. Of course I've already taken them out. Of course I've already forgotten. I sigh, blowing out a frustrated breath that sends my hair flying off my face.

"One of those days, huh?" Caroline asks.

I nod. I don't know what else to do. My brain feels foggy and unfamiliar, my limbs heavy and unyielding. It's like someone hit me with a bus. The bus has been coming around more and more often these days. I wish I could perk up—or at least make it seem like I'm not feeling conflicted and weird.

"You never answered my question."

"You go ahead. I just don't feel like it tonight."

That, at least, is the truth. I don't really feel like anything.

Caroline grabs her keys and opens the front door. I start to say goodbye, but she sticks her head back around the frame before I can.

"I'll tell Grant you said hi."

Flustered, I drop my measuring spoons, instead dumping distracted handfuls of spices into the bowl. If the bread turns out tasting like homemade soap, it'll serve Caroline right. As much as I've been avoiding thinking of that circle of chairs, I've been avoiding one chair in particular.

I've never been so wholly curious about someone before. I just want to know everything about him. I want to know if he ever feels like this, like his brain and body aren't communicating on the same frequency. If he ever feels like all of his body's wires are crossed.

That's why I'm not going tonight. The real reason. Because even though I've thought about him all week, I don't want to be feeling like a disheveled mess when I see him again.

As I knead the dough together, I wonder what medicine he takes. Another turn, and I wonder how old he was when he was diagnosed. As I cover the dough with a towel to let it rise, I wonder if we see the same doctor. Maybe we've been there at the same time. I wonder if he always sits with his legs straight out in front of him like he did last week. I wonder if he smiles at everyone the way he smiles at me.

"Is it bread time again already?" Mom rounds the corner into the kitchen, leaning against the fridge.

"Someone ate the last slice and neglected to tell me." I assume it was Ethan. When anything even mildly irritating happens around here, I assume it's because of Ethan. Mom lifts the towel off the bowl to sniff the dough. I swat her hand away.

"Is that rosemary?" she asks. "I should've named you Rosemary."

I chuckle, just barely. I'm starting to feel the impact of the beating I put my hands through to make the new loaf. Pain radiates up my arms and lodges in my shoulders. My wrists won't move, and my fingers feel like they're nothing but grating bones.

Mom moves to start cleaning up. She dusts the flour off the counter while I put my spices back in their proper places. I know this means she wants to talk. I put my last spice bottle up and twist it so the label is facing out.

"So . . . are you ready to go back to school?" Mom drops the last of the dishes into the sink, which is already full of foamy water, and begins to clean them.

I fight back a groan. The simple answer is no. I don't want to think about the more complicated answer.

"I guess so," I mumble. Giving up my lazy mornings and kitchen afternoons for wake-up calls and forced socialization is never ideal. I grab a towel and start drying the dishes Mom just washed.

"Are you thinking of going to the dance?" Mom stops washing, her hands just hanging at the edge of the foam.

"What dance?" As soon as the words leave my mouth, I know it's the wrong response.

I could've just said no. I've never spent a moment of my life thinking about going to *any* dance. Rory mentioned this one, I think, but that was a while ago and it slipped my mind.

"The back-to-school dance. I'm taking Caroline shopping for a dress this weekend."

I turn to put a stack of plates away, mostly to think about how I want to handle this.

"I hadn't thought about it." I don't even want to look up at my mom. I know I'll read too far into whatever is in her eyes.

"Well, you haven't done much with your friends this summer. I thought you might like to see them before school starts. Maybe even have some fun."

I sigh. For one thing, "friends" is a misnomer. The plural implies multiple friends, and I just have the one. For another, I haven't done *anything* with Rory this summer. At all. I haven't seen her since the last day of school. We've talked, we've texted. She's asked me to do things with her, but I've chickened out every time. So my friend situation is complicated at best.

Most of all, though, my mother's definition of *fun* completely contradicts my own.

"Don't worry. I'm sure I'll see enough of her at school."

That much is true, if a little sad.

It's not that I don't care about Rory. It's that, at some point, the piece of me that used to be my social battery just…had to be devoted to something else. Maintaining friendships seems to take energy I don't have to give anymore.

Mom leans forward, placing her elbows on the lip of the sink. The dishes are forgotten altogether.

"I'm worried." She takes a deep breath and releases it hard enough to blow her bangs off her forehead. "It just feels like you don't have much of a life outside of this house."

I desperately want to roll my eyes. Or bang my head against the wall. Or slide out of the room. I *don't* have much of a life outside of this house. That's not exactly deniable. What my mom isn't understanding is that I'm kind of okay with that.

We stand at the counter, looking at each other in the sort of awkward silence I always do my best to avoid.

"Is it because of your RA?" Mom winces as she says it, like the words make her mouth go sour. "I feel like things have gotten worse for you since then…socially, I mean."

"Haven't most things gotten worse, though?" I really try not to think like that—so negatively. I try not to spend too much time thinking about my illness at all. Thoughts like that make me feel like my joints are decaying faster.

But things *have* gotten worse. I'm more tired, achier. My brain doesn't work like it used to. I have to worry about medication and doctor's appointments and side effects and disease progression.

There's no way to consider my social life without thinking of all that.

"I guess that's fair." Mom sags; her head rolls forward like her neck just won't hold it up anymore. "I just worry about you. I can't help it."

Worry about yourself, I want to say. *You're sick, too.*

"I thought the support group would help, but you didn't even want to go back." She isn't talking to me now, not really. Her voice takes on this floaty, barely there tone that means she's just thinking out loud.

I freeze. "I thought the support group was for Caroline."

I don't know how I didn't see it before. I should've known Caroline didn't need me. She's never been afraid of going anywhere alone. I should've seen right through that excuse.

"We weren't trying to deceive you or anything, I promise," Mom says quickly. "Caroline really did want to go. I just thought it would be good for you, too!"

I don't feel deceived, exactly. I just feel like they conspired against me behind my back. On second thought, maybe that's exactly what deception feels like.

"No, you just thought I needed to go. Why didn't you tell me that?"

Mom gives me her signature side-eye. My parents always joke that it took words for Caroline to listen, and action for Ethan, but I always responded to just that look.

"I couldn't tell you that." Mom rises to her full height in front of me. She's so tall. I thought I'd catch up one day, but that ship has probably sailed. "You wouldn't have listened, and you wouldn't have gone."

I can't refute that. It's true, point blank. I still don't like this, though. I don't like that they thought me pathetic enough to warrant *social intervention*.

I shake my head, withdraw one step. The heat from the stove warms the joints in my hips and the muscles on the backs of my legs. It's kind of heavenly, despite this uncomfortable conversation.

"To do something for yourself, I had to make you think it was for someone else."

I look away. Mom's eyes are too probing. Too honest.

Across the open kitchen into the dining room, our Christmas card picture from last year hangs in a huge dark frame above the mantel. My parents are in the middle, arms around each other. Ethan sits on the ground in front, smiling so much it looks like it hurts. Then there are me and Caroline, on either side of our parents, flanking them like bookends.

Caroline stands strong and tall, one leg bent in front of the other like she models for a living. I stand, if you could even call it that, bent at the waist, laughing at something Ethan said. If I remember right, it was something about the snow seeping through his jeans. As if the decision to plant himself in the frozen wet grass was anyone's but his. I don't remember if my feet were feeling that chilled pain I normally associate with snow. I don't remember the schoolwork I missed that snow day. All I remember is the way I laughed.

I walk past that picture every day, and each time, I think about how rarely I see myself smile like that. Never with anyone else. Never alone in the mirror. Only with them. So, yeah. Maybe I do care about them more than I care about myself. That's not so bad. It can't be *that* bad.

"All you do is help other people," Mom says, sounding exasperated.

I tilt my head to look at her again. This is supposed to be what parents want: kids who care about each other.

"I'm grateful for that. I promise, I truly am. I just feel guilty that you're here all the time taking care of everything. It's like you're Cinderella or something."

"Oh, come on. If I scrubbed floors for hours like she did, I wouldn't be able to let go of the sponge!" I smile, because it's a joke. Mom laughs, but it's a pity laugh.

I'm not like everyone else. There's always going to be something different about me. Something I'm not comfortable sharing with the rest of the world.

Except here. Right where I am, with a view of Ethan riding his bike up and down the street, and the heat of the oven against the palms I'm resting behind my back. This is safe. This is *home*, and that has nothing to do with the beige walls and family photos. This is my fortress, and I don't relish the idea of leaving it—especially not for loud music and a friend I haven't seen in months.

"I don't know, Mom."

"Just think about the dance, okay? Wouldn't it be nice to see your friends? Have some fun for once, please?"

I see the begging and pleading in her eyes. I hear what she's not saying. It's there in the silence, in the negative space between her words: *For me.*

She's right about me. I wouldn't do this for myself, but I would do anything for her. Even this.

Every once in a while, even commoners have to go to the ball.

CHAPTER SEVEN

—————— • ——————

SAT, AUG 15, 9:09 A.M.

> Caroline: like this, but shorter.

> Ivy: Shorter? You know there's a dress code, right?

> Caroline: Oh I know I just don't care 😌

"Let's talk about my *vision*."

Despite looking at the back of Caroline's head, I can imagine the expression on her face: determination mixed with an excitement only brought on by the thought of racks and racks of clothing options.

She's up front and has both feet resting on the dashboard. I would never feel comfortable that way. Too much pressure on my hips. Too many thoughts of my legs crushing my ribs in the event of a crash.

"Okay, great. I'm glad you have a vision. Maybe we won't be there all afternoon." Mom hits her turn signal and pulls her huge SUV into the mall parking lot.

I'm actually minutely excited for this part. Shopping is reasonably comfortable territory. The mall closest to home is the biggest one in Charlotte. It's easy to get lost in. And it's easy to pretend the wall-to-wall display of taffeta and chiffon isn't tied to a massive social event I'm terrified to attend.

We all climb out of the car, and I stop on the way out, putting one hand on the door handle and twisting my body until I hear the satisfying cracks of tension leaving my lower back. I stand up straighter, because with just those few cracks, I feel like a different person.

There's a guy across the parking lot who has Grant's haircut. His hair's lighter than Grant's, but it's enough to bring Grant-related thoughts up to the surface. His hair isn't as pretty as Grant's. Maybe it's the color, or maybe it's the texture.

Maybe it's just Grant.

"I've done some research, and I'm thinking pastel. I haven't decided what color yet, but light, *not* bright." Caroline walks toward the store ahead of Mom and me, her shoulders back and spine straight.

"Why do you want pastel? It's not an Easter dress." Sometimes I say things just to hear Caroline's rapid-fire response. She always has one.

"Because I want something trendy. I want something I'll look at pictures of ten years from now and think was a bad choice."

I roll my eyes and walk through the heavy door that takes Caroline's entire body weight to hold open. Everywhere I can see, packs of teenagers weave through racks of clothes and frazzled adults try their best to follow them through the maze. Music floats through the store, but the lyrics are basically unintelligible over the dull roar of conversation.

We parked right outside, but we still have to walk through the men's department to get to the dresses. My hip starts to burn after a certain number of steps. It always does.

The hallway between racks past the men's department opens up into a huge, open floor. Long gowns hang on tall racks directly in front of us. Mom picks up something on a hanger. It's floor length and fire-engine red with too many straps. It's decidedly not Caroline's style, and so opposite of mine that I have to look away. That color red only belongs on children's playgrounds and sports cars.

"So what are we thinking, girls? Short or long?" Mom drapes the satin-looking fabric over her as if she's trying to see how it looks against her complexion.

"Definitely not that, and definitely short. It's still August. Anything long would be way too hot and way too formal." Caroline puts the dress back on the rack.

"What if I wanted a long dress?" I ask. I can just imagine it: me, waltzing down the school hallway toward the gym in a flowing gown.

"You're short. Every dress is a long dress on you."

I roll my eyes again. Caroline's not wrong. If I were to walk down the hallway in a flowing gown, I'd definitely trip.

Suddenly, Mom's eyes light up in a way that makes me think my policy of considering shopping *comfortable territory* is about to meet a swift end.

"I have an idea," she starts to say. Caroline and I both groan. "Just humor me, please. Remember when you were little, and you'd pick out each other's clothes?"

"Of course I do," Caroline says, her hands on her hips. "That's the last time she wore anything other than black."

"That's not true," I say reflexively. Caroline points at me and runs a line with her finger from my shirt to my shoes. All black.

"I think you should both pick something out for each other, and I'll pick out something for each of you. We'll meet back in the dressing room in ten minutes. Stay on this floor. Okay?"

Without waiting for a reply from us, she takes off, walking this mom-like power-walk and disappearing between racks of dresses. I look around. I don't know how she even expects us to cover this floor of the gigantic department store in ten minutes, let alone branch out to other floors.

"We should ju—*Caroline!*"

Caroline takes off in the opposite direction before I can even finish my sentence. Great. By the time I blink, I can't even see the tops of their heads anymore. I'm on my own.

I sigh, glancing around me at rows and rows of dresses in inky blacks and blues dark enough they pass for indigo. I want to hide myself among the skirts.

But I have to find something for Caroline. So I walk, things running lighter as I go on. I stumble upon the neon dresses, which she already said she doesn't want. For that, I'm grateful. They remind me of the '80s section at a party store—too bright and generally too much. There's also a rack next to me in varying shades of pink. It makes me think of Rory. I wonder what she'll be wearing to the dance. Something pink, I'm sure.

I sidestep to a rack full of neutrals. I run my fingertips over a tawny dress, thinking it's something I'd try for myself if it weren't covered in crystals.

I feel someone creep up behind me, this weird kind of awareness making the hair on my neck stand up.

"Two more minutes. Mine are already in your dressing rooms." Mom smiles so brightly it's alarming, like this is the most fun she's had in months. It probably is.

As Mom walks toward the dressing rooms, I stand on my tiptoes to try to spot Caroline. If she's in a sea of bright colors I wouldn't be caught dead in, I'm going back to the car. But they really do expect me to have something in my hands in two minutes, so I give up and go back to sorting through layers of fabric.

Five clanks of a hanger later, Caroline walks by. Her gait is so effortless it almost looks like she's skipping. Her arms are loaded down with dresses. It's a rainbow cacophony so loud it makes my eyes ache.

I'm not the overachiever that Caroline's always been. I wander back to the dressing room with only one dress. When I turn the corner, I find Mom sitting cross-legged on a padded bench in front of the rows of doors.

"She's already changing into my pick. You do the same." Mom points to the room directly in front of her. I take one step forward, then stop as the door next to mine swings open.

I try not to laugh. Really, I try. The murderous look on Caroline's face is just too much.

"Mom. This is ... not it."

It's pastel, she listened to that much. But the entire bodice is bedazzled, from the waist to the sweetheart neckline, and the skirt is overlaid with coral tulle. It's a pageant gown. Caroline's shoulders are hunched and her hands hang by her sides. She's the picture of physical discomfort.

"Oh, come on. Look at the sparkle!" I'm surprised Mom is even defending her choice. Caroline likes to be her own sparkle.

"Here, try this." I pass Caroline my pick.

"This is more like it." Caroline disappears behind her door and Mom gestures for me to follow her lead. The thought of putting on a dress even remotely similar to the one Caroline just wore is terrifying, mostly because I'd have a much harder time telling my mother I don't like it than Caroline did.

I step behind the door into the harshly lit square of space. A dress hangs from a hook to the right of the mirror. I change and step into it quickly—cubicles like this make me feel claustrophobic.

The thin fabric falls over me in a way I'm not upset about, but I can't get it zipped all the way by myself. I step out to where my mother is sitting, and her eyes light up.

I turn and let Mom zip up the last few inches. I watch in the mirror at the end of the dressing room hallway as the fabric comes to rest across my shoulders the way it should. This is definitely better than her pick for Caroline. It's crepe, I think, in a burgundy so deep it's almost maroon. It complements my skin tone and makes the brown flecks in my green eyes stand out. Even my myriad of freckles seems to dance across my face. On someone taller, it would hit mid-thigh, but it graces the tops of my knees. The skirt is flowy, and with the drapey off-shoulder sleeves, I feel decidedly more feminine than usual. It's nice.

I don't expect it, but I feel...pretty.

My bare feet take a few steps on the shaggy carpet toward the mirror. I want to see the dress up close, see if I can find something wrong with it. I spin around slightly, looking at myself over my shoulder. I look delicate, in a way that I rarely feel.

Another door opens and delicate and feminine gives way to confident and flawless. If I were a weaker person, I would have put Caroline in something else. My sister is just so naturally stunning, and the dress does nothing but amplify that. The light powder-blue silk-satin brings out the red tones in her auburn red hair. It's fitted from the high neck to where her fingertips rest at her sides, then it flares out into a dramatic ruffle just below her hips.

Caroline walks up next to me. She seems to take up all the mirror space.

"I love this, Ivy. I can't believe you picked it out."

"Thanks," I reply, sarcasm lacing my tone.

"That came out wrong." Caroline meets my eyes in the mirror. She's looking at me like she wants to say something else, but then Mom steps up in between us with a hand on each of our shoulders.

"So, what do we think?"

I think we look like we're going to different parties, but that's not unusual. Caroline always feels miles ahead of me in the fashion department, anyway.

"I think they're both perfect, don't you?" Caroline looks over at me, hope in her eyes.

I nod. I'm not going to find anything better than this. I don't want to take it off, and that must be a good sign.

There are more smiles and happy remarks, and we go back to our individual cubicles to change. Once we pass Mom the dresses and she leaves to go check out, Caroline is waiting for me outside my door. My leggings and T-shirt are infinitely more comfortable than the dress I just took off, but they don't hold quite the same kind of magic.

"You should wear the dress to support group next week. I'm sure Grant would love it."

Despite the idea of wearing a semi-formal dress to a gym being *unbearably* ridiculous, some part of me can imagine it. This dramatic, music-video moment where he looks at me and no one else.

"Yeah, right." I push past her, not willing to give this conversation any more thought. The idea is ludicrous. Laughable.

"You don't have to wear that, but you should come back." Caroline turns serious, and I never know how to handle that. Discomfort crawls its way up my neck and lodges at the base of my hair.

"Why?" I ask. If this is about a boy Caroline imagined having a crush on me, there's no reason to even entertain the thought.

"Because it's *good*, Ivy. Last week, I stayed after for almost an hour talking to Stella. We don't have the same disease, obviously, but I'd never gotten to actually talk about the whole journey with anyone before."

I wince. We don't talk about it, the time before Caroline was diagnosed, the time when everything she ate stole nutrients instead of providing them. Malabsorption turned to malnutrition, and she lost so much weight. It took months for her to bounce back from that kind of anemia.

"Why Stella?" I ask. Stella is the quiet one, the one who has sickle cell. There are more people there Caroline's own age, and Stella's closer to mine.

"I don't know." Caroline seems reserved for a moment, and seeing that is like an out-of-body experience. It's just weird. "She reminds me of you a little bit. She's quiet, and shy, but as soon as

I started paying attention to her, she just kept talking. She's been in and out of the hospital for her whole life, and you know that doesn't breed friendships. She doesn't have an older sister, either. I mean, she's like you, but without me."

"Is this what it's like to be the oldest? You just go around adopting younger siblings?"

"No, not really. I wouldn't adopt another Ethan, just another you."

Silence settles over us for a moment because I don't know how to respond to that. Saying that I probably wouldn't adopt another Ethan, either, seems like it would ruin the moment, so I don't say anything for a while.

"Is that why you're trying to push me with Grant?" I ask. "So I'll have someone to talk to?"

"Sort of." Caroline shrugs. She looks across the store to where our mom stands, talking to the cashier in her animated way. "I just think it would be good for you to relate to someone who isn't us."

I sigh, my limbs feeling suddenly heavy. I don't know how I'll ever need anything more than them, but it is a fair point.

"Besides, he kept staring at the empty seat next to me. It was weird, like he thought if he looked hard enough, a portal would open up and you'd step through it." Something in my stomach turns. That can't be true. Caroline's perception has to be exaggerated.

We start to walk toward Mom. She hands us each a hanger

covered in a plastic garment bag. I'm not hearing anything around me. My mind is in the gym, sitting in the seat beside my sister, looking at him. I'm trying to see what Caroline saw. .

Something bumps against my shoulder.

"While we're here, we should go get pretzels," Caroline says from far closer than I thought she was.

"You can't eat pretzels," I reply, my brow scrunching up. From somewhere behind us, Mom laughs.

"Just checking to see if you were paying attention."

I'm definitely not. I don't even remember the drive home. My consciousness is taking a trip outside my body to places unknown. The way I see it, there are two choices. I can trust Caroline's assessment of the situation without any proof. Or, I can go back to the group and determine it myself.

CHAPTER EIGHT

•

SAT, AUG 22, 8:17 P.M.

Mom: Have fun! Call me if you need me to bring you some sensible shoes.

Ivy: I won't need shoes. But thanks.

The walk down the school hallway is undeniably satisfying. No one is here to witness it, but it's my big dramatic moment in my fancy dress and heels.

I love this dress. It's flowy and demure and possibly prettier than anything I've ever worn. The heels are *definitely* prettier than anything I've ever worn. Still, by the time I reach my locker, I can feel every joint below my ankles.

Caroline strides ahead of me. This is her first walk down this hallway as a senior, and I can tell she's loving every minute of it. The curls our mom spent an hour on are bouncing against her back, reaching almost to the waist of her dress. Judging by her stance and general confidence, Caroline isn't having any trouble marching in her heeled nude sandals.

I can hear the music blasting. Dancing is one thing, but we haven't even gotten there yet, and my feet are already screaming. I should have just listened to my mom when she tried to talk me out of the heels. *It's perfectly normal for a high school junior to want to wear heels to a dance.* That was my argument. *But what about your feet?* my mom had shot back in the middle of the shoe store. Like my feet would shatter if I put them in something with an arch.

Needless to say, I bought the shoes. Four inches of chunky black heel in a classic pump shape. They could be Prada knockoffs. They were too perfect to walk away from, and I wanted to look like everyone else. Just this once.

As we reach the door to the gym, the bass thumping through the hardwood floors beneath my feet, Caroline is instantly off. The seniors congregate together on one side of the room, acting like they own the place. For the next year, I guess they do.

I scan the room, looking for Rory. I haven't seen her since the last time I walked these halls, back when we were still lowly sophomores. With any luck, she won't be here, and I'll be able to find a nice dark corner to chill in until Caroline's ready to go home. I wonder if I could stuff myself in my locker...

I spot Rory right in the center of the dance floor. I'm glad she's facing me, because I wouldn't have recognized her from behind. Her hair was a foot longer when we left school last year. She had glasses then, too. She must have gotten contacts. She's part of a group of three wearing the same shade of spring green. Either that's a coincidence, or there's a bride around here missing her wedding party. They're dancing in a line, even though the song playing isn't a line dance.

The green is surprising, somehow even more than the hair and the contacts. I don't think I've ever seen her wear it before.

As I get closer, I realize who the other two are: Brooke and Sloane, Rory's soccer friends. When we started high school, Rory and I gravitated toward each other because we were the same kind of weird: both loners who didn't really belong anywhere. We were in all the same classes, but none of the friend groups. So we sort of made our own.

"Ivy!" she yells. Rory throws her arms around my shoulders, wrapping me in a tight hug that almost knocks me off-balance and shifts my low bun out of place. "I didn't think you were coming!"

It never really occurred to me to tell her. It should've, though. We could've gone shopping for dresses together, theoretically. If I'd asked. If I'd actually just talked to someone for once. Being the one in the non-green dress is what I deserve.

No one says anything after that—at least, I don't hear if they do. They all go back to moving to the pulsing music. I'm rarely comfortable in social situations, but I am never comfortable in social situations where *dancing* is involved. I never know what to do with myself, and all my limbs start to feel extraneous and awkward, like I don't know how to control them, like they're not a part of me anymore.

But Rory takes my hands, and suddenly we're making this weird kind of spinning circle that no one else is allowed into. We dance like we're kids on a playground. As awkward as I feel, as much as I didn't want to come, this is actually kind of fun. My heart pounds to the music, my feet move in unexpected ways.

Rory smiles, and I realize that being a part of this—our friendship—is something I should never have willingly let go of.

Songs fade in and out, slow and fast. We don't care; we just keep dancing. I have no idea how much time has passed, and I haven't thought of anything besides the four-foot square of space I'm occupying. There's a weird timelessness about environments like this, where it's too loud to think.

As soon as I stop moving, I regret everything.

The subtle awareness of the joints in my feet turns to pain. A new song starts, the beat of my heart and the throbbing ache joining in time with the bass. I freeze, biting my lip and willing it all to go away. But I feel the pain crawl up my legs, above my ankles, past my knees. It lodges in my hips, festering until it's a tension so strong I don't know if I can move. Every step on my heels feels like daggers. I let out a tiny gasp.

My mind races back, counting the songs I've danced to. I lose count after fifteen. It's breathtaking, how I allowed myself to be pushed so far past my limits.

Rory catches my eye. She doesn't know my biggest secret—no one here does—but she can still tell when something is wrong.

"Are you okay?" she mouths.

I nod in response, pointing to the girls' locker room door in the corner of the gym. I take a deep breath, square my shoulders, and attempt to force my way through the throng of people. I'm too short for this, too timid. I'm not meant to bust through a crowd; I'm not meant to be in a crowd in the first place. I catch sight of Caroline's powder blue dress. I was hoping I'd be able to escape without worrying her.

Once I make it to the locker room, I can breathe deeply again. Immediately, I wish I hadn't. The locker room smells like it hasn't been cleaned all summer. Gross. The disgusting tile floor is probably older than both my parents, and it is *so* not the place to take off my shoes. I do anyway. I just can't walk another step on those sword heels.

Barefoot, I make it to a sink, where I attempt to fix myself. The bobby pins holding my updo together threaten to fall out, auburn strands already framing my face. My cheeks are bright red—from the dancing or from the flare I brought on myself, I'll never know.

Deciding they're doing more harm than good, I tear at each and every pin until my hair flows around me in haphazard, messy waves. I roll my neck in circles, pop my knuckles. It's like waking up in the morning: taking inventory of how much everything hurts, and what I need to do about it.

I slide to the ice-cold floor in between the sinks, my back against the wall. I extend my legs as far in front of me as they'll go, stretching everything from my hips to my toes. It makes me think of Grant, how we both sat that way in group. It makes me think of what my sister said, too, about how it felt to actually talk about this stuff...illness stuff. Instead of running, instead of hiding.

Mom's words echo in my head, reverberating in the space between my thoughts. *It just feels like you don't have a life.*

The door slams open hard enough that it bounces against the wall.

"Ivy?" I hear Rory call. She's looking under stall doors for feet.

"Over here," I mumble.

"Oh, you're...okay, that's not what I was expecting." She turns around, tilting her head like she can't figure out why I'd be willingly sitting underneath locker room sinks. "Are you okay?"

"Yeah, I'm..." I want to say *fine*, because that's what people say, but for some reason I feel like she won't believe that fine means fine this time. "I'm good."

"Kind of overwhelming out there, huh?" Rory gestures toward the door. She tucks a strand of her new hair behind her ear. It's too short to stay there.

"Mm-hmm." I nod. "Just loud and...thumpy." I don't know what I mean by that, whether it's the bass thumping, or the hundreds of feet thumping, or my own heart thumping against my ribs.

"Yeah..." Rory nods. She picks at an imaginary wrinkle in her pale green dress. It looks darker in the dim light of the bathroom. The wispy fabric looks almost eerie.

It goes quiet, as quiet as a bathroom attached to a school dance can be, and the awkwardness sucks the air out of me.

"Are you sure you're okay?" she asks again, her brows tightening up and her fingers beginning to tug on the ribbon sash at her waist. "You don't need me to stay for another minute?"

"I'm sure." I try to smile and create the illusion that I'm totally okay and normal and not in any pain at all.

Rory smiles back, and as I watch her leave, I lean my head back against the chilly tile wall and close my eyes. Everything is so much cooler in here. At first it was soothing. Now I'm starting to shiver.

Eventually, through the closed door, I hear the volume go down until the music is barely background noise. Someone's voice takes over. It's muffled enough that I can't tell who it is, but I hear that they're getting ready to play the last song.

I stand up, slowly, using the wall behind me for support. Waves of pain shoot through each of my joints, even the tips of my fingers holding onto my shoes. I take one tentative step, and it feels like the balls of my feet are twice the size they should be. I probably couldn't put my shoes back on if I wanted to.

Once I make it to the door, I use the last of my energy to pull it open. Caroline meets my eyes as soon as I emerge, and then she's briskly walking me out. I must look as terrible as I feel.

She leads me to the car. Heavy sadness fills my mind.

I shouldn't have come in the first place. I should've told Rory the truth when she came to check on me.

I should've just admitted that I couldn't wear the heels.

CHAPTER NINE

— • —

MON, AUG 24, 7:03 A.M.

Mom: Have a good first day!

Ivy: you too! Give someone
some good advice for me.

"I already hate History," Rory says, slamming her tray down next to mine on the table. The impact makes me jump, and I nearly spit out the apple juice I just sipped. We've only been back in school a morning, barely enough time to learn where our new classrooms are and how fast we have to walk from one to the next without being late.

Rory is a classic overachiever, and I'm willing to bet that this sudden hatred for her favorite subject has a lot to do with Mr. Bowery not responding to her aggressive question-asking. He's boring, and of the opinion students should be seen and not heard. I warned her to raise her hand a little less this year—a friendly warning—but I think she took it as a challenge. That's just another thing I messed up.

"We have a paper due next week. I'm going to do it in Chicago style just to impress him. Not even Turabian, either. Full.

Chicago." Rory pulls out her two-inch-thick planner and a neon green pen. She flips until she hits the dog-eared page marking today. "Actually, I'm going to see if the library has a Chicago Manual first. It's so finicky. If I mess anything up, I'll look *ridiculous*."

"I think he's just a bad teacher, and I'm pretty sure you're every bad teacher's worst nightmare," I tell her seriously. She's wearing yellow today. It's still weird to see her in anything that isn't pink.

"What do you mean?" she asks, brows pinching together again like in the bathroom during the dance.

"I mean you're his worst nightmare. A student who actually wants to learn."

"Oh." Her face brightens up, then turns contemplative. "That's kind of sad, though. Isn't it?"

"Yeah." I take a bite of my sandwich. No one ate much bread this week, so it's on the verge of going stale. "There should be more Rorys and less Bowerys."

"He *is* pretty abysmal. Did you read the syllabus?"

"No," I mumble, because she knows I didn't read the syllabus.

"There's basically nothing on the Nineteenth Amendment or the Civil Rights Movement."

For a second, I just blink at her, holding my sandwich in front of my mouth like I'm in suspended animation. "Am I supposed to know what the Nineteenth Amendment is?"

"Yes." She rolls her eyes. "It gave you the right to vote."

"I'm seventeen," I say to hide my embarrassment. "I don't have the right to vote."

She rolls her eyes again, then picks up a French fry and throws it across the table at me.

"Okay, okay," I say, crumbling the fallen fry up with my trash from lunch. "Be mad at me if you want, but don't take it out on the food."

She laughs and I laugh, and people are starting to wonder what we're giggling about. But then we settle into one of those silences again, just like we did in the bathroom during the dance. I start to sweep nonexistent crumbs off the table just to have something to do with my hands. I need to have somewhere else to put my eyes for a second.

The moment passes after a few tense seconds, and Rory heaves a deep sigh. She does this when she's about to change the subject. That deep sigh is her reset button.

"Hopefully Mr. Bowery's not all bad. We're going to need recommendation letters for college soon. I bet I could get him to write me one." Rory raises an eyebrow thoughtfully. "You know, eventually. After I've won him over."

This is the eternal dichotomy between us. Rory's aimed for straight As since preschool. She sees school as a vehicle to her future soccer career, a goal she decided on recently. Before that, she just wanted to be the best. I do the bare minimum to pass with something above a C, and I don't stress over it. Actually, now that I think about it, I should probably care more.

"I need all the help I can get if I'm getting into Chapel Hill," she murmurs under her breath. She doesn't like to let people see this side of her—the insecurity she pretends she doesn't feel. The UNC-Chapel Hill women's soccer team is like the most successful college team ever. Everything she does is with that light blue jersey in mind.

Me, on the other hand, I haven't thought about recommendation letters, or majors, or touring schools. I haven't even fully decided if I want to go to college. Charlotte has a pretty great culinary school, and cooking is the only thing I can imagine myself doing for the next four years, or the next forty. It's hard to think that far ahead, though.

I know that Rory can be found dribbling a soccer ball in her driveway before the sun comes up and long after it goes down. She's so determined to reach the successful kind of life she's aiming for. I'm just determined to survive.

"Ivy? You in?" Rory asks. She has to nudge my elbow off the table to get my attention. First of all, ouch. Second, I don't even know what we're talking about.

"Sorry. What?" It's blatantly obvious that I haven't been paying attention. But that isn't unusual—it's as commonplace as me getting lost in a book, or in a pot on the stove.

"I'm going hiking on Saturday. Want to come with?" Rory asks, explaining what I have apparently missed. "I'm stressed already. I need to see a mountain or something." She closes her planner and actually starts eating, even though there are mere minutes left in our lunch period.

I fumble for an excuse. I wish she hadn't asked. *She doesn't know*, I tell myself. *She wouldn't ask stuff like this if she knew.* I try to imagine it, going on a hike with her. As competitive as she is, it would become a race. Definitely not a leisurely walk where I can make my own pace. Definitely not something I could just stop doing when my battery inevitably runs out. I'd push myself too far trying to keep up, and I wouldn't be able to move for days. I'd miss classes and fall behind.

There's no way to justify any of that, even if I *did* want to spend hours walking around in southern humidity.

"So...?" Rory pokes at my arm. I know she wants me to go—if she didn't, she wouldn't have asked. Shame creeps into the recesses of my skull, hiding behind my brain.

"Hiking sounds...fun. When?" I hope my voice is convincing enough. I hear the weird inflection.

"Saturday afternoon," Rory replies. Her eyes are hopeful. I swallow a golf-ball-sized clump of guilt.

"Actually. I...uh...I have to take Ethan to baseball practice Saturday." That isn't a lie, exactly. Ethan *does* have baseball practice Saturday...but Mom is taking him.

"Oh! Well. Maybe next time." Rory smiles, although I can see she's disappointed.

"Yeah, sure. Next time."

After the lunch bell rings, I walk toward my next class with dragging feet. My fingers are starting to ache. I sit down in the chem lab with a huff of exhausted breath.

I'm going to have to keep lying to her. Unless I want to tell her the truth about my illness, there's always going to be this barrier between us. But I can't tell her. Not after what happened last time I tried with somebody.

It might be a new year, and everything might feel different, but nothing is ever going to *really* change.

Actually, maybe that's not true. There is someone who I wouldn't have to lie to. There is someone who wouldn't ask me to go hiking, because he knows I can't.

Grant.

I wouldn't have to lie to him.

CHAPTER TEN

—— • ——

TUES, AUG 25, 6:23 P.M.

> Dad: How long was I supposed to leave the casserole in the oven, again?

> Ivy: 30 minutes at 350.

> Dad: So, let's say if I, theoretically, heated the oven to 450 how long would I leave it in?

> Ivy: Oh my God.

> Dad: 🔥

"So who went back to school yesterday? How was it?" Lilah isn't as sunshine-bright as she was last time. Even her clothes are more subdued.

I'm not sure how I got here, honestly. At some point after school yesterday, I made an executive decision to come back to the gym for support group. Caroline just knew, somehow. She showed up in my doorway an hour ago asking if I was ready. Physically, I was. Emotionally, I can't be sure.

There's a beat of silence that flows through the circle.

"Actually, I'm going to answer my own question." Lilah sits up straighter, speaks louder. I've always admired people who speak to strangers with ease, and Lilah is definitely one of those people. She seems so open, so free. "I graduated high school early, so last year was my freshman year in college."

Lilah leans back, and Parker rests his arm on the back of her chair.

"You're supposed to live in the dorms as a freshman, but everyone thought I was too young and too sick, so I got an exemption. I decided to move into a dorm this year. It felt like a good way to try being independent—like a trial separation from home."

Lilah sighs, and on either side of her, Parker and Avery tense. I get the sense that those three are almost a core group of their own. They seem connected on a different level.

"It's not going well," Lilah finally says. Her face wrinkles up as if the words pain her to say. "I mean, it's not *bad*. It's just... *hard*."

"Hard how?" Avery asks.

"I don't know how to explain it. My roommate is nice and all, but we've never talked about anything that matters. How am I supposed to tell her I might wake up one morning with blood all over my sheets? Or that I always have to keep my heating pad plugged in by my bed? All the doctor's appointments. The pharmacy of pills I had to bring with me from home. I don't know how to put that on someone else."

There's a shroud of silence over the room, but everyone is nodding and digesting Lilah's words. I take a deep breath. I don't *talk* about it, but I *think* about this kind of thing all the time, how a roommate would end up hearing a speech. A speech about what I can't do. About everything I have to do just to function.

The immunosuppressants. The side effects. The creaking stiffness I can't control. Lower life expectancy. Higher risk for cancer and heart disease. Increasing decay and decreasing mobility. I don't know how to put that on someone else, either.

"I'm not asking for a solution." Lilah speaks again, not looking at anyone in particular. "I don't think there is one, besides just telling her. I just wish it wasn't so hard to explain."

Silence reigns again, but it isn't uncomfortable. It's the silence of understanding, the quiet that means we all know what she's going through, and that there's no easy way around it.

"Okay, Grant. I know you're dying to talk." Lilah's bright smile is back, her white teeth showing in Grant's direction.

I take a shaky, ragged breath. My fingers tense around one another where they're sitting intertwined in my lap. I've been actively trying to ignore his presence in the room, because I'm not ready to acknowledge it yet. He sits there directly across from me, and I'm pretending he's somewhere else. Somewhere away from me. It's like I feel it every time he moves. As if I can hear it every time his body shifts.

I don't want him to think I hate him. I just can't find the right compartment in my mind to put him in. That's not his fault.

The group's attention moves to him. Now he's unignorable. I look up. If my entire existence is going to be attuned toward him, I might as well look.

Grant has this windswept brown hair curling over his ears. I noticed it before, but now I consider the color. It's ash brown with golden streaks, and suddenly I know it so well I could probably pick out which box of drugstore hair dye is the closest shade to his. It looks so perfectly messy.

His features are angular, defined, with thick dark eyebrows and amber eyes that brighten with the attention on him. He glances at me, his smile warm—and just far enough beyond *friendly* that it makes my stomach flip.

I like it. It's kind of uncomfortable, actually, how effective that smile is.

He is definitely a *handsome young man*, a term my mom uses when she tries to set me up with the sons of her friends. But more than that, he's *cute*—unbearably so. He's class-clown cute, wouldn't-hurt-a-fly cute, is-probably-nice-to-servers-at-restaurants cute. He's cute enough he'll probably be my textbook definition of cute for years to come. He hasn't even said a word yet, and I'm already charmed.

"School sucks," he says.

Everyone laughs. It feels like he's flirting with both the entire room and only me.

He doesn't wait for anyone else's response before he continues. The gym is his stage, and this is the opening monologue of his one-man show. "It's so much of the same. Same people, same place. Same locker, same classes. Junior year feels like being last in a race. You know you aren't going to win, so you're just looking for the last-lap flag to fly. And it's taking too damn long."

Several people around me chuckle. I look around. Everyone is enraptured by him. At least it's not just me. Grant is so obviously convivial that it practically hurts to look at him. The indisputably social energy he exudes is almost too much for my delicate sensibilities.

"And everyone's healthy. They're running down the halls or doing backflips in the grass. It's annoying to be around. This is why I have sick friends, because healthy people are annoying."

More people laugh. I think I might, too, but then his face morphs into something serious. His eyebrows turn down, and he crosses his arms over his faded Nirvana shirt.

"I don't know," he says, shrugging. "Going from being around only people who understand for months, and then going back to normal people—whatever normal people are—just feels..."

"Like you're pretending to be healthy."

I don't know where that came from. I thought it, and then it escaped out of my mouth without permission. I clap a hand over my lips so I don't make the mistake of speaking again.

"Yeah. Exactly like that." He looks at me, and a current of something passes between us. I wonder if anyone else sees it, this invisible flash of something unidentifiable.

Even after someone else starts to speak, I can still feel it. It's this weird pull.

The girl two chairs down from me, Stella, talks about her first day. Caroline chimes in a time or two. I don't absorb much. I'm too preoccupied with staring at a point on the wall just east of Grant. I'm so busy doing it that I don't realize the whole hour is up until Caroline stands beside me. I'm supposed to do that, too, I guess. Caroline hugs several people, and then she asks me if I'm ready to go. I nod, but I'm not comfortable hugging anyone. I've only met them twice.

As I rise, I can feel Grant looking at me. It's this warm glow that settles around me and makes my insides gooey and my nerve endings sparkle.

We leave, exiting our emotional oasis in the gym for the world. For some reason, I don't want to cross that line: I don't want to step back into the world where we all have to go to school tomorrow and deal with our annoyingly healthy friends.

The sun has just started to set, and it blares against my eyes. At the last second, I turn and look over my shoulder.

Grant's eyes are right there, looking at the same setting sun. He smiles at me. It's milder and shyer than before, yet somehow more potent than anything I've ever felt.

My smile back doesn't feel like enough. I can't possibly give something so little in return for that heart-stopping twitch of his lips.

Caroline opens the gym's front door. I hear the bell chime. It breaks the spell in an instant, and the harsh humidity flowing in hits me right at the base of my neck. Grant is still looking at me, never breaking eye contact.

I raise one hand, waving my fingers just enough for them to start to creak.

I want to bottle this one sun-kissed moment, so I can keep it forever.

CHAPTER ELEVEN

———— • ————

SAT, AUG 29, 8:39 A.M.

Rory: I didn't go all the way to the mountains, but we're at the lake.

Rory: u missed a great view!

Ivy: next time!

An open kitchen window. A steaming mug of black coffee. Herbs, spices, fresh produce. Three tiny birds fighting for space on my mother's feeder in the front yard, their high-pitched chirps all I can hear. There are few things I love more than Saturday brunches.

I wrap my tense fingers around my mug, letting the heat warm them over. I expected soreness today, a few days before the medication cycle starts again. Even holding the coffee cup is intensely painful, so when I pick up the knife again, it's definitely not better.

I gently put it down and shake the tightening numbness out of my hands. Looking at my cutting board, I can see the decline in the quality of my juliennes. I started with the red bell peppers, fresh-handed, but by the time I got to the potatoes, my dices came out uneven and jagged. I have to whisk the egg mixture next, but first, I need a longer break.

I cup my mug again, humming a wordless melody I'm making up as I go. Everyone else is still asleep, so I'm trying to be quiet. Both my parents need their sleep, my mom because she's perpetually exhausted, and my dad because he works weird night-shift hours at a manufacturing plant, which is it's own kind of constantly exhausting.

The world moves all around me, and I operate in my domain. It's just a hundred square feet of my own territory.

After I crack my knuckles loudly enough to scare off one of the birds, I go back to my frittata. I whisk with all the vigor my hands have left, breaking yolks and stirring in cream until it starts to foam. This is one of Grandma's recipes, one of the few that didn't require modification.

I'm so focused on the task at hand, I don't hear the dragging footsteps until my mom is all but in my face.

"Oh God. Mom." I let go of my whisk and set my mixing bowl down on the counter. I run my eyes over my mother's face. The fatigued eyes and dark circles are normal. The raised rash covering her cheeks in the shape of butterfly wings is not. It's always been her most visible symptom, a sure sign that she's done too much of this or not enough of that. Too much inflammation, not enough medication. Too much sun, not enough rest. More than anything, it's lupus's hallmark symptom. It's the surest sign of internal destruction.

"I know, I know," Mom says, raising her palms in surrender. "I must have been outside too long yesterday."

"Why were you outside?" I ask. She works in an office for a reason, an office deep in the dark recesses of a school. She even keeps the overhead lights off because of her photosensitivity.

"A couple of the teachers went home sick. They needed me to cover recess duty."

I sigh. It's always like this, Mom sacrificing her health for the greater good and paying the price later. I don't blame her, though. She didn't have much of a choice.

"Do you need any help?" Mom asks, poaching a handful of diced red peppers.

"No, I'm good." I smile, and Mom turns to leave the kitchen. "Hey, wait. Why don't you let Caroline and me take Ethan to practice? You don't need to be out in the sun."

"I can't ask you to do that," Mom says.

"You didn't. I was going to go with you anyway, just to get out of here for a while." That's not the whole truth, but she doesn't need to know that. I was going to go because I told Rory that's what I'd be doing today—because I couldn't tell her that hiking would basically physically kill me.

"What about Caroline, though?"

"They have those SunDrop slushies she likes. She'll be fine."

<hr />

Ethan sits in the back seat of Caroline's car; his baseball bag rests diagonally across his chest like a second seat belt. We tried to make him put it in the trunk, but he wouldn't let go of it long enough.

"I was hoping I wouldn't be with the kids I was with last year," he says. I look back at him in the rearview mirror. He's fiddling with the zipper on his bag.

"Why?" Caroline asks. "What's wrong with them?"

"Nothing." Ethan shakes his head. "We've just been on the same team since we were in T-ball. Jace's always going to have a weak arm, and Dallas is never going to be able to hit. I just want to play with new people, you know?"

I don't know. I don't fully understand the concept of introducing yourself to new people when you have perfectly fine, well-understood people all around you.

Caroline parks the car, and Ethan is out the door before I even get my seat belt unbuckled. Caroline chases after him like a good older sister, but I lag behind. I watch Ethan hang a left and run through the open gate at the fence, kicking up dusty gravel. Caroline sighs, turns, and gestures me toward a seat on the lower level of the bleachers.

When I finally sit down next to her, she has this terrifying, glee-filled expression of deviousness on her face.

"What?" I ask nervously.

Caroline crosses her arms and turns her head back to the field in front of us.

When I do the same, I notice someone waving in my direction. Not someone. *Grant.*

"Oh my God," I whisper under my breath, involuntarily. At least I think it's under my breath. Caroline chuckles.

"This just got a lot more interesting," she says, nudging my shoulder.

Now that I've noticed him, I can't stop. I can't remember if I waved back, but he's already gone back to talking to the coach, so if I haven't, I've missed my chance. Grant's bright white Converse high-tops seem out of place on the field, like they're just asking to get dirty. He and the coach are wearing matching baseball shirts, white with red sleeves. SLUGGERS, they read across the front, in that typical, loopy baseball font.

He's the one who taught Ethan how to slide. He's the one who said all the bad words. He's the reason Ethan came home the other day with the dirty face.

Grant's the bad influence.

They start the practice in a huddle, then the boys run laps. I can't help but watch Grant: the way he stands, the way he laughs at something the coach just said.

I keep watching his hands...his fingers, his forearms, his wrists. I know that the joints there are decaying just like mine. He pushes himself away from the fence, and his left knee doesn't cooperate when he puts weight on it. He winces, and I do, too. I know that exact pain, that exact situation.

As if he can feel the tune my consciousness is humming, Grant looks up at me from across the field. He smiles, a smile so wide I can see all his sparkling molars. All I can do is smile back.

It's different to see him like this, out in the real world, where we mix in with healthy people and try not to stick out too much.

Grant doesn't stick out at all, not in that way. He's clearly acquired a band of supporters in the team. Each kid looks at him with awe, like he's a special kind of fascinating. I know the feeling. (Now I'm emotionally relating to pre-teen boys. Fantastic.)

They're all in a circle, throwing in a random pattern. A boy two down from Ethan throws in Grant's direction, and he catches it with ease. He throws it back to a different kid in the circle. His arm is a perfect arc. The motion was so natural and familiar, as if he'd been born to throw. At that moment, I realize something. Grant is even more interesting out of context—out of our group.

After an hour, practice ends the way it started, with a huddle, and Ethan starts running back in our direction. Caroline stands and sucks the last icy bit of slushie through her straw. She checks the time on her phone and spins her keys around her pointer finger. "If we head home now, we can catch Dad before he leaves."

I stand, too, stretching out my back and shifting just enough to get my hips to pop. My SI joints shift back into place, and I start to move. I thread my fingers through the links in the fence as I go. Ethan bursts through the gate so fast he nearly knocks me over, and a second later, Caroline bumps my shoulder again. Apparently, they both want me to end up face-first in the dirt.

"Look," she whispers. "Something cute this way comes."

My stomach twists. I'm not ready for whatever this is, and part of me hopes he'll just keep walking. But he doesn't. He stops just short of us on the other side of the fence, and the fingers

I have wrapped around the wire flex as if they have a mind of their own.

"I didn't know there were more of you," Grant says, pointing to Ethan at Caroline's side, who is swinging his baseball bag around.

"Yeah, well. We don't talk about the healthy one." Caroline shoves at Ethan's shoulders.

I laugh and let my head fall forward against the fence. That's probably an incredibly inappropriate thing to say, but I don't think Grant minds.

"Come on, I wanna see Dad before he leaves," Ethan whines, already taking backward steps toward Caroline's car. Caroline follows him, and, alone, I'm stuck not knowing what to say. I drop my hands to my sides.

Grant looks like he doesn't know what to do, either. He just stands there, shifting his weight from foot to foot like he doesn't know which leg will hold him up.

"I guess I'll see you Tuesday," I say, taking a step away from the fence. I actually convince myself to look him in the eye.

It was worth the convincing.

"Yeah. Tuesday." He looks me up and down, and suddenly, I wish I'd made more effort. My oversized T-shirt and cropped yoga pants aren't ideal; if I'd known I'd end up this close to him, I'd have worn something that actually matched.

I take two steps away, turning on the heels of my worn Birkenstocks.

"Hey, Ivy?" he calls. He actually sounds nervous, which isn't doing anything to ease my *own* overactive nervous system.

"Yeah?" I turn back around, take a step forward. There's that pull again, completely invisible, and completely nonsensical.

"Let me give you my number," he says, scratching the back of his neck. "In case there's a baseball emergency, or whatever."

Something inside of me glows. Something else, inside my stomach, squeezes.

"Right." I hand over my phone, and my fingers just barely brush against his as he does the same. I don't know what I expect, but his fingers are too warm and just the right amount of rough.

I type my number into the screen, but I actually struggle to remember how to spell my last name. Harding. Like the president who died in office. H-A-R-D-I-N-G. His last name is my last name. It's not hard, but somehow it is.

He passes my phone back and I can still feel the heat of his hands on the back. There he is on the screen. Grant Deluca. I don't think I even knew his last name. I wave again, because I can't make my brain and mouth communicate long enough to form words. Thank God my feet, at least, decide to move.

By the time I get to the car, Ethan's already taken the front seat.

"So . . . what was that about?" Caroline asks, devious grin in place yet again.

"Nothing. It was nothing." I look out the window to avoid meeting her eyes in the rearview mirror. The engine revs to life and the field disappears.

"Ivy?" Ethan asks, turning in his seat to face me. That's not safe. I want to turn his shoulders back around.

"What?" I reply, sure he's going to ask me to make something weird for dinner.

"I know Grant gave you his phone number. Can I have it?"

"No. Absolutely not," Caroline says, taking one hand off the wheel to turn Ethan back around. Thank God. "Why do you want his number anyway?"

"I don't know." Ethan shrugs. "He's just so cool."

"You can't have his number," I say rationally. "It's for emergencies only."

Caroline scoffs.

CHAPTER TWELVE

———— • ————

TUES, SEP 1, 4:59 P.M.

Rory: what kind of potatoes do you use to make your mashed potatoes again?

Rory: my mom wants to know.

Ivy: red. Hold on, I'll send her the recipe

Rory: wait, there are red potatoes?

Ivy: you've never seen a red potato

Rory: yeah but I thought it was rotten

Ivy: you...what

I collapse onto my bed, sprawling my limbs out as far as they'll go, then curling them all back in as soon as they start to hurt. I'm convinced I've never been this tired. I might even be persuaded to say I've never hurt this badly.

There's no way it's only Tuesday. Judging by the exhaustion weighing me down, it's got to be Thursday, at least. That's how the medication cycle works—it makes the good days and the bad days predictable. Now, the days almost run together, because they all feel bad.

Nothing has ever been as heavy as the weight that's settled across my chest. I place a hand right below my collarbones, right across the top part of my rib cage. The joints there are palpable, so inflamed I can actually feel them. That explains why I've been struggling to breathe through the tightness that's squeezing the life out of my lungs.

There's a knock on my slightly open door, and Caroline sticks her upper body through. I envy the way she moves, with the elegance and grace of someone who doesn't have the connective tissue of the Tin Man.

"I was going to ask if you're coming to group with me, but you look *bad*." She walks closer and sits on the corner of my bed, none too gently. "I mean, no offense," she adds at the last second.

"None taken." I roll over. I pull my comforter tighter around me. Strands of my hair fall over my eyes, and I make no effort to brush them away.

"Are you sure it's just a rough day?" Caroline asks. That's what I told her in the car on the way home from school, when I hadn't said more than two words. *Just a rough day*. It's a classic chronic illness excuse for naps, canceled plans, and other general disappointments.

This doesn't feel like that, though. It feels like something more. It's like a rough day with the volume turned up.

"I don't know," I say, squirming around, trying to get comfortable. One way I turn, my hands and wrists feel better, but my ankles hurt worse. The next, my hips and knees are okay, but my elbows and shoulders aren't.

"Is Mom home yet?" I ask. Mom will know what to do. She'll know if this is a flare or something else to worry about. She'll tell me exactly how to make it easier.

"She's staying late to meet with some parents about something." Caroline shakes her head. She stands up. "I gotta go. I'll tell everyone you said hi."

I smile at her retreating back. I rearrange myself again, and then give up. If my mom isn't home, then no one is using her electric blanket. I practically crawl to the living room, every joint in my body locked in a tense ache.

My dad is in his recliner, flipping between channels. I claim the couch, flopping down and sinking in. The overstuffed fake leather is cool against my skin, and somehow the most comfortable sensation ever. If anything happens to this couch, I'm going to be devastated. I curl myself into a ball again, draping the wired blanket over me and turning it on high. My head rests on the back of the couch near my pulled-up knees.

"You okay, Iggy?" Dad asks, swiveling around in his chair to face me. I smile at the nickname. Apparently, when I was a kid, they tried to get me to say my full name, but Ivy Grace came out Iggy. He's never called me anything else.

"I don't know," I say, again. There's not anything else to say, really.

"Your cheeks are red." His brows knit together in concern.

"Flare-up fever," I reply. I can feel it now. The chills, the burning cheeks. I run my fingertips over my legs, knees, ankles, feet. They're all blazing hot.

Dad stands up and tosses the remote onto the arm of the couch. I don't want to come out of my blanket cocoon to retrieve it.

"You find something to watch. I'll go order pizza."

Reluctantly, I wiggle one finger out from under my blanket and flip until I hit the Food Channel. They're showing old *Iron Chef* battles. I live for this, the best chefs in the world battling it out under ridiculous circumstances. It's Michael Symon versus Cat Cora, because that's just my luck. Give me a break. (The secret ingredient is chocolate, which is also rude, because I don't have any and can't try their recipes until I go shopping.)

I don't like episodes like this, except I really do. Normally, they have good chefs challenge Iron Chefs, and I always want the Iron Chef to win. Now, right in front of me, are my two favorite Iron Chefs competing against each other. I don't know *who* I want to win.

Here's the thing: I want to be Cat Cora. She's the first female Iron Chef, and the first woman to be inducted into the American Academy of Chefs Culinary Hall of Fame. She's also a mother of six boys, which sounds a lot harder than anything she's ever done in the culinary world. Just the sight of her pristine, light-blue chef's coat is enough to make me feel better. She runs around the kitchen like an Olympic sprinter. Alton Brown can barely keep up his commentary, and he speaks as quickly as an overexcited kid. Cat's making duck confit because she's a genius.

On the other hand, though, is Michael Symon. He's such a joy. No one has more fun in the kitchen than him. He's smiley and chaotic and messy. The real kicker is, he has rheumatoid arthritis! He's living my dream, *with* my disease. There's no way I can't love him.

I make an executive decision to be Switzerland. I will not root for anyone. I will judge them objectively, as if they aren't my literal role models.

"Why do you watch these episodes you've seen a hundred times?" Dad asks, stepping back into the room and falling into his recliner.

"To learn," I say, even though I haven't seen this episode specifically. I'm always transfixed watching these. Every knife cut and every sizzling sauté pan matters. It makes a difference, and I absorb it all.

Inside my blanket burrito, my phone buzzes. Rather than subject my hands to open air, I duck my head under the blanket. The screen lights up, and so do I.

Am I allowed to text you if it isn't a baseball emergency?

I can't help but smile. Under the cover of my electric fort, it almost feels like we're having an actual, private conversation. I've almost texted him at least ten times since I decided not to go to group tonight.

But now I have to text him *for real.* I panic for a few seconds, my thumbs resting just above the screen, awaiting orders from my currently malfunctioning brain.

Yes, I type.

I should say something else—something cute, or flirty, or funny. I should give him something more than a one-word answer. At least I used the right word, though. I could've said no.

Wait, I start typing again. Shouldn't you be in support group?

Yeah, but Caroline came in without you and I wanted to know why.

I smile again. The air in my blanket enclosure is turning stale, so I stick my head out. I can feel staticky hair sticking to my face. Cat Cora stuffs white chocolate ice-cream base into a piping bag and pours it into a bowl of liquid nitrogen.

Why didn't you ask her?

It's a legitimate question. By all accounts, Caroline is easier to talk to than I am. She's better at it, and she actually enjoys the process of human interaction. She doesn't stammer or panic or forget words. If he were anyone else, I'd actually want him to talk to Caroline instead. He's not anyone else, though. He's Grant.

Because she's all the way over there.

He sends a sneaky picture of Caroline from where he sits, directly across from her. She was talking animatedly with her hands on either side of her face. Always the conversational exhibitionist, my sister. It's eerie to see my own seat empty, like maybe no one would notice if I just stopped coming once and for all.

I shoot back: And I'm all the way across town.

My phone is silent for a few solid minutes, the rhythm of our conversation interrupted. Michael and Cat are trash-talking across their stations, her southern accent versus his Cleveland drawl.

No you're right here.

Attached is the same picture of Caroline, with a poorly drawn stick figure in the chair beside her. I suppose the reddish orange squiggles of hair are what make it me.

If I stopped coming to group once and for all, Grant would notice.

The bow in my hair is a nice touch.

A half second later, another chime.

Seriously, though. You okay?

That he just assumed something is wrong shocks me. I thought he'd ask where I am, or what I'm doing. I thought he'd ask the same things other people would if I kinda-sorta stood them up. I don't know how to answer. I don't know how to explain it. If he were one of my classmates, I'd lie through my teeth. I'd say I have too much homework to do, or that I have to help Ethan with his. I'd say I'm grounded, even though I've never been grounded in my life. But I don't feel like I can lie to Grant. He'd know. He already senses something is off. I might as well just tell him the truth.

I feel gross. Maybe it's an arthritis emergency.

That's much more likely than a baseball emergency.

Honesty is kind of refreshing. It's unbelievably freeing to just be able to admit that I feel like human garbage, that my body is crumbling.

Oh. Been there.

That he's not trying to make it better, or apologize, solidifies that he's undeniably different from anyone that I've ever met. He can commiserate, and empathize—and up until this very moment, I didn't know how much that's worth.

Somewhere in my chest, I feel the realization that Grant just might be worth his weight in gold.

Shit. Ave and Li caught me. Talk later.

I giggle through a bite of my pizza. It's not Cat Cora's duck confit, or her ice cream with liquid shortbread, but it's greasy and cheesy and comforting just the same. Even though I know Caroline isn't home, pizza still makes me feel guilty. It's the only gluten we allow in the house, and only when Caroline isn't around.

Keys jangle in the door, and Mom steps in. Her bags drop to the floor, and she nearly follows.

"The girls gone?" she asks Dad from across the room.

"Only one of them," I say, popping my head up.

She leans down over the back of the couch and kisses my forehead. She stands back up again, but bends down to press her hands to my reddened cheeks.

"You're warm," she says. She walks around the couch and waves a hand at the legs I have sprawled out over the whole thing. "Move over."

She slumps down, taking over the cushions I vacated. She leans her head on my shoulder.

"How was your day?" Dad asks. On the screen in front of us, judges deliberate as to which plate is best.

"It was fine. Just long. I had some parents who couldn't meet with me during the day, so I had to schedule after hours. There's always growing pains at the beginning of the new year, you know that."

Mom turns her head on my shoulder to look at me. "Why didn't you go with your sister?" She's not judging, I can tell. She just seems curious, and a little concerned. I've always hated that look, like I'm someone who needs to be taken care of. I am, right now, but I still don't like it. I'd rather it be the other way around.

"I just don't feel good." It's the most accurate description. Nothing feels good. There's a flu-like ache that has settled into my bones, and the crushing fatigue makes everything feel heavy, like I'm walking through neck-deep snow.

"I can tell," Mom replies. She looks me up and down. "Does anything hurt more than anything else?"

This is our usual protocol for things like this. Lupus and RA aren't too different—joint pain and fatigue are an unfortunate part of both. So, this is how we operate. If anything hurts more than anything else, we try to fix it, like plugging the biggest leak in a sinking boat.

"No, not really." I survey my body, two bilateral joints at a time. Shoulders, barely achy. Elbows, hot but manageable. Wrists, hotter, less manageable. Fingers, might be withering away, I can't be sure. Ribs, possibly burning. Hips, nearly dysfunctional, as usual. Knees, tight. Ankles, stiff. Feet, swollen beyond belief. So yeah. Something hurts worse than everything else.

"Maybe my ribs," I concede. I run a hand back and forth up the center of my chest, putting as much pressure on the palm of my hand as I can. Pressure makes it easier to breathe.

"That worries me," Mom says, holding her head up to look me in the eye. I hate this, being worried over. It's more uncomfortable than the aching tightness in my ribs.

"We might need to talk about making the jump." Mom runs her hands over the crown of my head. She pushes an errant strand of auburn hair behind my ear. "You're almost eighteen, anyway. And I don't think you're being treated aggressively enough."

I shudder. I don't want to be treated more aggressively. The chemo drug I've been on for a year is plenty aggressive for my tastes. I don't want to mess up my medication cycle. I don't want to admit it's not working.

More than that, though, I don't want to make *the jump*. I don't even want to talk about it. Switching to a new medication, with new side effects, probably administered with an adult dosage... well, it means everything gets more serious, more real.

And it's related to my birthday. I hate my birthday. I don't even want to think about it. I don't even want to acknowledge the milestone it is.

"I think it's just a flare," I insist. It's nothing for anyone to be concerned about. It'll just be a few days of particularly bad pain and the heaviness of debilitating fatigue. It has to be. I'll feel better soon. This definitely, 100 percent isn't the progression I've been afraid of since I was diagnosed.

"It's nothing," I reiterate, burrowing deeper into my warm blanket. *It's nothing*, I think again.

It has to be nothing.

On the screen in front of us, the music rises dramatically as the end of the episode approaches. I'm not guessing who's going to win. I love them equally, like they're my children. I'm not even comparing their dishes. The lights lower, and the Chairman's voice gets more and more intense.

Michael Symon wins.

CHAPTER THIRTEEN

— • —

FRI, SEP 4, 11:11 A.M.

Grant: What's your favorite color?

Ivy: Blue spirulina.

Grant: Idk what that is, but okay.

Ivy: It's the prettiest blue.

"Why do you keep smiling at your phone?" Rory asks. She's not, like, mean about it, but her tone conveys that the question demands an answer.

"Oh, it's nothing. Just reading."

I don't smile when I read, at least I don't think so. Hopefully Rory doesn't know that.

"You've been all weird the past few days. Is something going on?" Her tone isn't unkind, but her questions are getting more and more suspicious.

"Nothing's going on, really."

I hope my face doesn't betray that I'm completely and totally lying. I don't remember ever making a conscious decision to lie; it just happened. There's a reason I'm smiling at my phone, of course, but I don't know if she's safe to share it with.

I *want* to, on the one hand. I want to tell her I've been texting Grant all day, and all of yesterday, and that he's sweet and funny and he swears too much. I want to tell her his favorite color is the blue in the Atlanta Braves logo and that his favorite class is English, because it's the one he can argue with people in.

I want to talk about the way he looks, and the way he looks at me, and how I met him when I never expected to. I want to talk about him relentlessly.

Just...not with Rory. That would mean admitting everything. I can't explain Grant without explaining where I met him and how we're the same.

So I deflect—I ask about her. It's the easiest way to get the topic of conversation off of me.

"How's soccer going?" I can tell that's what she wants to talk about, anyway. She loves soccer as much as anyone loves anything.

"I'm still trying to push Coach to let me start, but she always gives those spots to the seniors! Ugh. I guess I'll just have to wait another year."

"Right," I mumble in response, stabbing a fork into my left-over chicken. I didn't even bother heating it up. It wasn't worth waiting in line for the microwave. I marinated it for hours in my homemade marinade; it's even good cold.

"At least we're finally supposed to get new uniforms. We've literally had the same ones for twenty years. *Twenty. Years.* My mom played soccer here, and she probably wore the same shirt I did."

"Didn't they promise you new uniforms last year?" I ask,

because I think I remember having this conversation before. She's probably said these exact words to me, during another lunch period just like this.

"Yeah, but there was budget stuff. I've decided: we're getting new uniforms this year if I have to sew them myself."

I look up at her. I don't think I've done that since I came back to school, really looked at her. She's never sounded this formidable. She's never had this determined look in her eye. When I met her, she was timid, quiet, and gentle. We'd sit in class together and talk about homework. We did every group project together. And when we met up outside of school, we never did anything too high octane. She likes to overprepare for tests the night before, and the flashcard method she taught me has probably saved my grades. If it wasn't a pre-test day, we'd go shopping, because she loves to try on clothes she'd never actually wear, and I love to look at stuff I'll never buy. Or sometimes I'd go to her soccer games, so it wasn't just her mom there cheering her on.

Now, she has the new haircut. The sharp, choppy bob that ends right at her chin, that makes her look older and smarter and more daring. I bet she can't even put it up for soccer practice. And she got rid of her glasses, too. Without them, her dark eyes are more expressive.

I don't know how it's taken me so long to realize it. Rory came back to school this fall a completely different person.

It's all my fault. The distance. The way I don't recognize the person I still thought was my best friend. She's texted; I've blown her off. She's reached out; I've chickened out. I've accidentally distanced my way out of the only friendship I've ever had in the first place. Did the illness take it from me, or did I do it all myself?

I noticed that she looked different, of course. I'm not so clueless that I missed a foot of chopped-off hair or absent glasses or a rainbow of new clothes. I just didn't think they meant anything. I thought it was just a haircut. I thought they were just clothes.

"Would you really do that?" I ask. "Make new uniforms yourself?"

She nods immediately, like a reflex. "If I had to, yeah."

We sit in silence for a moment, because I don't think I know how to talk to this new Rory. I suddenly feel like I'm sharing a lunch table with a stranger.

My phone buzzes in my back pocket, but I don't move. I think Rory hears it over the volume of the lunchroom, somehow, because her eyes shift. They go soft, almost sad. It's an expression that would've looked right at home on the old Rory. On this new, sharp Rory, it looks out of place.

My phone vibrates again, and I take it out and hold it in my palm, because I don't know what to do.

How's school?

It's Grant. Of course it's Grant. Telling her feels weird . . . and not telling her feels weird, too. I flip my phone over.

"You know, if something is going on with you, you can tell me. Right?" Rory says, her brows wrinkling up.

"Yeah," I say with what I hope is a smile. "I know."

I put my phone away without another word.

CHAPTER FOURTEEN

·

SAT, SEP 5, 6:46 A.M.

Caroline: I might've told mom about Grant. Oops.

Ivy: This is why I can't have nice things.

It's possible I used too much vanilla, I think as I sniff the air. It's heavily scented, like cheap shampoo. But the waffle batter is all mixed. (I used a mix because I'm low on energy, but it's my own homemade mix, because there was a point I wasn't so low on energy.) The kitchen is, of course, an incredible mess. There are eggshells on the countertop, and the milk is open beside the stove. I almost forget to spray the waffle maker before I pour in the first of the batter. Another disaster narrowly avoided.

As the waffle maker turns liquid to solid, the vanilla scent is replaced by the aroma of buttery carbs. I check on the bacon I have on multiple cookie sheets in the oven. It's the only way I make bacon anymore, because there's no popping grease and leftover fat. Besides, Ethan eats his body weight in bacon nearly every weekend—if I had to fry it one piece at a time, I'd never get anything else done. I take one tray out of the oven early, because

Caroline likes her bacon chewy, not crispy, like the rest of us normal people.

Then I crack more eggs. I'm cracking them too fast, actually, and they're dripping all over my hands. I don't care. I whisk them until I can't anymore, then add in a splash of milk and what I deem to be enough salt and pepper.

I toss some oil into my biggest skillet and let it heat up. Check the bacon again, take one tray out. Flip one set of waffles out and start another batch. I walk so smoothly between the oven, the counter, and the stove, I feel like I'm skating. (I don't have the balance for actual skating, so this is as close as I get.) It's the same routine for a while, stir eggs as they firm up, flip waffles as they brown, move bacon out of the oven at just the right level of crispness.

I remove the last of the waffles from the waffle maker. Today's brunch is less of a production than last week's; no quiche Lorraine, no baked eggs en cocotte, nothing fancy. I don't have an abundance of energy, so I've stuck with the basics. Now the kitchen smells like a cheap diner, and I love it.

"Food's ready," I call down the hallway.

Mom walks in and pulls the maple syrup out of the cabinet. I should've done that already. Ethan slides into the room, his socks propelling him so far forward he nearly collides with the counter.

"Calm down," Mom hisses. "And hurry up. We're going to be late."

Behind her back, I roll my eyes. Mom is known for being

criminally early everywhere she goes. Punctuality is tardiness in her book. We have an hour before baseball practice starts, and it won't take more than ten minutes to get there.

Ethan grabs three waffles and floods them in syrup. A literal flood: syrup spills off his plate and onto the counter. Mom puts a dish towel into his shirt collar like a bib. It won't help.

Mom takes one waffle and eats it dry, a sign that she's nauseous. She won't admit to it, but I can tell. Any Saturday brunch where she leaves bacon untouched, she's nauseous. I make a plate for myself, then one more for Caroline, and another for Dad. I leave theirs by the microwave and take mine to the farthest end of the counter, putting the greatest distance between myself and the syrup flood that I possibly can. I'll probably still get syrup all over me, somehow.

I love Saturday brunch.

As the time to leave grows nearer, I start to sweat. I've been texting Grant all week, but I'm not sure I'm ready to *see* him again. Texting is easier. It's one-dimensional, and I don't have to figure out what to do with my hands. I don't have to worry about weird eye contact or wet palms.

If I could, I would keep texting him forever. I didn't think there was a path through time and space where I'd wake up looking forward to speaking to someone I'd just met, even if it was almost entirely digital. This thing with Grant—whatever it is—is new, and strange. There's a warm tingle of excitement in my stomach, despite my nerves.

I have to bicker with Ethan for the front seat, and we get to the field painfully early, just as I expected. I don't think anyone else is here. The parking lot is empty except for one car parked in the back. But when I open my door, I hear the unmistakable clanking of a baseball hitting the chain-link fence.

I squint my eyes against the bright sun, and I spot someone on the field, so far away he's barely visible.

I know exactly who it is. The natural grace of that pitching motion is so distinctive. He picks up another ball from the bucket beside him and throws again. The ball flies over home plate and bounces off the fence, right where a catcher's mitt would be, had there been one.

"He's so cool," Ethan whispers reverently, whizzing by where I stand.

"Is this *the boy?*" Mom asks, standing next to me as Ethan runs to join Grant on the field.

"What boy?" I ask. I don't want to believe that Mom knows what she thinks she knows.

"Don't 'what boy' me. The support-group boy. The one you've been texting all week."

I roll my eyes and resist the impulse to stomp my foot and run away. I'm never telling Caroline anything again.

"Yes, that's him."

Mom starts to walk toward the field, and I immediately follow. I'm not willing to let Mom approach him first. There's no telling what she'd say. By the time we reach the fence, Ethan stands at home plate, catching every pitch Grant throws. Mom veers off abruptly, setting up her chair and umbrella near the bleachers without saying anything to Grant, thank God. She looks perfectly comfortable, shaded and smiling. I know better, though. The sun is going to take a toll on her, sunscreen and shade or not.

I stand at the fence with my fingers through the hexagonal shapes of the wire. Grant stops throwing, and my heart starts to thud in my chest. (Combined with my inflamed rib joints, it kind of sucks.) He's wearing the same Sluggers T-shirt he had on last week, and jeans, but this time, he has a baseball cap on backward over his disheveled hair.

He says something to Ethan that I can't hear, and Ethan takes off into the outfield. Grant walks toward me, his gait effortless in a way mine will never be. He tosses a baseball from one hand to the other, his glove left behind on the pitcher's mound. It's like the baseball orbits around his gravitational pull.

"Feeling better?" he asks once he's close enough. He catches the ball one last time and relaxes his hands at his sides. Grant is almost dazzling like this, backlit by sun, eyes brightened by the dedication he clearly has for the game. He smiles just enough that I can see his vampire teeth. They're dazzling, too, because of course they are.

"A little," I admit. I was able to get out of bed easier today. That's something. I probably look pain-free. I hope so, anyway.

"Where's Caroline?"

My face falls. I don't want him to ask about Caroline. He's not looking for Caroline, though—he's looking at me, like I'm someone worth talking to.

"She's sleeping off whatever fun she had last night." I don't know much more than that (and if I did, out of loyalty to my sister, I wouldn't spill it).

He laughs, just barely, and I feel myself smile. I like that, I think, making him laugh. It makes me light and floaty inside.

Maybe I have a shot at being the axis he spins on.

A few more cars have pulled in. A group of kids and parents is headed our way. The bubble we seem to be in is about to pop.

"Are you sure you're okay?" he asks, leaning in just the slightest bit closer. I feel my sharp intake of breath in my damaged ribs. "You just look like everything hurts. I mean—not that you look bad or anything. I just meant that—"

I manage to laugh.

"Everything hurts, but I'm okay. It'll pass." I smile, and I hope it conveys that I'm telling the truth. I want it to be the truth, anyway.

The team starts to assemble behind Grant. He's going to have to step away from our quiet conversation. I should want him to. That's my MO. Talking to people in the real world is uncomfortable and anxiety-inducing and generally to be avoided, especially when that person happens to be a boy.

Grant's different, somehow. He walks backward away from me, just a few steps, then turns around. I catch the Atlanta logo on his dark blue baseball cap. I've never met anyone like him,

I realize—someone who doesn't make me so afraid. Lines are starting to blur, and he's begun to take up more space in my head than I ever decided to allow for.

I walk back to the bleachers, planting my feet under me and trying to get comfortable on the near-melting-point metal.

"I've never seen you have a conversation like that," Mom says, looking at me from behind her sunglasses.

"What do you mean? A conversation like what?" I ask.

"Where you didn't look like you'd rather be anywhere else."

CHAPTER FIFTEEN

—— • ——

TUES, SEP 8, 6:13 P.M.

Grant: you're coming to group tonight right?

Ivy: Yep. Why?

Grant: just wanted to see you.

Caroline opens the door to the gym ahead of me, and a rush of cold air and muffled music hits me right in the face. For some reason, I absolutely love it.

I've never cared about a gym in my life, but this one has a sense of safety about it because of group, like it's a place anyone can belong. We wave to the guy behind the desk. Over his head is a display of those S&F Fitness shirts. I kind of want one. One of the black ones, of course. Red isn't my color.

"Hey, Ivy. We missed you last week." Avery comes out of the women's locker room as we pass it, wearing that same S&F shirt. Even in an oversized tee, she looks so put together. I don't feel that put together in *anything* I wear.

I walk in between Avery and Caroline as they talk about their weeks. They're both several inches taller than I am, so I don't have to make an effort to stay out of the conversation—they just speak over my head. I go to sit down and nearly trip on the leg of my chair. Great, just *fall* in front of everyone. That's exactly what I'm trying to do.

I'm being watched. Grant's looking at me, but not like I'm embarrassing. He looks at me like there's nothing else in the room worth looking at. I smile at him and mindlessly tuck a strand of hair behind my ear.

More people file in; seats fill. I keep my gaze in the center of the circle, a point on the floor near Grant's shoes. I can still feel his eyes on me. It's painfully clear that he just appreciates the opportunity to look at me. I realize that even if I *had* fallen, he wouldn't judge me. No one would.

The hour passes in a blur. I melt into this sense of comfort I rarely feel anywhere but my home. I'm safe here. I don't have to hide when I shift positions to keep my joints from stiffening up. I don't have to make awkward small talk. I can talk about things that matter, or I can just listen when talking feels too hard.

The biggest bonus, though, is that there's someone sitting across from me who's a gentle kind of enchanting.

My entire life, I've sought out things like this—people, places, and things that turn the volume down on my anxiety. And yeah, okay, maybe I didn't want to be a part of this whole support group thing at first, but now it's become one of those soothing things.

All too soon, the group breaks up and the spell is broken. I can't remember a thing anyone said—I went into this vegetative zen state. I feel like I've been meditating, letting the feeling of community settle into my bones. By the time I stand up, my very cells are calmer. It's rejuvenating.

Stella walks up to say goodbye to Caroline, and I stand awkwardly next to them. It's a strategy I use a lot in my life, standing just outside conversations so I don't get dragged in. It's an effective strategy for preventing social contact.

I notice Grant getting up out of the corner of my eye. All his usual effortlessness is gone today, replaced by a certain...awkwardness. Am I the cause of this slip in his easygoing extraversion? He's walking toward me. But maybe he wants to talk to Caroline. Maybe he wants to say he likes her shirt. I don't even know what shirt she's wearing, but maybe he likes it. Maybe he wants to say that he missed her at baseball practice. That's it, I'm sure.

Then he stops in front of me. His hands are in his pockets, and he's not completely meeting my eyes. He's looking at my face, but it's like he's chosen a single freckle to focus on.

I don't know what to do with that. I *just* got used to the bold, filter-less Grant who speaks everything he thinks. I don't know how to handle whoever this...nervous person...is. I should identify with this kind of demeanor. It's been my hallmark my entire life. I don't, though. Not on him.

"You look really pretty today," he says.

I'm taken aback. I was so not expecting that. Everything in me ramps back up until it feels like my body is powered by a jet engine.

I start to respond—with what, I don't know—but he speaks again.

"That's not what I meant. I mean—I didn't intend to start out that way. Although, honestly, I wanted to say that the first time I saw you, but I didn't think anyone wanted to be hit on during support group. That seems really weird."

He stops to take a breath, and I know I need to say something. I just have absolutely no idea how to verbalize a response.

"I'm sorry. I'm being weird." Grant stops looking at me altogether.

"No, no. Don't apologize." I grab his arm, but realize that I don't really have permission to do that. My fingers tingle when I unwrap them from his wrist. I probably have the same charge as a D battery in each of my fingers.

We stand there in silence, half a breath away from each other, neither one of us sure how to bridge the gap. I don't know what to say to get us back on whatever track we've been on.

"I feel like I should leave," Caroline says out of the blue, "but I've kind of been eavesdropping, and I don't think what's supposed to happen here will actually happen if I leave." I hadn't realized she was still standing so close. There are apparently other people in the room. I forgot.

Awkwardness freezes me, and I'm stuck. Grant doesn't speak, either.

"So," Caroline starts, placing a gentle hand on my shoulder. "I think Grant here is trying to ask you out. Right?"

I turn my head to look at her. I hadn't thought that's where this was going at all.

But Grant looks at me hopefully. He nods.

Holy crap. Oh my God. This is happening.

"Okay, great," Caroline says.

I'm not sure how to feel about her intrusion, but I often rely on Caroline's innate social ability to help me interact with the world, so really, this isn't unusual. It seems like it might be for Grant, though. In the group, he's always been the one to break the awkwardness with something unexpected and funny. Now, he stands in front of me completely silent. All his social prowess seems lost.

"Now that we all know what's going on here, and you"—Caroline looks at Grant—"don't look like you want to throw up anymore . . . I'm going to leave you to it."

Caroline slips away, and I feel a rush of cold air hit my side in her absence. The circle has emptied, and it's just us. Oh God. It's just us. Just Grant and me. It's just Grant and me, and he's asking me out. At least I think he is. Maybe he's already changed his mind.

"Let me start over," he says.

My blood suddenly feels like it's made of lead. Awkwardness weighs me down like a brick.

"Okay, so, I was trying to ask you out, but I wasn't really doing a good job."

I chuckle a little, but I can't look at him. His nervousness is palpable, and it's making mine worse. I've never been asked out before, especially not in this prolonged, fumbling way.

"What I *meant* to say," he starts again. I glance up at him, his voice too compelling not to. If this really *is* happening, I don't want to miss it. "What I meant to say is that I like you, and I want you to go out with me. But only if you want to. That kind of sounded pushy, and that's not what I'm going f—"

The idea that he's so nervous over *me* is absurd. It's completely unbelievable.

"Grant?"

"Yeah?"

"You're rambling again."

He finally laughs at himself, and I do, too. Some of the intensity of our awkwardness fades away. This must be how people feel when they're being proposed to, honestly.

Grant takes a deep breath, like he's really psyching himself up.

"Ivy, will you go on a date with me?"

I feel myself grin, wide enough that the apples of my cheeks press against the bottoms of my eyes. My face is so scrunched up that I probably look like the amalgamation of one giant freckle.

"Sure."

"Good." He grins at me, this twinkly, beaming smile that makes my blood turn from lead to liquid gold.

"Good," I whisper back.

CHAPTER SIXTEEN

———— • ————

FRI, SEP 11, 5:03 P.M.

Grant: Do you still not want to know where we're going?

Ivy: Nope. Surprise me.

Grant: IKEA it is, then.

Ivy: Don't tease me. I would love that.

I stand with a hand on each closet door, staring at what my wardrobe has to offer. I want to lean forward and let the dark mass of fabric absorb me. I'm still in my don't-give-a-crap school clothes, and I know I have to change.

I run my fingers over the smooth fabric of the dress I wore to the dance, wishing I could separate the way I felt in it from the way I felt at the dance. Behind it is the dress I wore to my eighth-grade graduation, something white and lacy that is definitely not my style anymore. Everything I touch is saturated in memories. That's why I can't decide what to wear.

"So what's your outfit?" Mom asks, walking through my open door and falling onto my bed. She lies on her stomach and hangs her feet in the air, kicking them back and forth like a little girl at a sleepover. (That's a weird image, actually.)

"I don't know," I say, flopping down beside her. I've been staring into the depths of my closet too long; everything is starting to run together into a mostly black ocean.

"Where are you going?" Mom asks.

"I don't know that, either," I admit. I haven't asked. If I knew, I'd just overthink and stress more.

"Well, I have to meet this boy before you leave, make sure he's not a bad egg." That's Mom's counselor voice. It's the one that inspires her students and scares her children.

I groan.

"You've met him, Mom. He's helping to coach Ethan's baseball team. How bad could he be?"

"You never know. I need to look him in the eyes, make sure he won't hurt my little girl." She points two fingers at her eyes, then turns them on me. She's always watching. That message was received before she sent it.

I stand up again, bouncing from one foot to the other. I rise up on my toes. I'm trying to get another angle of whatever it is that I'm going to wear.

"I never expected this when I saw that flyer, you know. The group wasn't some ploy to set you up with someone."

"I know that." I turn around to look at her. "You couldn't have known there'd be anyone there worth setting me up with."

"It's not just that—it didn't even cross my mind. Sometimes, when you have a sick kid, it feels like they're the only one in the world. Like no one else will ever be able to relate."

My head tilts to the side, my brows pulled together. "No offense, but that doesn't make any sense." I stand facing her, hands on my hips. "I get what you mean, but you're sick, too. So is Caroline. In this house, more people are sick than healthy."

Mom shakes her head.

"I know, I know. I just feel guilty, though. When I saw that flyer, it was like a light bulb. Why hadn't I tried that? Why hadn't I tried to help you interact with other people who have similar illnesses? I'm a counselor, why didn't a support group occur to me?"

Mom has her hands at her temples, like she wants to pull her hair out. I move them. Lupus does enough hair pulling on its own.

"I don't know, but it doesn't matter. Caroline and I have a safe place to talk now. Isn't that all that counts?"

Mom nods. "You're right." She pats my arm. "And you found a nice boy."

I turn back toward my closet so I can roll my eyes in peace.

"What's wrong with him again?"

I let my head fall forward and bang it against one of my closet shelves. "You can't just ask what's wrong with him, Mom."

"He has RA, like her," Caroline says, appearing in the doorway. I should've closed the door when I had the chance. Caroline takes up the rest of the space on my bed, lying across my pillow in the same position Mom is in. Apparently, this is a party.

"You're not dressed yet?" Caroline asks. "Isn't he picking you up at seven?"

"Yeah, why?" I don't even turn around. I start tossing clothes behind me in a sort of fabric tornado.

"It's six-thirty. Hurry up." Caroline crawls over the bed and joins me in the closet. She starts throwing clothes, too. Me, methodically. Caroline, frantically.

"Do you wear anything that isn't black?" Caroline picks up a long skirt and throws it. It hits me directly in the face.

"I try not to."

The mattress springs squeak as Mom gets up. "I'm going downstairs. I need to take note of how early he is."

I roll my eyes again.

"Have you figured anything out at this point? Or are we just working with a blank slate here?" Caroline pulls out a lavender top I haven't worn in years.

"Black."

"Ugh." Caroline grabs a black miniskirt with silver buttons all the way down the front. She throws it at me. "Here, start with this."

I take it into my bathroom.

"Go ahead and do your face and hair," she calls. "I'll figure out the rest."

I look at my minuscule collection of makeup on the sink. It's early fall, but that doesn't mean the southern humidity has stopped. If I were to put some on, I'd probably just sweat it off. I untwist my hair, unraveling my falling-apart braid. The waves fall against my neck and down my back. It looks nice like that, but I know there's no way I'll be able to stand a second in the heat with it down. I raise it up into a high ponytail and pull down a few strands to frame my face. There's a knock at the door, and it cracks open before I can respond.

"Here," Caroline says, passing me a deep purple high-neck sleeveless top. "Tuck it into the skirt."

I put it on and step out. I don't have a full-length mirror in my room, but Caroline does. I follow her across the hall.

As I stand in front of the glass, Caroline stands behind me. She wipes imaginary dust off of my shoulder. I look at my reflection, trying to figure out why I'm not nervous. There's an odd expression of peace on my face, and a casual aspect to my posture that is rarely there.

Weird.

I have to admit, Caroline's outfit is the right choice. The top's high neck covers my weirdly pointed collarbones and takes attention away from the fact that my chest isn't proportional to my hips. The short skirt makes my legs look longer, too. I almost feel like I can pass for average height.

"Don't do anything I wouldn't do," Caroline advises, passing me a pair of black earrings. I snort. There's *plenty* that Caroline would do that I wouldn't—ever.

I hadn't thought there was anyone in the world I'd actually look forward to going out on a date with, though, either. Maybe the Caroline side of the world isn't bad. I think maybe Grant's on that side, after all.

I put the earrings in and take a deep breath.

"I'm serious, Iggy. But have fun. Be wild and ridiculous."

"I don't get why I don't feel worse."

Caroline interrupts me with a laugh.

"I mean it," I insist. "I don't like people. I don't willingly go out with people. But he asked, and I said yes without a second thought. The actual asking-out was uncomfortable, but I haven't freaked out since. This kind of calm is just...inexplicable."

Caroline smiles and sets her hands on my shoulders.

"All the best things in life are."

CHAPTER SEVENTEEN

———— • ————

FRI, SEP 11, 6:54 P.M.

Dad: Make sure this boy treats you right.

Ivy: I don't know how I'm supposed
to respond to that.

Dad: Me either. I just had to say it.

"Come on, we need to rescue him," I say, taking the stairs two at a time, Caroline right on my heels. By the time I hit the middle of the staircase, I can hear voices. I didn't notice the doorbell ring, so Mom must have been *watching* for him. Great.

"How do you like coaching?" I hear her ask. I speed up. My footfalls on the stairs are so loud, I probably sound like a Clydesdale.

"It's good—different than I thought it would be. The team is fun to be around, and as long as I'm around baseball at all, I'm happy."

I can't see him yet, but his voice is relaxed and calm. He sounds much less nervous talking to my mother than he's ever been talking to me.

"Hey, Grant!" I hear Ethan say. Perfect, now my date has become a full family affair. At least Dad's at work.

"What's up?" There's a loud smacking sound. I can picture them high-fiving like they always do at practice. I'm mentally crossing my fingers that Ethan is just passing through and isn't planning on hanging around.

"If you love baseball so much, how come you don't play?" Mom prods.

I roll my eyes. The reason he doesn't play is obvious to me, and I don't want him having to answer that question out loud. I take the last step into the kitchen and keep walking. I grab my purse in one hand and Grant's shoulder in the other.

"We're-leaving-Mom-see-you-later." I push Grant out the door and shut it behind us, heaving a sigh when we're on the other side.

"I'm sorry about her," I say, almost wincing. "She shouldn't have asked you that."

"It's okay! I get asked that all the time." Grant laughs.

"Yeah, maybe, but not by people who should know better."

We walk toward his car and he opens the door for me. I didn't expect it. But I didn't expect him to entertain my mom's third degree, either.

I climb into the passenger seat and buckle my seat belt. As he does the same, it occurs to me that we've never really been alone before. The tiny, enclosed space of the car feels intimate and personal. Though, now that I look at it, it's not really that tiny. It's a big SUV, sort of like the one my mom has. Impeccably clean, too.

There's an ID badge hanging from the rearview mirror that just says **MEDIA**. I wonder what that's about.

Grant turns his head to back out of the driveway and he narrowly misses hitting Caroline's car. I didn't have a chance to look at him before, and now, stealing a peek, I don't want to look away. He's done something to his hair; it's not as unruly as it normally is. I want to run my fingers through it and mess it back up, restore it to its disheveled default setting.

We're out of my neighborhood and nearly on the interstate. Still, neither one of us has spoken, and I don't know how to fill the silence. Maybe I *should* have been nervous. I still don't know where we're going, so there's no way to know how long this car ride is going to last.

My mind starts to race. Maybe there was more Mom said to him that I didn't hear. Maybe he's regretting asking me out. Maybe there's somewhere else he'd rather be, someone else he'd rather be with.

"Can I ask you something?" I break the silence before it breaks me. I have to. It's starting to press on my chest like a too-tight hug.

He looks over for a brief moment, one hand on the wheel and the other on the console between us.

"Sure," he says.

"Why can't you talk to me?" As soon as I say it, I cringe. I didn't mean for it to come out that way—so rude, so accusing.

He laughs. It's a weird laugh, like a chuckle getting run over.

"That's not what I meant," I clarify quickly. "You just talk to everyone, like it's easy. Everyone at group, all of Ethan's team, even my mom." I realize I'm disjointed, but I can't stop. "You talk like it's breathing—like you just talk to live. And then you get around me, and...nothing. I mean, maybe a little—at the ball field, on the phone. But not when we're alone."

"To be fair, I don't breathe much around you, either," he says quietly, almost inaudibly, but I hear it anyway. I try not to smile. "I don't know. It doesn't make sense, but you're right. You make me nervous."

I have to laugh. "It's just hilarious. That I do this to someone. Nervous is my natural state."

He laughs, too, and some of the tension in the air dissipates. "Well, I hate it."

"It's not my favorite thing, either."

Grant turns his head to back into a parking space. I don't even recognize where we are. In the mirror on my door, I can see a giant white screen and groups of people spread out on blankets. A makeshift drive in!

We walk to the rear of the SUV, and Grant opens the back hatch. The seats are folded down, and blankets line the entire rear of the car. He climbs in and holds out his hand. I take it without thinking, wrapping my fingers *just barely* around his. I climb in gently, trying not to fall on my face or accidentally flash anyone who might be walking by. I carefully arrange myself next to him, extending my legs in front of me like I always do at the gym.

"I didn't know we had one of these here." I look around at the people on the field below us. Kids run from blanket to blanket, diving at the ground like it's a ball pit.

"We come all the time," Grant says, actually looking into my eyes for once. "There's this food truck here that has the best tacos, too. When the support group was just the five of us, we always came over and got them after a meeting."

"What was it like when it was just y'all?" I think about it a lot, what the group was like before me and Caroline, before Stella or Holden, any of us.

"Loud." Grant laughs again. "Parker and I fought a lot. We still do."

"*Really?* I can't imagine you fighting." I feel my eyes widen.

"Yeah, we're … aggressive sometimes. The group wasn't as official as it is now, so we really got into things. Like, we just *talked*, for hours, and sometimes we didn't."

"Do you miss it?" I find myself asking. I don't want him to. I don't want him to prefer a world I'm not in.

"A little." He looks up at me, more intensely this time. "I mean, I like everyone in the bigger group, especially you. It just feels different."

I understand that. "Do you think everyone else feels that way?"

"No." He sighs. "Avery's the reason we started the new group. In her mind, the more people, the better. Lilah, too. As long as she can help someone, she will. Parker wants whatever Lilah wants, and Manny and Holden are joined at the hip. He'd never talked to someone else with an insulin pump before…" His voice trails off.

"I'd never talked to someone else with RA," I say quietly, like it's a secret.

"I wasn't expecting that," Grant says. "You, I mean. I wasn't expecting you."

His voice is quiet, too, so quiet it feels like it's just for me.

The earlier awkwardness is gone. I find myself wanting to ask him question after question, just to hear him keep talking. I've never been so interested in someone else's words before. Whether he talks about baseball, or the group, or types of dirt, I'll listen. I want to bottle his voice up and carry it with me, have it read me each step of a recipe like Siri, so it feels like he's there in the kitchen with me.

I'm thinking of something to say in response that doesn't sound pathetic, but the giant screen flashes to life, neon green. It's so bright it hurts my retinas. I raise one hand up to shield my face, and Grant does the same.

"It looks like aliens are landing out here," he says. I giggle.

The horror of green goes away, replaced by a Netflix home screen. The quality looks as if someone is streaming it directly from their phone; it's pixelated and too spread out. What they're doing here might not be technically legal. This is like explaining the nuances of the internet to my dad, watching someone do something they are terminally ill-equipped to do. They must have chosen not to invest in the commercial-free streaming, either. The first commercial is at volume so booming, I can't even figure out what it's for. Then, I hear something all too familiar. *Our patients inspire us in how they triumph over rheumatoid arthritis.*

I can't help it: I laugh.

At first, it's just this little puff of air I'm trying to hold back. Then, as the commercial keeps playing, Grant laughs, too. Soon we're both cackling. I laugh so hard I snort, and tears stream down my face. I'm glad I decided against the makeup. I saved myself the raccoon eyes.

People in the cars on either side of us look over, like they're missing the joke. They are. It's right there in front of them, the size of the side of a building, and they're still missing it.

"I fucking hate those commercials!" Grant cries, still laughing.

"Me too!" I wipe my eyes, but my lashes stick together. "I'm not triumphing over anything!"

"They're always building playgrounds or going on safaris. The people who film these have *definitely* never actually met anyone with RA."

"And they gloss over the part where the drug will make you sick for six months solid and maybe end up giving you cancer."

We laugh again, one last time. People around us really are starting to stare.

The movie starts, the first *To All the Boys I've Loved Before*. I've never seen it, despite the modern-classic status. Grant extends his legs out in front of him, mirroring my position. It's just like in group, except he's never this close in group. I can never feel the heat emanating from him in group. He bumps his right shoe against my left, worn Vans to worn boots. He shifts his shoulders closer. I move my hands so they're at my sides, rather than behind my back. I do this for no particular reason, obviously.

"Hey, Grant," I say, whisper-quiet.

"Yeah?" He turns to look at me again. His hand drifts over mine.

"I didn't expect you, either."

CHAPTER EIGHTEEN

———•———

SAT, SEP 12, 7:21 A.M.

Grant: HAPPY BASEBALL DAY!!! ⚾ ⚾ ⚾

Ivy: It's so early for this kind of enthusiasm.

Grant: happy baseball day

Grant: ⚾

Ivy: happy baseball day.

It's the Sluggers' first game of the season, and judging by the atmosphere in the car, it might as well be the World Series. We've all acquired Sluggers shirts. Our family hasn't worn matching shirts since we went to Disney World when I was seven. Dad has the day off, and he's undoubtedly the most excited. He and Ethan are talking back and forth as he drives, making eye contact in the rearview mirror.

It's an early game, which is criminally disappointing because I didn't get to make brunch. But I was too spaced out to be trusted with knives, anyway—too preoccupied replaying last night over and over again. I keep thinking about the way Grant held my hand, even when he was driving, and how he didn't let go until we got to my door. I keep remembering the way saying goodnight felt like the actors in a play taking their final bows. The show was over, but I just wanted to go back to the beginning and watch it all again.

Still, I dread the moment this car stops. That means a matching family of five will descend on Grant. I can only hope they'll behave. If last night is any indication, they won't.

Even *if* they behave when it comes to *Grant*, they won't in general. My parents are the kind who scream from the stands no matter what: win, lose, strikeout, home run. All of it. Ethan could run off the field in the middle of an inning and they'd probably cheer. I would, too, I guess.

Dad presses down on the brake to park, and I briefly wonder if I should've stayed home.

The game is much more official than practice. There are umpires on the field talking to one another, and more people running the concession stand. There are more people in general, all over the bleachers on each side of the field. Ethan pushes me out of the way to get out of the car. That's just what I need right now, to eat dirt in front of everyone. He runs off ahead of us and joins his team on the field. He probably doesn't even care if we follow. We could go home and I could make brunch. As long as we're here to pick him up when the game's over, he wouldn't notice a thing.

"So, which one's the boy?" Dad asks, hands on his hips. He's broadening his shoulders in an attempt to appear intimidating.

I want to roll my eyes. There's only one person in my field of vision who looks even remotely close to my own age. Everyone else is either twelve, or old enough to be friends with my dad. It really shouldn't be difficult to pick out Grant, even if your vision doesn't seek him out in a crowd like mine does.

Grant doesn't make a move to walk toward me when he notices my presence, and for that, I'm grateful. I don't want to subject him to whatever my parents might have to say. He does wave, though. It's a wild, uncontrollable wave that makes my stomach somersault around in my abdomen.

As I look at him, I realize that in wearing a Sluggers T-shirt, I'm not just matching my family—I'm matching him, too.

"That's him, huh?" I hear Dad whisper in Mom's direction. I turn my head to look at them both, trying to make my face appear annoyed and menacing, like there will actually be consequences if they keep *literally* talking behind my back.

"They're starting. Turn around." Mom nudges my shoulder. She's traded her umbrella for a floppy hat and a copious dose of sunscreen. I still worry.

The Sluggers are the home team, so they run out to their positions in the field first. The Sliders gather in their dugout. The team names are so close, if their shirts weren't different colors, I wouldn't have been able to tell the teams apart. Ethan takes his place at first base and pounds his glove against the dirt like it owes him money. Caroline and I shake our heads. That kid has always had too much energy for his own good.

After the first batter, I stop flinching at the metallic clink of the bat connecting with the ball. I relax some, and I'm actually kind of impressed. Ethan even makes a double play, something my dad calls a 4-6-3. My parents clap so loudly behind me that I almost fall off the bleachers. Caroline has to reach out and steady me.

By the fifth inning, the Sluggers are up by three runs, and I'm actually enjoying myself. I've been going to Ethan's games for years, but I've never really paid attention. I cheer when everyone else does, but I never fully understand what's going on. There's something different about this time, though, something electric that makes me keep my eye on the ball, from the pitcher, to the batter, out onto the field.

It's the first batter in the sixth inning. The kid at bat swings early at the first pitch and misses. The second pitch seems lightning fast, so fast I can't find the ball until I hear the loud rattling of it hitting the bat. It goes foul, and I lose sight of it again until the crowd's collective volume starts to rise. I swear time moves in slow motion. The ball flies right toward where Grant stands behind third base. It's like a heat-seeking missile; I know it won't miss him. My muscles tense, and I can't make my voice work. I try. I have to warn him. Over the crowd's roar, I hear Caroline yelling for him to look out.

I watch with bated breath as he hears. Recognition crosses his face, and I expect him to run. He does, sort of. Time is still crawling, and his motions seem slack and almost imperceptible. Two steps back, and he raises his arms like a boxer fending off an attack. I can almost hear the smack as the ball hits him just above his right elbow.

All at once, time speeds up again, and I have to move. My vision blurs, and all I can see clearly is him. I brush past Caroline and jump off the bleachers. Pain lances through my feet. Subconsciously, I realize I shouldn't have done that—but I still keep going. We are on the first base side, but I move fast enough that as Grant comes through the fence, I'm there to meet him.

"What was that?" I ask, watching him run his left hand over his probably damaged elbow.

"I don't know." He winces. "I guess I wasn't paying attention."

I guide him to the bleachers by the third base side. There's an empty corner on the lowest level, and he sits down right on the edge.

"Hold on, let me go get you some ice." Without waiting for him to respond, I take off again and head toward the concession stand. The woman behind the counter must have been watching: She hands me a bag of ice before I ask. Maybe they just keep them ready for any potential injuries.

The game continues around me, and I head back to Grant.

"Let me see," I say, rolling up his shirt sleeve. His arm is already red and swollen, and there's no doubt it's going to bruise. He winces again as I run a finger over the mark. I can practically see the imprint the stitches made on his skin.

"Why weren't you paying attention?" I ask, sitting down next to him and holding the ice to his arm.

"Let me do it," Grant says, covering my fingers with his. "I don't want the cold to hurt your hands."

"Like it's not going to hurt yours," I shoot back. "That's some luck, getting hit in the joint that hurts the worst."

His face wrinkles up in an adorably confused way. "How'd you know my elbows hurt the worst?"

"You're always holding them, or your arms are crossed to keep the air off. Been there, done that."

He tries to smile, I think, but it looks like more of a grimace.

"What's yours?" he asks.

"My hips. Wait until I stand up, I'll crack like a glow stick."

Grant laughs, and something in my chest loosens. As much as I want to bottle his voice, I want to make a vinyl record of his laugh and play it again and again until the needle breaks. A line of players walks along the fence; only then do I realize the game is over. I faintly remember that they only play seven innings in this league.

"I should've gone back. If no one's coaching third, no one knows when to run." Grant winces again, moving the ice to survey the damage.

"Then this was a good opportunity for them to use their own judgment."

"How are you so positive right now?" he asks, looking at me seriously.

I shrug. "I didn't get hit by a baseball."

I'm not as even-keeled as he thinks I am. Not now, and not in the dark moments, either—the unforgiving mornings.

"Well, you don't quit baseball just because you get hit once in a while."

"See, that was positive," I say with a half smile.

"But I did quit baseball, so..."

I roll my eyes. It was *almost* positive. Out of the corner of my eye, I see my family approaching. Mentally, I groan. I hadn't even thought of them when I jumped to make sure Grant was okay. I'd almost forgotten they were here.

"Well, that was eventful," Caroline says. She's just like Grant, sometimes, saying whatever she has to to break the tension.

"I've never actually seen someone get hit before," Ethan says. His eyes are wide with wonder, like he's glimpsed a unicorn in the wild. "Would've been more hardcore if it was on your face."

"Ethan!" Mom exclaims, giving him one of those pointed-eyebrow looks that says he better shut up for his own good.

But Grant laughs. "I'll leave my arms down next time, if you want."

"Hopefully there won't be a next time," Mom replies. Grant looks at me, and I can tell what he's thinking. That's where the positivity comes from. He's right.

We say our goodbyes, and Dad even tells Grant he hopes his arm feels better soon. All that false bravado, wasted. The ice is melting in the heat, but Grant holds it to his arm anyway. I take two steps away, my family already ahead of me.

"Hey, Ivy?" Grant calls out. I turn around and look at him over my shoulder. "Thanks for taking care of me."

CHAPTER NINETEEN

●

TUES, SEP 15, 1:03 P.M.

Grant: want to get dinner tonight?

Ivy: Sure.

Grant asks me out again. I'm not expecting it. Not so soon, anyway. I'm not used to dating, but I'm *really* not used to midweek dating. I never have anything to look forward to after school but my afternoon nap.

It's Tuesday, so I would've seen him at group, anyway, but this is more...official. I'm determined not to make a big deal out of it. I'm just going to ignore the rising anxiety. If I see my hands shaking, *no I don't*. It's just dinner before group, a last-minute thing. I'm not even going to change. My leggings and T-shirt are just going to have to do. I don't have the energy to handle much else.

He comes to pick me up, and it's so early that it doesn't even seem late enough for dinner. He's driving a different car this time, a small blue one. (That's all I can tell about it: I don't know cars.)

"What's with the ride?" I ask, instead of saying hello or something normal.

"I drove my mom's last week. If I'd driven mine, we would've had to watch the movie in the trunk. I've heard girls don't like being put in trunks on first dates."

"It could be argued that no one wants to be put in a trunk ever."

"Fair." He waits a beat before adding, "Also, hi."

"Hi," I reply. Grant seems less nervous this time. We've switched back to our correct seats on the anxiety seesaw. He's on the ground, and I'm high in the air. I watch his arms move and flex as he drives, trying to see how he's feeling. Finally, I just ask. "How's your battle scar?"

He's wearing one of his old baseball-style Nirvana T-shirts, the one with sleeves that come down past his elbows. He shifts his hands on the wheel so he can push up his sleeve. When he does, I resist the urge to gasp. The angry red I saw only days ago has morphed into a ring of dark purple. I run my fingertips over it absentmindedly, like I can make it go away with some kind of gentle magic. It crosses my mind that I don't have permission to touch him like this. My fingers fall away.

"Looks terrible, doesn't it?"

I nod. "Despite what Ethan said, I'm glad it wasn't your face. That would've been much worse."

"My face is all I have left." He smiles, turning the wheel to pull into our destination, and my stomach flips.

"You mean besides your natural personability?" I open my door.

"You think I'm personable?"

"No, I find you completely repulsive, that's why I'm here."

Okay, so maybe I didn't mean to let that slip out. Maybe he's not ready for my sarcastic side, innate personability or not. But his face breaks into this heart-stopping grin, and I freeze where I stand in the doorway of the diner we've arrived at, completely mesmerized.

He's gazing at me, too. The way he's looking makes me uncomfortable, or, maybe, it makes me uncomfortable that it doesn't. "What?" I ask.

"Nothing, I just didn't expect that."

We sit down in a shiny vinyl-covered booth, and I shift back and forth, trying to get comfortable. My hips are screaming at me, and there's no way to arrange myself in this booth where they don't hurt.

"Put your feet up here," Grant says. He pats the space next to him on the vinyl. "You know you want to."

I kind of really do want to.

I pick my legs up and set my feet on his side of the booth. They're just long enough to reach. Grant rests his right hand across my ankles, right at the tops of my sneakers. Some kind of tingling sparkle flutters across my legs.

But then . . . conversation doesn't really start. I notice, for the first time, that he seems a little down.

"Are you okay?" I ask. Looking closely, I can just tell he's not himself. All of the natural, glittery brightness of his personality seems muted.

He looks at me then, and I almost wish he hadn't. I've never seen him actually look upset, and it makes something in my chest sink all the way to where his fingers are splayed out against my feet.

"I don't know," he says. "Sorry. Things are . . . hard."

"What does that mean?"

A waitress in a retro diner uniform skates over. Her skirt is so poofy it almost looks like she's wearing a tutu. The fabric is so obviously synthetic it looks like it came from a costume store. Grant orders a Philly cheesesteak and onion rings. I think that's probably one too many onions. I order a burger and fries, the only acceptable diner food. When the waitress skates away, he starts talking again.

He takes a deep breath. "It's baseball."

I wait for him to keep going, swirling my straw around in my sweet tea with too much ice.

"The season doesn't even start until January, and they're already talking about it. They're saying this freshman is going to be the starting pitcher and that makes no fucking sense."

I'm not used to this, him just unleashing a full stream of consciousness on me. I'm not used to the irritated bite of his voice, either.

"I could literally wipe the floor with that kid, except I can't. No matter how many posters in the locker room claim hard work pays off, or how many motivational speakers say you can do anything you put your mind to, sometimes you just *can't*."

The brutal honesty shocks me.

He's right, of course. I know that. But hearing words that I've thought time and time again in his voice is eerie.

"I mean, I like coaching and all—"

The waitress skates toward us again, a tray of food-filled baskets resting on one hand. I admire her balance. I'd have fallen on my face a hundred times by now.

"It's not the same, I know," I say when the waitress leaves. I try to pick my burger up in a way that won't send lettuce and tomato falling all over my hands, but then I look over at Grant and he already has peppers and onions all over his, so I guess it doesn't really matter.

"It's just... frustrating."

That, I know all too well. I nod.

Grant keeps talking around bites of his food. I usually think it's gross when people do that, but this tiny slip in his usual politeness is actually kind of cute.

"There are professional athletes with chronic illnesses, playing in Super Bowls and winning gold medals. They're fine. And I can't even play high school baseball."

"I know what you mean. Trust me." I smile at him in a way I hope is encouraging, or at least not weird.

"I know you do."

We eat in silence after that, until Grant looks at his phone and realizes we're going to be late for group. We pay and rush over so fast I don't have time to worry about what everyone is going to say when we walk in together.

When we get there, Caroline is waiting for us, leaning against a wall with her arms crossed over her chest. She looks slightly menacing. "Dad grilled burgers and forgot to season them. It was like eating a wad of wet paper towels, and it's your fault for abandoning us."

"Oh my God! Bless his heart." Being in public, I try to repress a laugh. It comes out a strangled chuckle when I want to double over and cackle.

Grant looks at me like I'm the most curious thing he's ever seen.

Everyone else is already in their seats, talking among themselves and stealing glances at us. Great. This will definitely end up being a whole thing. If Grant sits next to me, they'll assume something is up. If he sits in his seat, they'll think something is up and we're trying to hide it. There really isn't a way to win, so I kind of want him to just sit next to me.

All of this feels painfully childish, like we're playing a game of extremely important musical chairs.

Caroline sits down, and I do the same. I haven't felt Grant move away yet. He's stuck in my personal space, as if by magnetism. This invisible connection is always there.

He sits down in the chair next to me. Instead of looking past my feet to his, I can bump his right foot with my left if I shift by a couple of inches. I like it.

"So before we do anything else, we should talk about the lock-in." Avery's voice carries through the whole gym, past the circle and out into the open space.

My head snaps up. I vaguely remember hearing about the

lock-in before, but only in the broadest of terms. Last time I checked, it was a hey-we-should-have-a-lock-in kind of thing. It was theoretical. It wasn't something that's actually happening.

"That's next Friday, right?" Caroline asks.

Avery and Lilah nod at the same time. If Grant and I have an invisible connection, so do they. They're telepathic.

I hadn't realized the lock-in was happening so soon. I haven't even mentioned it to my parents. It's a novel concept, a lock-in, where everyone stays overnight in a place like this. I think it's the kind of thing that normally happens at, like, churches and schools, but whatever. We're not normal.

It's also just occurred to me that I'll be locked in here all night with Grant. My sister and everyone else will be here, too, but still... Grant. He'll be there to see my slept-in hair and my worn-out pajamas. I start to panic at the thought.

"We need to talk about food. I was thinking we'd just order pizza, but that doesn't seem completely safe, right, Caroline?" Avery asks. She's approaching it so well, straightforward but gentle, like we're talking about the weather.

"Yeah. Some places offer gluten-free crust now, but you never know if it's been cross-contaminated. I'd rather not take the risk."

Caroline looks over at me.

"Ivy can cook," she says, smiling a wicked grin.

"We couldn't ask you to do that," Avery says, meeting my eyes. She says it like cooking is a chore, like she'd be asking me to drive her to the airport.

If the choice is between being out here in the open with everyone else for hours and spending half the night in a kitchen, there's not even a choice.

"No, I'd love to—really." I don't know how else to articulate *please let me do this.*

"Are you sure?" Lilah asks.

"I could make pizza. That way everyone gets what they want. No one has to eat anything that might hurt them."

Everyone starts talking at once, excitedly, and I feel my cheeks burn. Grant bumps his elbow against mine.

"I didn't know you like to cook," he says.

"You went on two whole dates with him and didn't mention cooking at all? What did you talk about?" Caroline says, leaning too far over toward me.

"To be fair, I did most of the talking," Grant replies.

I roll my eyes, trying to fight off the wave of embarrassment washing over me. That this conversation is happening in front of everyone is making stomach acid burn my throat.

"Okay, pizza sounds good. You can cook everything in my apartment. I'll help so you know where everything is. That's all I'm good for, though. I'll mess up any food I touch," Avery says. She's probably not as hopeless as she makes herself out to be.

"I'll help, too," Caroline says.

"I'll do the dishes," Grant says. He actually raises his hand like he's in school. Everyone looks at him like they want to check him for a fever. I kind of want to, too. "What? I like doing dishes."

Caroline giggles under her breath and I elbow her in the side.

The conversation moves on to other subjects, but I tune out. By the time the meeting is over, my mind is spinning in dizzying circles. We all get up from our chairs and break up into smaller groups on our own, saying goodbyes and making plans for next weekend.

I pull on Grant's shirt sleeve. Something about the way we left our conversation at the diner isn't sitting well with me.

"When I told you earlier that I understood what you meant, I did," I say.

"I know," Grant replies. He looks slightly, adorably confused. I realize I'm just going to have to come out and say it if this is going to make any sense.

"I didn't tell you why, and I should've. There's this Iron Chef who has RA, Michael Symon. He runs restaurants, and films TV shows, and writes cookbooks. Then there's my mom, and she spends all day in her office or running from classroom to classroom counseling kids. There are all these people in the world who can do whatever they want to, and I can barely make it through school without falling asleep."

I take a deep breath. This must be how Grant feels all the time, I think, empty and bereft, like the words he just said took everything he has.

"So I promise," I say, after another deep breath, "I know what you mean."

CHAPTER TWENTY

———— • ————

THU, SEP 17, 5:41 P.M.

Avery: When you say basil, do you mean fresh or dried?

Ivy: Both, preferably.

"You haven't mentioned the lock-in to them, have you?" I ask Caroline. I check the potatoes I'm boiling to see if they're done. They're not. They're hot enough to burn the tip of my finger, but they're not done. Mashed potatoes were the first food I ever learned to make, but apparently, in all that time, I still haven't learned how to make them without burning myself.

"No. I wasn't really planning on it...Why?" Caroline pulls plates out of the cabinet to my left. She doesn't have to stand on her tiptoes to do that, but I do.

I roll my eyes.

"Sure, we'll just not come home one night and that won't be a problem at all."

Caroline rolls her eyes back.

"I was going to tell them, just not yet." She starts tossing forks onto the plates, making the loudest clacking noise I've ever heard.

"Tell them when? When we're on our way out the door?"

"Yeah, probably."

"We are very different people," I murmur.

"Fine, we'll tell them at dinner." Caroline leaves the kitchen. Sometimes she's just so loud.

I check the potatoes again, and in minutes, I've turned them into the mashed potatoes that are arguably the best thing I make. They don't even have a recipe card. Grandma taught me to make them before she died. They're an unwritten urban legend. I carry the bowl to the table where everyone else is already sitting. This is rare, having us all together for dinner. If Dad isn't working, then someone usually has a club to go to or some kind of practice. I try to set the bowl on the table, but Ethan intercepts it before I can. He puts a giant scoop on his plate, and only then does he let anyone else have any.

"So the support group is having a lock-in at the gym next weekend," Caroline says casually. There's no preamble, no small talk. No asking about anyone's day, nothing.

"That sounds like fun," Mom says.

"Ivy's going to cook."

"That was nice of you to volunteer, Iggy," Dad responds.

"I didn't volunteer." I point my fork at Caroline. "But I don't mind."

"Will this boy of yours be there?" Dad asks. He puts his silverware down and everything, a sure sign he means business.

"He's not mine, and he has a name," I reply. I have to keep my cool, even though talking about this still makes me *so* viscerally uncomfortable. This whole conversation is my fault. I should've just taken Caroline's advice and told them as we're walking out the door.

"Yeah, it's Grant." Ethan puts his fork down, too. At least the founding member of the Grant Deluca Fan Club will be on my side.

"Yes, he'll be there. I'll keep an eye on them, Dad, don't worry." Caroline looks over at me ruefully. Every once in a while, her piercing eyes get genuinely terrifying.

"That doesn't help as much as you'd think, hon." Mom caught the look in Caroline's eye. I hate this conversation and my life. But it's probably too late to duck under the table and live there forever.

"I don't know how I feel about you going to a sleepover with your boyfriend." Dad looks painfully serious, and I feel my face flame up like my favorite burner on the stove.

"He's not my boyfriend, and there are going to be like ten other people there."

I'm not sure if my math is right, but it's the thought that counts. All I'm thinking right now is that I want his to be over. That, and I'm almost certain Grant isn't my boyfriend. Even hearing that word makes my mind short-circuit.

We've only been on two dates. That doesn't make us anything. How did I end up having a conversation about whether or not I'm someone's girlfriend with my entire family? Grant happened way, way too fast. I still haven't caught up.

"I guess it's okay. Just no funny business." Dad picks his fork back up and jabs it in my direction. I'm counting how many steps it'll take to get out of here. Seven, maybe eight.

Caroline raises her hand, that mischievous smile back in place. "Can you define funny business for me, please?"

I chuckle, and Ethan laughs so hard he spits mashed potatoes across the table.

"That's something you've figured out for yourself." Mom's eyebrows are low, almost threatening.

This is going further and further off the rails. I know I won't be able to gain any kind of control now—if I ever had any in the first place. Thankfully, I'm done with my food, and I want to get a head start on the dishes, so I pop up. (Washing up used to be someone else's job in our house, but I always make such a mess that it's only fair I clean it up. Maybe if I didn't turn the kitchen into a disaster area, I wouldn't have to do so many dishes. That's something to consider.)

I load the dishwasher and then fill the sink with warm, soapy water. My good pots and pans are dishwasher safe, but I always wash them by hand. It feels more like taking care of them that way. For a minute, I let my hands rest in the borderline too-hot water. It feels nice, just letting my joints relax.

This is what I told Grant about . . . this feeling of my body being on the edge of a breakdown; a complete malfunction. Everything aches so much it feels as if all of my connective tissue is going to spring apart.

I lean my elbows on the cool metal of the sink and let my head fall forward. A strand of auburn hair falls out of my bun and drags in the foam. I don't care. I roll my neck around, trying to alleviate some of the tension there. I flex my shoulders back and forth.

"You okay, honey?" Mom asks from the doorway. She has two dirty plates in one hand and a completely empty bowl that used to contain mashed potatoes in the other. Seriously, the bowl is empty, not a visible speck of potato to be seen. Ethan must have actually licked it clean.

"Yeah, I'm good. Just tired." But I realize I don't have to pretend around my mother. She knows this kind of tired better than anyone. It's just the easiest excuse, the one that flies off my tongue without my brain's permission.

My entire being, my entire soul is exhausted. If my body breaks apart like Jenga pieces, I won't even have the energy to put myself back together. I stand up straight again and take a rag to the first pot in front of me. Mom steps in to help, drying as I wash.

"Hey, Mom?" I ask.

She *mm-hmm*s in response.

"How do you know your medicine isn't working?" I plunge my hands into the soapy water, grabbing all the silverware at the bottom of the sink.

"I don't know, sweetie." She sighs. "I think it's just something you have to learn—what your baseline symptoms are and what a flare feels like. What's normal bad, and what's bad bad."

I nod.

"Do you feel like your medicine isn't working anymore?" she asks, dropping the dish towel on the counter and turning to look at me.

"I don't know." I shrug. "I feel... bad. But maybe I'm just supposed to."

"No." She pulls me into a hug. "You're not supposed to."

My hands are wet, so I can't really hug her back, but I wrap my arms loosely around her and rest my head on her shoulder.

"So tell me about Grant," she says. Internally, I groan. I've had enough badgering about him for one evening. "No, I really want to know. You've never seemed interested in dating before. I want to know what makes him different."

That, in all fairness, is true. I've never dated anyone before. I've never wanted to. People are foreign to me. I've always felt like I was born on another planet, like an alien in human clothing. Boys, especially, were not on my radar. Then, one day, there was a blip. It was just the tiniest sound, a small green dot on an otherwise completely clear map. I thought Grant was going to be someone I noticed because I *had* to—someone I noticed in order to *avoid*. But he's special. And I still don't know why.

"So..." Mom says, bumping my shoulder with her own. "Tell me about him."

I don't know where to start.

"He likes baseball." That's the obvious place. Mom knows that much already. "And he talks a lot. Like, a lot. He lives with his mom, and he doesn't have any brothers or sisters. The first time we went to the support group, he was the one who broke the awkward silence."

That's it, I think. Grant's breaking the awkward silence of my life. He reached me.

Up until this very moment, I hadn't realized how much I like him. Up until now, I've been in this sort of bubble, floating in a haze above reality. But then I said yes when a boy asked me out, and soon I was saying yes again, running toward him when he got hurt, resting my feet on a booth next to him, grabbing his arm, tugging on his shirt sleeve. Being honest with him.

"I don't know why he's different," I say faintly, reverently. "He just is."

There's a seismic shift in my world. This is monumental. This is an oh-shit-what-have-I-gotten-myself-into moment I never expected in a million lifetimes. I have this indistinct feeling that when I come out on the other side of this, whatever this is, things will never be the same.

It's not a bad feeling. Actually, it's sort of the best.

Grant's right there. He's in the chair next to me at support group. He's at my brother's baseball practices. He's texting me every morning and night. He's opening doors and making sure I'm comfortable, and I am. Even though he's a person and a boy and I'm never comfortable around either of those things, I am.

He's right there, smiling and laughing and talking entirely too much.

Grant's right there, and I really, really like him.

CHAPTER TWENTY-ONE

•

FRI, SEP 25, 3:36 P.M.

Grant: I got new Braves pajamas. Prepare yourself.

Ivy: *clutches pearls*

I don't think I'll ever be ready for this much social interaction at once, but I walk into the gym anyway. They've already closed for the lock-in, so the front is completely dark. Even the electronic bell over the door is turned off. Something about this feels wrong, like Caroline and I are sneaking in somewhere we shouldn't be. My footsteps are quiet, like I'm afraid of getting caught.

"I hope you plan on starting dinner soon, because I'm starving," Caroline says loudly. Apparently, she's not bothered by the darkness at all.

Inside, everything looks different. There's a sheet hung up on one wall and a projector in the middle of the room. There are mats everywhere, the floor completely lined with them. Caroline and I take our shoes off and toss them into the haphazard pile near the wall.

People are already scattered about on the mats, rolling out

sleeping bags and tossing pillows back and forth. I'm surprised I don't feel more anxious when I see them. Our circle isn't here, but *we* are. Everyone has something in common, and no one has anything to hide.

I breathe in a lungful of sweat-and-detergent-scented air. Over toward the back of the room, Parker is wrestling on one of the mats. He has someone in a headlock.

"That's why I'm glad we only have one brother," Caroline says drily.

"God, I know," I reply.

Then they stop, and I see who he's wrestling. Grant stands up and adjusts his clothes. They're all rumpled from Parker's attack. I'm sure that's what it was, an attack. I'm sure Grant didn't start it. I'm about to say something—I don't know what—when Avery comes through the door behind the boys.

"Would you two knock it off, please? I can't hear myself think. I'm trying to get my shit together before Ivy gets here and realizes I have *no clue* what she put on this list." Avery hasn't noticed I'm standing right here.

I laugh, and she looks over.

"Shit," she says. "Pretend I didn't say that. And pretend I didn't swear. I'm trying to do that less."

"Do y'all do . . . *this* . . . often?" Caroline asks, pointing to Grant and Parker, the latter of whom is still on the floor. It's a valid question, one I'd like the answer to. Grant told me he and Parker fight a lot, but childish wrestling wasn't exactly what I pictured.

"Fight? Yes," Avery answers for them. "If you want to come back and start cooking, feel free. It's a mess, but I tried."

Caroline and I drop our stuff and follow her. I've never been in her apartment behind the gym before. Avery and her mom live here. It seems weird to me to live where you work, but Avery likes it just fine. She'd probably be okay if she never left this place again.

It's not a mess, not really. It's perfectly homey, in a lived-in way. There are clashing styles at play, though: dirty sneakers and an expensive-looking blazer hanging by the door; perfectly arranged pillows on the couch next to a pile of laundry on the floor.

We follow Avery into the kitchen and Caroline takes a seat on one of the stools in front of the tall counter.

"Okay," Avery starts. "So what do we do?"

"Are you starting already?" Lilah asks. She's appeared from somewhere down a hallway I can't see much of.

"Yes. We don't know how many attempts it's going to take to make something edible," Avery replies. O, ye of little faith.

"One attempt. I promise." I try for enthusiasm, but it's not my natural approach. In the kitchen, I'm more of a Gordon Ramsay than a Pioneer Woman.

Grant peeks his head in the door.

"I tried to tell Parker he needs to ice his knee, and he told me to fuck off. So maybe someone else should give it a try."

I've learned that out of all of us, Parker is the most reluctant to take care of himself. The display I just witnessed is more proof. Lilah takes off.

Grant steps in the opposite direction, closer to the kitchen where I stand. There's that odd magnetism again. It flares to life, and so do I. I haven't seen him since my groundbreaking revelation that I actually really like him. Now every detail about him seems better. Everything seems sharper, crisper. It's like I've been seeing him through the lens of an old Polaroid, and now I'm seeing him in crystal-clear HD.

"So," I say, trying to take back control. "I think we should split up. I'll make the gluten-free crust, Avery can roll out and cut the regular crusts, and Caroline can chop up the veggies. Does that work?"

"Yep," Caroline says. "I don't want to hear any criticism on my knife cuts, though. You hear me?"

I nod. She's the one person the Gordon Ramsay in me hides from.

All the ingredients I'd put on the list are in a pile in front of me on the counter. I take out one of the cans of pre-made pizza crust and pop one open. "Avery, can you cut these into…" My voice trails off as I count people in my mind. "Three pieces each and put them out on baking sheets?"

Avery nods.

"I'll work over here." I point to the opposite counter near the oven. "In the gluten-free zone. Anything I touch, no one outside the gluten-free zone can touch. There shouldn't be any cross contamination, but we really can't be too careful."

Avery scoffs. "You're right. I know about careful, trust me. I bought extra mats so everyone would be comfortable, and made sure they were all sanitized, old and new. I cleaned both locker rooms top to bottom. I screened the movie for photosensitivity. I got extra blankets and fans, because who knows how many people we have out there with temperature issues."

"Wow," Caroline says. "You really went all out."

"It's not something you can half-ass. Everyone deserves to be comfortable."

With just those words, I'm impressed at Avery's fierceness. She's the kind of phenom Caroline is, all strong personality and deep feeling. It can be intimidating, but her assertiveness is rooted in caring for other people, and that makes her softer, somehow.

"Someone"—Avery points her half-open can of pizza crust at Grant—"got sick from something in my gym once, and it's not happening again."

"You don't know I got sick there," Grant says, crossing his arms.

"Listen, all I know is you came here one day and the next you looked like you were dying. How many other explanations can there be?"

I think about it, about what Grant could've been doing in this gym that might or might not have made him sick. Sicker than his normal sick, that is.

"Easy. I went on an escalator at the mall and licked the handrail," Grant offers.

Caroline laughs, and I would, too, but the mental image of him doing that is so disgusting, I can't.

"Grant, that's so gross," Caroline says between laughs.

"Look," I say. This is already the strangest kitchen experience I've ever had, and we haven't really even started. "Not that this conversation isn't riveting, but we really should at least make an attempt at getting food on the table."

Avery pulls out baking sheets and I start measuring out ingredients.

"Wait." I stop them all. "After that conversation, everyone needs to wash their hands. Grant, wash yours twice."

I wash until my hands smell like lemon soap. We work in silence for a while, the noise of clanging pans and Caroline's knife hitting the cutting board filling the apartment. This is what I love about cooking. There's a rhythm to it—a steady beat that makes everything work. The grinding chop of onions falling apart, the metallic shifting of Avery pressing dough onto pans... it's almost melodic. I can feel it like it's *tangible.* It's culinary harmony, and there's nothing better.

"Okay. Got the first few pans ready to go." Avery picks up a pan in each hand. I arrange them to where some of hers and some of mine fit in the oven.

We go back to our rhythm, and soon, pizzas flow in and out of the oven, and people begin to flow in and out of the apartment, choosing toppings and taking slices. This pizza bar was a good idea, even if it was mine. Everyone gets exactly what they want, and my sister doesn't have to be in misery.

The sink fills up with dirty cooking things, and Grant becomes part of our harmony. He stands next to me; I pass him utensils and he washes them, me watching from the corner of my eye. This moment is so simple, but I don't think I've ever paid anyone this much attention.

He's wearing one of those S&F shirts, this one black and long-sleeved. The sleeves are rolled up to his elbows, and I'll never understand why I find that so attractive. They're just forearms… but they're such perfect forearms. His hands are soapy, and he smiles at me every time he looks over. Every time, it makes my stomach lurch. I have to remember there are other people in the room.

The four of us eat last, although not much is left. The toppings are almost picked clean. No one's taken any of the ribbons of basil I chopped myself. That's a chiffonade wasted.

Grant's behind me, leaning over to decide what else he wants on his pizza. He keeps slowly creeping into my personal space.

"Hey, wait. Why didn't we get pineapple?" he asks. I try not to look at him like I'm personally offended.

"Because that's disgusting," I say, completely deadpan. All he has on his pizza is pepperoni, and he was actually going to put *pineapple* on it, too. That's genuinely repellant. (Parker chose ham and black olives, though, so Grant's not the one with the worst taste.)

"All right, sorry I asked."

I giggle. He has to stop making me giggle like that, so obnoxiously, because I sound like I'm exaggerating. Laughing too loud and too long on purpose because I want him to think he's hilarious.

I lead the way back out into the gym. It's quieter now, everyone settled into their spots and eating. I walk to where Caroline has set up our sleeping bags in the corner.

"Seriously, try this crust," Caroline says, tearing off a piece of her pizza and passing it to Stella. The sight of Caroline sharing food in public is so strange. Even though I made it with my own hands, I mentally flinch.

"When you open a restaurant, let me know!" Parker says to me from across the room. He's stolen some of Lilah's pizza with my celiac-friendly crust. I guess I can consider that recipe perfected. I'll have to move it to the complete box when I get home.

"Same," Holden says, his mouth full of barely chewed pizza.

"What kind of sauce is this?" Manny asks.

"Homemade. Ivy did that, too," Avery says. That recipe is already in the completed box.

All the attention makes me want to crawl into my sleeping bag and never reemerge. Everyone's looking at me and it's making my heart race. There has to be something else I can do back in the kitchen—something else I can clean up. There has to be somewhere else I can be where no one is looking at me.

"Are we watching a movie or what?" Grant asks. He winks at me. He actually winks, somehow with his whole face.

Avery jumps up and starts fiddling with the projector.

"Thank you," I whisper to him. Not everyone understands.

Having someone around who is more than willing to be an attention vacuum is undeniably convenient.

The lights around us go down, and everyone shifts to get comfortable. I scoot back toward the wall, resting against it and stretching my legs out in front of me. It's like support group, but without the chairs. Everyone is still in a makeshift semicircle facing the screen on the wall. Grant settles next to me, mirroring my position, as always.

He's so close I can smell the clean cotton scent of his shirt and feel his shoulder pressed against mine. He has one foot crossed over the other, and he keeps shifting them back and forth, rocking on his heel.

The movie starts. I don't even catch the name. Avery picked it because it's set in a hospital and it's supposedly full of medical inaccuracies. Everyone around us is all but yelling.

"They got that IV on the first try? Yeah right!"

"That oxygen tubing isn't even connected to anything!"

Grant laughs, and I feel the rumbling vibration in my own chest. The dense weight of exhaustion is settling into my limbs, though. A day's worth of kitchen time makes my heart lighter, but my body completely and thoroughly fatigued.

Whether I mean to do it or not, my head comes to rest on Grant's shoulder. I can't remember a time I've been this comfortable. I wrap my hands around his arm and rest my fingers near his elbow.

I hear, and feel, him inhale, and he presses a barely-there kiss into my hair.

CHAPTER TWENTY-TWO

●

FRI, SEP 25, 11:28 P.M.

> Lilah: This is your friendly reminder that I want that pizza crust recipe.

> Ivy: SuperSecretPizzaCrustDONOTSHARE.doc

I've never really been the sleepover type. I'm the socially anxious type, and those two are kind of mutually exclusive. Sleep is inherently vulnerable, private. It's not something I want to do around other people.

Add in rheumatoid arthritis, and it becomes a huge nope. Basically, if there was a college degree program somewhere where one could major in RA, the first class would be called Joint Stiffness 101: Mornings Suck. Essentially, I'm not really able to move for the first fifteen to thirty minutes of my day. Even if I had ever been a fan of sleepovers, I wouldn't be now, just for that reason. It's not a pretty thing to witness, and if sleep is private, my waking-up ritual is sacred.

The gym is a safe place, I know that. That's why I'm here. But I'm still not looking forward to the morning.

I wash my face. I brush my teeth. I put my hair up in a weird, complicated bun so it hopefully won't look like a rat's nest in the morning. As I look in the mirror, I feel a twinge of regret for bringing my blue fuzzy pizza pajama pants. I'm so embarrassing sometimes.

Theoretically, I am ready for bed. Physically, I'm past ready. I could probably sleep standing up at this point—it wouldn't be a great idea, but I could do it. Emotionally, however . . .

Most of the other girls are gathered around me, chattering our way from the women's locker room to the sleeping-bag circle. I'm extra quiet. I don't have the mental space for verbal communication. My battery ran out long, long ago.

Caroline and Stella take their places near the half wall, and I do the same. Grant is in the opposite corner talking to Parker and Lilah. He really is wearing Braves pajamas—a set with blue pants with a blue button-down shirt. He's so adorably strange.

"I'm taking the spot next to Ivy," I hear him say.

"Excuse me," Caroline says, whipping her head around in his direction. Her hair flies into my face. "That was a statement that should've been a question."

Grant smiles, already walking toward me. I know I have basically none of my faculties right now, but my God is that smile disarming. I let my head fall against my pillow, turning my heavy eyes up at him. My vision's already gone blurry, and he's little more than a hazy silhouette and a fuzzy feeling.

"Ivy," he drawls my name, soft and slow. "Can I take the spot next to you?"

Sure, I want to say. I want to mumble, at least, but I'm so tired, all I can do is nod.

<hr>

I don't remember falling asleep. That's not too strange—chronic fatigue and all—but being the first one to fall asleep at a sleepover isn't ideal. The first thought that registers in my mind when I wake up is that someone could've put whipped cream in my hand and tickled my nose, or something else juvenile like that. But then I remember I'm between Caroline and Grant, and there's really not a safer place to be.

After the anxiety fog clears, all I can register is this all-encompassing stiffness. I'm the Tin Man without his oil can. I'm one of those dollar-store paper skeletons, the ones whose bones are held together by metal brads that just won't move. I expected this. I should've, at least. Everything I did yesterday left its mark. I can't spend a full day on my feet and not pay the price.

I feel the backs of Caroline's feet on my calves. If she kicks me again, I'm kicking back. I'm just about to start my stretching routine when I feel the tiniest tickle on my palm.

I turn my head in Grant's direction. It's essentially all I can move. He's walking two fingers up and down my hand, from my fingertips to the inside of my wrist. He's so intently focused, it's like he has X-ray vision and he's trying to tell which joints in my hand are the most damaged.

"What are you doing?" I ask, my volume low. I can't tell who else is still asleep. The entire room is illuminated, even with the half wall acting as a guard from the sun. There are too many windows in this gym.

"Seeing if you're awake," he says.

He looks soft and rumpled and smaller than normal, his shoulders hunched and his knees curled against his chest. He always has this one cowlick curl on his forehead, and more strands have joined it there. Grant has these skyscraper eyelashes, and he bats them at me. My joints might not be awake yet, but the nerves in my stomach burst to life like confetti from a canon. More confetti flutters each time his lashes touch his cheeks. They're such dark lashes.

"You couldn't have just asked?" The stiffness is becoming more and more painful. If I don't stretch and crack a few bones soon, I'm going to be in for a rough day.

Grant sits up all at once, curling his legs underneath him.

"Whoa, what was that?" I ask without thinking, because there's no way he can just do that when I can't even move.

"What do you mean? I sat up." He seems genuinely confused. Welcome to the club.

"You only woke up a minute ago, and you can just sit up like that?" It's almost laughable, how absurdly fluid the motion looked, as if he doesn't have a dysfunctional joint in his body.

"Yeah. What else am I supposed to do?"

"Unthaw, like I do."

"Unthaw? What does that even mean?"

I think of my morning routine. It's a slow process, letting my joints warm up at their own pace, stretching just a little at a time until every bone is cracked and every joint is moveable. It's a way to assess myself and my pain.

"It means not moving when you first wake up. You know how in therapy they'll teach you progressive muscle relaxation? Where you relax all your muscles in groups, starting from your head and moving down to your toes?"

It occurs to me mid-sentence that not everyone has been to therapy, and not everyone would have a clue about what I'm talking about. It's possible this wasn't the best way to start this speech. Still, I go on.

"I do the opposite. Move all my joints in groups. Hands first, because my knuckles always need to crack." For the added sound effect, I bend my fingers into fists.

My approach is the equivalent of defrosting my frozen joints in warm water. His approach is just hacking away at them with an ice pick.

"Then I move my toes and ankles." I do so, my squirming visible under my sleeping bag.

Slowly, I sit up, knowing this is going to be the grand finale in the bone-cracking show. Both of my hips pop, one after the other. It's so loud I actually think Caroline might wake up.

"Holy shit, that was your hip?" Grant asks, his eyes wide.

"RA isn't visible, but sometimes it is audible." I chuckle.

Grant laughs then, too, and I feel it in my chest. The sound wraps around me like my sleeping bag, warm and soft and fuzzy.

Avery appears and walks in our direction. Her shirt is covered in splotches, some that look like flour, and others that look like a baby spit up on her. She looks like she's living out the worst episode of *Hell's Kitchen* ever. "So, I tried to make up the pancake batter, but it fully took control of the situation. Help."

I try not to laugh, but Grant laughs next to me, loudly enough that I know he didn't even attempt to hold it back.

"I'll be there in a minute," I say. I need to at least brush my teeth and comb my hair. "Coffee wouldn't be out of the question, would it?"

By the time I make myself presentable, bags under my eyes excluded, I still haven't done my full fifteen minutes of stretching. I feel stiff, but I'll just have to push through.

This is the time I thought would be awkward, when everyone wakes up groggy and starts snipping at each other. But no one's snipping. Manny and Holden have taken over some of the machines in the gym, and Caroline and Stella are snapping pictures. That's the difference between my sister and me: the confidence required to take early morning woke-up-like-this photos.

The early-morning light is more palatable now that I'm fully awake. As I make my way back through the gym to Avery's apartment, a subtle kind of contentment washes over me. It's a fragile peace I've never experienced outside of my home.

When I walk through the open apartment door, it smells like rich, black coffee. Grant hands me a steaming **WORLD'S BEST DAD** mug.

"You good?" he asks.

"I'm good."

CHAPTER TWENTY-THREE

—————— • ——————

SUN, OCT 4, 11:32 A.M.

Rory: Any plans today?

Ivy: Not really. You?

Rory: Nope.

The thunder is loud enough that the floor Grant and I are walking on actually shakes. We live in the biggest city in North Carolina, with plenty to do, but somehow we still ended up at the mall. The original plan was to go back to the park where we had our first date, because I've yet to have these incredible food truck tacos I've heard so much about, but Mother Nature decided to bless us with a particularly intense thunderstorm instead.

I can see the people below us walking around on the ground floor. None of them seem bothered by the pounding rain and the periodic flashes of lightning. I can tell Grant is bothered, though, to say the least. As soon as the rain started, his posture shifted completely. I want to hold his hand, but I don't want to make either of us hurt worse. All our joints tense up as the rain gets worse, and neither of us needs to explain why. I have a feeling we're both putting on a show for the other's benefit, and it eats away at me that we're not past that kind of pettiness. Maybe that pretending-I'm-fine mindset is so ingrained that we'll never be past it.

I feel like we're made of glass, like the giant skylight above us. If the rain gets any worse, we'll break completely. Still, we keep walking. We don't have a destination in mind—at least, I don't. I just know that if we sit down anywhere right now, I'll have trouble getting back up. If the first class in the RA degree program is about how hard mornings are, the second one should be about how day-ruining rain can be.

A group of younger kids walks past us going the other way. They look about Ethan's age, and there are so many of them that they take over all the floor space in front of Bath & Body Works. I'm so distracted by the sickly-sweet lotion smell (and being pushed and shoved around by kids who *really* shouldn't be taller than me) that I almost don't see her. There she is, coming out of the video game store.

Rory.

Somehow, her gaze meets mine through the chaos.

She told me she didn't have plans today, and yet here she is with Brooke and Sloane and some of her other soccer friends I barely even recognize. I told her the same thing, and yet, here I am with Grant. She's wearing pink today, and somehow that makes this all worse. I pull my hands into fists before I think about it. After tiny pinpricks of pain shoot through all my smallest joints, I realize how bad an idea that was.

"Ivy?" Grant asks. I hadn't realized it, but I'm frozen mid-step. I reach for him, for something. I can't let them see each other. I can't let the awkward weirdness I've felt with Rory lately touch the perfect new contentment I feel with Grant. And how could I even explain him without spilling *everything*?

"Are you okay?" Grant turns me so I meet his eyes.

I don't know what to say. I don't know whether to fight, or run, or stay frozen where I am. My autonomic nervous system keeps my heart beating and my brain buzzing, but nothing else happens.

I turn my head again. Rory is closer this time. My heart rate speeds up and my palms start to sweat. I wonder if Grant can feel them. There's an escalator a little behind us. I decide on flight. I pull Grant's wrist as gently as I can—I won't hurt him, no matter how dramatic this moment might feel. I lead him to the escalator and only turn back around when we're halfway to the ground floor.

Suddenly the crowd noise and the hammering rain and the music blaring out of Hot Topic is all too much. My breath speeds up and I think my chest might actually cave in with the pressure.

"Okay, what the hell's going on?" Grant asks. His eyes are wide and he keeps looking behind us like he's expecting us to be chased.

"I promise I'll explain, I just—" I look around for somewhere to hide. I need an exit door, or a store she'll never go in, like one for babies or old ladies. I can smell frying oil and the gross stuff out of a can that the pretzel place calls cheese.

"Hey, Ivy." Someone taps on my shoulder from behind, and I flinch hard enough I think my feet actually come off the ground.

It's Rory.

I don't know how she beat us down here. She must've taken the elevator, or some set of stairs I don't know about. If I don't get out of here, I'm either going to pass out or throw up.

"Who's this?" Rory points at Grant.

I open my mouth to say something, probably his name (or something completely unrelated, who knows), but nothing comes out.

"I'm Grant," he says. He smiles. Sometimes that innate agreeability is useful.

Everyone but me has questions in their eyes. I'm sure mine are filled with terror.

"Hi." She waves. "I'm Rory."

"We were just about to leave." He puts one hand on my shoulder and steers me to the nearest exit. I thank all that's good in the universe that he can read me so well. "It was nice to meet you," he adds.

"You too," she says to our backs.

We walk down a long hallway toward a rain-splattered glass door. My heart begins to slow. I take deep, deep breaths, hold them in, let them go.

We reach the end of the hall and Grant takes my jacket from my hands. He puts the hood over my hair and I take over from there. My brain is beginning to function again. Some of my fine motor skills are coming back. The worn cotton of my hoodie feels good on my elbows and wrists. Everything has turned cold.

I know I have to say something to him, explain this monumental problem somehow. He walks ahead of me into the rain. The thunder has quieted, but the showers are still heavy. We make it back to his car just in time for the rain to slow to a stop. We're both drenched, and I can't even bother to take off my soggy sweatshirt. The sensory input of the gross-feeling fabric will keep me from drifting too far away into my own head.

"Are you good?" Grant asks. He looks completely baffled, and I don't blame him. I don't know how this all happened, how the rain came down and melted all my worlds together like layers of different-colored cotton candy. Grant was blue like the sky. Rory was Pepto Bismol pink, nice and sweet.

Now they've all entirely dissolved into a dirty purple, like a bruise.

"So..." Grant starts to say, once the silence and the humidity and our rain-soaked clothes settle into the most stifling hot mess of an environment I've ever been in. "What was that about?"

He's not looking at me, because he's driving, which is the ideal scenario here. I don't want him to be looking away from the road, obviously, but I also don't really want him to look at me. I have this thing where if people look at me when I'm upset, I burst into tears, and I'm holding it together by the skin of my teeth right now. So one look at me thrown over his shoulder and I'm done for.

"I . . ." I try to say something, grasp for words that mean anything. "I don't know." I finally sigh.

He eases onto the brake at a stoplight, and he does the worst possible thing he could. He looks at me.

There's no way I can explain this. Not without hurting someone, me or Rory or him—or I could end up hurting us all. I could end up ruining everything, just by opening my mouth.

Honestly, though, I could end up ruining everything without even speaking. I can't imagine what they're both thinking right now, the thoughts that are taking root in their minds.

Grant doesn't say anything for a while, and I just look out the window at the passing scenery. For once, there's not any traffic, and the trees move past the window so fast they run together.

"I don't know how to explain what just happened," I admit finally. "But I will, eventually."

He still doesn't say anything, and we're just sitting in my driveway in silence.

"Is that okay?" I ask, terrified of the answer.

"Yeah," he looks over at me again and shrugs. "It's kind of weird, but it's okay."

CHAPTER TWENTY-FOUR

———— • ————

MON, OCT 5, 3:51 P.M.

> Dad: Are you sure you don't need me to come home?

> Ivy: No. I can handle it, as long as nothing else goes wrong today.

When Caroline and I got home from school, Mom was already here. She came home sick. She's flaring so bad it's more than visible when I look at her. Her ever-present butterfly rash is a brighter red than ever, and her hands, legs, and feet are swollen beyond belief. Her blood pressure is probably through the roof. Worse, the instant we were inside, Caroline doubled over in pain, clutching her stomach like she'd been hit. Now I'm running from room to room, trying to take care of them both.

This is bad. It's DEFCON 1 bad. It's Red Alert bad.

"Has anyone seen my baseball bag?" Ethan asks, shouting down the hall.

"It's in the garage!" I shout back. Then I remember. He has a game tonight. Dad is at work, and everyone who can drive is currently incapacitated.

Everyone but me.

I could take him…but that would mean coming home in the dark, and I'm a nervous driver who cannot *stand* driving in the dark. Besides, I can't leave Mom and Caroline alone right now.

I let myself into Caroline's room, carrying a glass of water and one of Mom's Zofran tablets. She has the kind you don't even have to swallow, which is good, because Caroline doesn't look like she could keep anything down right now. I put a palm against her forehead. She's not warm.

"You had to have come in contact with gluten somehow." I hand over the water and the strawberry-flavored dissolvable tablet.

Caroline holds the pill out in front of her like she's trying to determine its genetic composition.

"Oh shit," she says.

"What?"

Caroline groans. "I had really bad cramps in Biology this morning, and my lab partner gave me some Tylenol. I was cramping so bad I didn't even think to make sure they were gluten-free. That's such a rookie mistake!"

She curls up in a tight ball with her knees to her chest, and I rub her back. Periods and chronic illnesses don't always peacefully coexist.

Caroline gets up and staggers to the bathroom. I hurry back across the hall to Mom's room.

"Do you need anything?" I ask.

She's loaded up with blankets and heating pads, but she still looks tragic. "I'm good. I promise. It's just a flare-up; you know how it goes." Mom tries to smile, but it looks like more of a grimace. "How was your day?"

I haven't even thought about my day since I got home, but in all honesty, it was grim. (That's the thing about being a sick kid in a sick family—sometimes there's no time to dwell on yourself.)

"Truthfully, it sucked." I think about it for a moment, about Rory and yesterday, about how it feels like I don't belong anywhere at school anymore. I even sat alone at lunch. Dark.

I collapse onto Mom's bed and feel exhaustion pull at my limbs.

No. I still have problems to solve, homework to do, dinner to make. I run my hands through my hair and resist the urge to pull handfuls of it out.

"I'll be right back." I try to smile so Mom will think I actually have things under control.

I walk the few steps to my room and close the door behind me. I take my phone from my pocket, then shift it from one hand to the other, unable to stand still. Talking on the phone is gross. It's one of the pillars my life is based on: *dodge phone conversations at all costs*. I avoid them like the plague, and being immunocompromised and all, I *really* try to stay away from plagues.

I chew on my thumbnail. Finally, I dial, then raise the phone to my ear. I try to time my breathing to the call: breathe in, ring, breathe out, ring. I'm breathing in when he picks up.

"Ivy?" He doesn't say hello. He mostly sounds surprised.

I let myself exhale in relief. The sense of calm that washes over me at his voice is almost tangible, like pulling the covers over my shoulders after the world's longest day. His voice is warm, and safe, and as comforting as the robin's egg blue walls of the room I'm standing in.

"Hi," I say.

"Hi."

"Can I ask you for a huge favor?" My stomach clenches again.

"What's up?"

I look at my alarm clock again. Maybe it's too late. Maybe he's already left.

"Can you take Ethan to the game? I know it's short notice and—"

"Yeah, sure. I'll be right there."

Of course, just like that. I breathe out another sigh of relief.

"Thank you," I say, trying to convey as much meaning as I can over the phone. "I really appreciate it."

"No problem."

After I hang up, I wander down to the kitchen just to have something to do with my hands. I need something that I can control. Within minutes, I have the entirety of the vegetable crisper in front of me and my favorite chef's knife in my hand. I don't even know what I'm making, but I chop on anyway. I lose myself in the rhythm of the knife hitting the cutting board, and I almost don't hear the doorbell.

"Ethan, Grant's here," I yell. I realize a moment too late that I probably shouldn't have; Mom or Caroline could be asleep.

Ethan comes running out of his room in his uniform, his baseball bag dragging behind him on the floor.

"Don't say anything weird, okay?" I say, drying my hands off and making my way to the door.

"What does that mean?" Ethan asks.

"It means I know you, and I don't trust you not to say anything weird."

I open the door before I can talk myself out of it. I can't help it; I throw my arms around Grant before I even give him a second glance. (It could've just been someone vaguely Grant-shaped, for all I know.) I breathe him in, and everything calms down. Somehow, he's just the kind of stillness I need.

"Whoa, okay," he says. His arms come around my back. "That was unexpected."

"That's gross." Ethan pushes past us and his baseball bag hits me right behind the knee.

Grant laughs and leans into me just slightly, but he doesn't let me go. I don't want him to.

"You seem . . . scrambled. Are you okay?"

That's what I am, scrambled like an egg. Today was a lot. Tonight will be a lot. I've been thrown from my shell into a hot pan I can't find a way out of.

"I'll be okay." I hope that's believable.

"We better get going. Don't want to miss first pitch."

Grant lets me go and I try to think of something valuable to say, something worth saying, something worth hearing.

He turns away to follow Ethan to his car.

"Grant?" I find myself saying.

"Yeah?"

"Be careful."

I feel strangely vulnerable here, watching him watch me. I wring my hands together and think about how I probably have discarded vegetable peels clinging to my shirt. My feet feel heavy and I don't think I'll be able to move until he's out of sight.

He smiles, and all of my bones go soft.

CHAPTER TWENTY-FIVE

●

MON, OCT 5, 7:46 P.M.

Caroline: Can you make me soup? I want soup.

Ivy: What kind of soup?

Ivy: I hope chicken noodle is fine, it's already simmering

"They're back," I whisper to myself. I see the headlights through the kitchen window.

Ethan's footsteps clatter on the wooden steps to the front door. His cleats are so loud, I think he might actually break through one of them. That would be great, the last healthy one of our generation in this family breaking a leg on our front porch. I can just see it now.

Ethan comes barreling through the door, not bothering to take his dirty cleats off before he tracks caked clumps of dirt through the house. Grant stands there at the door, like he's waiting to be invited inside. He probably is, knowing him. Suddenly, I just really want to hug him again.

It's not that he can't come in, but we'll have more privacy outside. I lead him to the set of matching rocking chairs on our front porch. They're worn from years of weather, and the wicker backs are all but falling apart, but they make this swinging squeak when they rock that I love. We sit down, and a heavy silence descends.

I look at him, just because I want to. But I hate having these kinds of talks—messy ones where feelings have to be heard and felt.

"Are you dumping me?" Grant asks abruptly.

I physically recoil. I almost fall off my chair. That's the last reaction I expected. I don't even think I have the power to dump him: that would mean we're in a relationship capable of being called off.

"No," I manage to say.

"Oh, okay. Good. You're just acting weird, and I thought—"

I don't let him finish.

"Oh, no. God, no. Hell no." That, I'm vehement about.

Grant smiles a wondrous grin that brightens up a dark night. "I don't think I've ever heard you swear."

"You swear enough for both of us."

I smile back at him. There's so much I want to say, so much I don't know how to.

"Give me your hand," he says, gently.

"Why?" I ask. I don't care why, and I shouldn't have asked. I should've just given the boy my hand like I want to.

So I do.

"You're an anxious mess, and it's stressing me out, and I want to hold your hand." He wraps his fingers around mine and traces the faint veins on the back of my hand with his free hand. I want to end the conversation here, and just let him keep running the gentle pressure of his fingertips over my skin.

"I didn't want to talk to you because I want to break up," I say softly. "I just wanted to say thank you. Today was chaotic and messy and I felt like I was on my own, but then I called you and you just…helped."

"You're welcome, but it was just a baseball game."

"No, it wasn't. Not to Ethan. Not to me. I don't have people who just help whenever they can, because they want to."

His brows knit up, and I wait for him to say something about my pathetic social life—or laugh at it, perhaps. I imagine him saying something about how I'm a dumpster fire of a person that he definitely shouldn't be hanging out with, let alone dating.

"That's what friends do, Ivy. That's what people who are… more than friends do."

"I know, I know." I run my fingers through my curls. "But not my friends. Not for me. I think…I think I don't let them."

"What does that mean? You don't let them?"

"Rory. She's been my best friend all through high school. I think I've pushed her away." I sigh, because realizing this is one thing and talking about it is another. "She's changed and I've changed, and I think she wanted us to change together. It's my fault we haven't."

"Well, then you need to let her be your friend."

I scoff. He's so deadpan about it, like I could actually wake up one day and decide to embrace total vulnerability.

"Yeah. As if it's that easy."

"What? Isn't it?" He's serious. Damn.

"Okay. Listen." I turn my whole body to face him, sitting sideways in the chair and pulling my legs up, knees to my chest. I wrap my fingers around them and dig my nails into the fabric of my leggings.

"I'm bad at this," I say, like that one sentence explains everything. "In case you haven't noticed, I'm social garbage. Anything that requires me to speak to anyone who doesn't live in this house is *terrifying*. Borderline impossible. So, yeah, maybe I don't exactly let my one friend... be my friend... but if I'm sitting with her at lunch, I'm not alone, and that's enough for me. That's all I can handle right now. I wouldn't know how to fix a friendship anyway. If it stops working, I'm just... lost."

I take a deep breath, wishing I could fill my lungs with aerosol strength. I don't mention that Rory and I are not, currently, sitting together at lunch.

"Everywhere that isn't home is intimidating. So home is where I stay. People need me here. Here, I cook, and I take care of people when they're sick and help them find things they lost when they're not. Home is safe. Everywhere else is agonizingly unnerving... Everyone else is, too."

I whisper the last part. I've never been able to admit that out loud, how petrifying the rest of the world is beyond this porch.

"That doesn't make any sense," Grant says. I can't look at him anymore. "No, I mean it," he prods, when I don't respond. "I don't get it. You didn't seem nervous to talk to me. I was more nervous than you were."

Part of me was hoping he wouldn't put those particular pieces together. I rock back and forth, trying to think of a way to explain this to him, trying to think of a way that my neuroses make any logical sense.

"I have social anxiety, Grant. It doesn't always make sense. I wish it did." I pause. "Okay, so I had this recurring dream as a kid. I'm skating on this really thin ice, and it's awful. I'm off-balance, and freezing, and nothing feels safe. And no matter what, I can't stop. The ice just keeps going on and on, and it never runs out. That's what being outside of this house feels like for me: thin ice."

I look up at him, trying to see if there's even a speck of understanding in his eyes.

"It gets better the more I know people, but they're still ice. It just isn't as thin."

He nods.

"One night right before I stopped having the dream, I ran out of ice. I don't know what happened, but I slid straight off and onto this field of grass. It was warm, and sunny, and my skates were gone. All I had needed was dry land. I felt like I could breathe again."

I have to force myself to say this part, because it feels so big coming out of my chest. It feels like it means too much to say with just words, but that's all I have left.

"If everyone else is thin ice"—I look up at him, blinking my lashes—"you're dry land."

He beams at me. He just...beams. He's incandescent. I've never had someone look at me like that, like I matter that much.

Grant's hand is warm around mine again, and then I feel that same warmth climb up to rest against my cheek. My autonomic nervous system forces me to breathe before I'm ready, and I can smell his shampoo. It's spicy, I think. Up this close, I can see the highlights in the one stray curl that lies over his forehead.

He leans just the slightest bit closer, and my eyes slide closed. Time slows down, almost to a crawl, as I feel him leaning even closer. Then his lips meet mine with a pressure so gentle I think I'm imagining it.

He's kissing me, and everything speeds back up.

I reach up for him with my free hand and find his shoulder. Everything about him is warm and steady, and as much as I've thought about this, I didn't expect it to *happen* like this, so naturally. I'd expected hasty movements, uncomfortable shifts into personal space.

What I didn't expect is this surge of feeling from every direction. I've heard about butterflies. These aren't butterflies. This is a kaleidoscope that's recruited the entire ecosystem to join the chorus. Honeybees. Dragonflies. Hummingbirds. Anything that buzzes in the forest. An entire food web floods my senses.

Grant tilts his head and his teeth bump against mine. It's just enough of a jolt to knock me back into reality, to make me realize I'm on my front porch, kissing him. It's enough to make me realize any one of my family members could walk out here at any moment.

I pull away, just enough that air passes between us. His hand still holds my face. My fingers are still bunched in his shirt.

I blink a couple times, trying to get my eyes to look at something besides him. They drift up to meet his of their own volition, the traitors. I can't read all the emotion there. It's part satisfaction, part exhilaration, and part *holy shit what just happened.*

CHAPTER TWENTY-SIX

— • —

FRI, OCT 9, 12:17 P.M.

Mom: Do we have any more flour? We're almost out of bread.

Ivy: Mom, please go to bed. I'll make the bread when I get home.

Mom: Fine, but only because you asked so nicely.

All I can think about is home.

A couple of days have passed since our initial Red Alert situation, and no one is feeling much better. Caroline is still incapacitated, so Dad drove me to school. Mom's stuck at home, too, and I feel like I left part of my brain there with them this morning. It's probably on the counter with my unwashed breakfast dishes.

I hate days like this more than anything, days where I could be home, in my safe place, taking care of people. Instead, I'm sitting alone in a dark corner of the cafeteria, avoiding the one friend I have here.

My phone buzzes.

I think Mom's trying to make bread. Did you tell her not to?

Caroline's such a snitch sometimes. I appreciate it.

She's really physically incapable of resting. Are you resting, at least?

Yep. I've watched half a season of America's Next Top Model already.

Good.

Enough lunchroom misery. I rise and leave through the cafeteria doors, heading outside where the sun is much brighter than the dark corner I've been hiding in. I pass Rory on the way, and she looks at me for a split second before she averts her eyes to the floor. I recognize that move. I practically invented that move, and that means I have no idea how to respond to it. I could go back there and talk to her, but even thinking about that makes me want to cry. So, I keep walking. I glance back over my shoulder: she kept walking, too.

Once I breathe a lungful of fresh air, my fingers tap against the screen, and Mom picks up on the third ring.

"Hi, honey. I didn't expect to hear from you today." Mom's voice is strong and sure. For a second, I consider making this a part of my daily routine, until I remember that she's not always home.

"Yeah, well, I hear you're still not resting."

"What, do you have cameras in this kitchen or something?"

"No." I smile. "Caroline's there, remember?"

"Oh, right. I should check on her."

"No, Mom!" I huff. "You should *rest*. Sleep, or at least be horizontal somehow. You would tell me to do the same thing."

"I know," she sighs. "I would, of course I would. And I know that's what I should be doing. It's just...hard to rest sometimes, you know? I shouldn't be putting this on you, anyway."

"It's okay. I get it, I promise. Just...take care of yourself, okay?"

"I will. I'll see you in a few hours. Love you, sweetie."

"Love you, too, Mom."

I lean against the wall just outside the cafeteria. My phone buzzes in my back pocket again; no one wants to leave me alone today. Then I see who it is, and I don't mind at all. Maybe being left alone is overrated.

Are you as bored as I am right now?

I read Grant's words like I can hear him speaking. I can imagine the inflection he'd say them with, how he'd lean forward, how that one curl would fall farther over his forehead. It's just one text, it's inconsequential, but I feel an easy smile grace my lips.

You have no idea.

I only have to get through two more classes, and it'll be the weekend. I can go home to Mom and Caroline, and not come back here for two whole days. My mind starts to drift as I overhear chatter from the picnic tables a few feet away. The one thing ringing through my mind is this prevailing sense of exhaustion. Mentally, physically, emotionally, every cell in my body is drained.

I don't have it in me to make mindless comments to contribute to the conversation. The Grant-caused easy smile fades. Instead, his earlier words reverb through my brain, what he said the first time I saw him: *Healthy people are annoying.*

It's there when I go to Chemistry and my lab partner spends

the entire period discussing how uncomfortable the track and field team's new uniforms are. *Healthy people are annoying.* Then, I overhear a conversation in the bathroom about the girl who broke her ankle in gym class. They're saying her crutches make her look clumsy, as if she chose to wear them like an accessory. *Healthy people are annoying.* The senior World History teacher was in a car accident last week. People in the hallway think she's "being dramatic" about it for taking off work this long, even though she literally ruptured her spleen. They have literally no idea how important an intact spleen is. *Healthy people are annoying.*

By the time I slam the door to Dad's car, it's all I can hear.

"Please get me out of here," I say instead of hello.

"I was going to ask how your day was, but that answers that."

I take a deep breath. I don't know why everything is bothering me so much today.

"Did something happen?" Dad asks, one hand on the steering wheel and one elbow resting out the open window. There's just the slightest chill in the air, the wind making it actually, finally, feel like fall. A storm is brewing, though. I can feel it in my bones, in my joints.

"No," I say, even though everything has. "School just sucks."

I sound like Grant, and that gives me an idea.

"Hey, Dad?" I ask, suddenly nervous. "Can I invite Grant over for dinner?"

He pretends to think about it for the distance between one stoplight and the next, which, in Charlotte traffic, is a long time.

This feels like a test, and I don't know who needs to pass, me or Grant.

"Sure," he finally says. "I don't see why not."

After a few more stoplights, we reach home and I check on Mom and Caroline with dragging feet. They're both alive and as relatively fine as they can be, so I head to my room. I barely kick my shoes off before falling into bed. With the last few moments of energy I have left, I fire off a text to Grant. *Do you want to come over for dinner?*

My eyes are closed before he responds.

Afternoon naps are a kind of bliss healthy people will just never understand. I roll over after I crack all the appropriate joints and check my phone. *What time?* I tell him to come over whenever, and head to the kitchen.

There are fresh vegetables I want to roast, and Ethan's been asking for garlic and herb potato wedges. With minced garlic and drizzles of olive oil, I lose myself in the rhythm of my happy place. Everything smells fresh and herby, and the late-afternoon light streaming through the kitchen window glints off the blade of my knife.

The doorbell rings, and my eyes drift to the clock blinking on the stovetop. It hasn't been more than fifteen minutes since I left my room.

"Hi," I say, pulling open the door. "I wasn't expecting you so soon."

"Yeah, well. To me, whenever means now." He smiles and steps closer. Grant waits there, a step away, as if asking for permission to touch me.

I wrap my arms around his neck, and he wraps his around my waist. I don't think I've ever been held so tightly.

"You smell like garlic," he says when he pulls away.

He didn't kiss me. That's probably why.

"Thank you?" I don't know how to take that, as accurate an observation as it is.

"Did you just wake up?"

I momentarily panic. I haven't even looked in a mirror, so I can only guess how bad I look. I thought I'd have more time until he was going to show up, time to cook and time to make myself look decent.

"Yeah, why?" I ask, as if I actually want to know.

"You have pillow marks on your face."

I groan. Great. Perfect. Pillow marks. They're probably connecting the dots between my freckles.

"That may have been something I should've kept to myself." He seems embarrassed, and I'm glad I'm not the only one.

He follows me into the kitchen and sits on one of the stools behind the island. I wasn't expecting to cook with an audience. I kind of feel like a hibachi chef, like I need to set something on fire or build an onion volcano. Seriously, though, this feels sacred, like I'm letting him into the deepest recesses of myself. In some ways, I am. This house, my family, they're everything to me. This kitchen is the direct center of my universe, and now here he is, sitting in it like he belongs.

"You don't have to just sit here and watch me cook. Ethan's here. You guys can practice if you want."

Grant looks down the hall. "You don't think he'll mind me just showing up in his room asking if he wants to play catch?"

I scoff and turn to face him. "Please. He thinks you hung the moon. Watch." I take two steps into the hallway and raise my voice. "Ethan, Grant's here."

Loud, reckless footsteps clatter down the stairs. I just barely move out of the way before he has a chance to barrel into me. Quickly, but not smoothly, Ethan slides to a halt and straightens, like he arrived at a socially acceptable speed.

"Hey," he says.

"Wanna throw around?"

Ethan runs away again instead of answering.

"Okay, I see what you mean," Grant says.

I bite back a chuckle. "Did you bring a glove?"

"There's one in my car."

Of course there is. They walk outside, Grant retrieving the glove, Ethan leading Grant to the side yard. There, they are away from the cars and all the fragile front porch furniture. I can still see them through the kitchen window. I stand at the sink, rinsing potatoes I'm about to peel. They throw back and forth, Ethan's motions less smooth and fluid than Grant's.

I try to gauge if this feels different, if he's still my mental dry land. I keep the thought in mind as I cook.

As we all gather around the table, I watch everyone carefully to see how they're feeling. Caroline doesn't look as groggy as she has been, but she's wearing the baggy T-shirt she only wears on gluten-bloat days. Mom's butterfly rash isn't as prominent, but she's not participating in the small talk as wholeheartedly as she normally does. Ethan, on the other hand, looks as if he's just been playing catch with a movie star, or someone who won the World Series. I wonder if that's what I look like after spending time with Grant.

"You're a pretty good coach," Dad tells Grant. I don't know how Grant does this, just charms anyone within a mile radius. It's fascinating to watch, and impossible to understand.

"Thank you," he says, taking the seat next to me. I briefly thought he wasn't going to, but that was silly of me. Of course he's going to sit next to me. We're, like, a thing.

"You know," Dad starts, "I'm glad those kids can't drive yet. They really like running through stop signs."

Grant laughs, and so does Ethan. I know I'm missing something, but I don't want to embarrass myself by asking what it is.

"Okay, okay." Mom takes the last open seat. "Everyone, eat."

Hands reach in opposite directions and forks clang against plates. Knives cut through chicken and people pass potatoes. More than the rhythm of the kitchen, I love the controlled chaos of the dining room. I love the way noise fades to silence as everyone eats, and then rises back into lively conversation between bites. I love when people grab seconds and speak with full mouths. I love when Caroline elbows Ethan in the chest for the last potato wedge, and when I catch Dad making sure Mom isn't too nauseous to eat. Then I look over at Grant and realize he really is sitting here like he belongs.

CHAPTER TWENTY-SEVEN

—— • ——

FRI, OCT 23, 2:55 P.M.

Grant: Can I ask you for a favor?

Ivy: You can ask me for anything.

"So where did this idea come from?" I ask as we walk farther down the pasta aisle at the grocery store.

"I don't know." Grant shrugs. I've noticed he does that when he doesn't know what to say. "Seeing you with your family . . . it made me realize that my mom does everything for me, and I never do anything for her."

I stop, right in the middle of the aisle. I agreed to this plan devoid of details, so I didn't know what to expect, but that answer wasn't it at all.

"What do you mean, exactly?" I stop looking at him and run my eyes over the jars of sauce in front of me. I don't have time to make it homemade, so I'll have to work with store-bought. Unless I make a brown butter sauce . . . My mind starts to drift.

"All of you take care of each other, like it's a two-way street. All my mom does is take care of me, and I never take care of her. She doesn't need me to, but that's not the point."

I love how thoughtful that is. When I think about it, though, all Grant has ever been is thoughtful. He's been careful, attentive. He's something else, something important.

"We need a dessert, too," I say, to keep from saying something else. "What does she like?"

Grant shifts his weight from foot to foot. Even thinking, he's cute.

"Um…" His voice carries through the whole aisle. "Cheesecake?"

I pull him toward the refrigerated section. On the way, we pass the produce aisle. The red potatoes are on sale. That makes me think of Rory, who didn't know red potatoes existed (?!?!), but thinking about her makes every feeling I have confusing. On one hand, I want to smile, because good Lord, how did she not know about red potatoes? Beyond that, though, I want to cringe at myself, at my own behavior. I want to apologize. I want to be back to where we were before, if that's even possible.

"Hey," Grant says, shaking me gently. "You okay?" I know he can tell I just went somewhere else there for a second.

"Yeah." I force a smile. "Cheesecake, right?"

He nods. That's easily the best thing he could've said. I throw cheesecake ingredients toward him and he picks them up when they land everywhere but the cart. He doesn't even comment on how bad my throwing is.

He completely charms the pants off the woman working the

cash register, because of course he does. She pulls out her cell phone to show him pictures of her son. She says Grant looks just like him. Her son is, like, twenty and has ginger hair and a face that is distinctly not Grant-like. She wishes her son looked like him. Grant smiles along and agrees anyway. That's something I'll never understand, the ease with which he speaks to people. He's just so effortlessly affable.

As we drive in companionable silence, my mind starts to drift again. I didn't think dating could be like this: having fun in a grocery store. I'd imagined stuffy dinners and awkward conversations. I hadn't imagined baseball and cooking and staring at each other across a circle of chairs in a gym.

"Are you coming?" Grant asks. I hadn't even noticed we weren't moving anymore.

I get out of the car and look around. His house is smaller than mine, which makes sense for just him and his mom. It's all bright white, the siding, the porch columns, everything but the gray front door.

I follow him. The grocery bags I'm carrying start to feel heavy, as if they're going to tear right through the joints holding my fingers together, but I say nothing. Grant opens the door, and we walk into a warm living room with pictures of him everywhere. *Everywhere.*

I lose myself in what is essentially a Grant museum in chronological order. He used to be blond; that's the first thing I notice.

Somewhere in between the last T-ball photo and the first pitching picture, his hair turned into the warm caramel brown I know and love.

In his expression is a parabola of happiness. The glossy photos go from the fair-haired little boy who radiates the easygoing energy I associate with Grant, to a frowning middle schooler who always has his arms crossed, to the dazzling, smiling human standing next to me.

Grant takes the grocery bags from my hands. There are things to do, I know that. There's plenty of cooking to be done. But this is much more mesmerizing. It's like a flipbook on a wall—I'm almost able to see Grant grow up in real time.

"I don't know why you're even looking at those," he says. He actually looks embarrassed. I didn't think he was even capable of embarrassment.

I gaze at him. In profile like this, he seems older. A strong jaw. Eyelashes so long they seem to brush against his brow. Undeniably striking.

I point one aching finger at a picture directly in between us, labeled SEVENTH GRADE.

"Is this about when you were diagnosed?"

"How'd you know?" His voice sounds closer than it was before. This seems startlingly intimate, being the only people here, looking at his past on display.

"It starts about here." I point toward a sixth-grade baseball photo. The action shots are less explosive, his body in the posed shots stiffer. "And this one... this one has the pissed-off look of someone who's just been told they're going to be sick forever."

He leans against the wall in front of me, replacing Grant-behind-glass with Grant-in-real-life. "How do you just... get me?"

"I'm your girlfriend. I'm supposed to get you."

My hand snaps up to my mouth. My reckless, out-of-control mouth! I blame the cute pictures for lowering my defenses. Those defenses are there for a reason.

I basically black out from embarrassment, and when my eyes focus back in, Grant is gazing at me intently. His fingers softly close around my wrist and pull my hand down from my lips. Our fingers tangle together. I stop breathing because the air in the room feels too fragile, like all of this will shatter if I move a muscle.

Finally, he leans in like he's going to kiss me again—and he does.

I think I actually sigh against his mouth because I'm so relieved. It's quick, and intense, and somehow nothing like our first kiss.

"Finally," I whisper. Oops. I don't think I meant to say that.

"We should, uh..."

"Yeah... yeah, we... should definitely..." Now, when I *try* to speak, my mouth isn't working.

We make our way to the kitchen. Standing in the silence at the counter, I realize he's waiting on me to give him some direction.

Obviously. That's why I'm here, to show him how to cook for his mom. I'm not here to kiss him against a wall.

I did, though. I fell into him without a second thought—and, admittedly, I have absolutely no regrets. I try to get my melting brain under control. What I can't control, though, is the faint smile on my face.

Wordlessly, I begin sorting through the groceries. I set the cheesecake ingredients aside, because I can make that myself while I tell him how to do the rest. That way I can be somewhere that's not right beside him. I need distance to clear my head. I'm not sure I haven't left the rational part of my brain behind somewhere in front of that wall.

"Okay, so . . ." I start, the reflexive art of cooking taking over my body. I can feel it—the way I stand up straighter and actually look him in the eye. I explain how to toast the pasta before boiling it for extra flavor; how to test the tenderness of hot noodles; how to brown butter. I've never had that *wow, I sound like my mother* moment before, but this is definitely a *wow, I sound like my grandmother* moment.

Once the kitchen smells like garlic, thyme, and sage, I can breathe again. All I'd been able to smell before was my lip gloss mixed with Grant's mint toothpaste–laced breath.

I'm checking on the chilling cheesecake when I hear stomping footsteps on the porch. It's not even six yet! Grant's mom isn't supposed to be here for another hour! I look at him. He's wide-eyed and as alarmed as I am.

Sharp shreds of panic pierce my chest, and I freeze, one hand on the spatula I've been using and the other gripping the countertop so tightly I think the corner might break off.

"You would not believe the story they have me working on!" We hear her before we see her. She's talking before the door is even all the way open. Her purse lands on the ground with a heavy *thunk*. "There was an accident at a construction site, and—"

She stops talking once she can see into the kitchen. I can see her wall of professionalism go back up immediately. Grant's mom reminds me of my own mom that way; the switch from consummate professional to mother and back again.

"Oh, hi! I'm Nicole." She smiles. Nicole is clearly who Grant got his previously blond hair from. "You must be Ivy."

I don't know how to respond. I am indeed Ivy, but words aren't really happening right now. Just social anxiety things.

Awkwardness descends, and it stifles me. Nicole is still too far away for a handshake, or a hug, or any of that other stuff people like to do when meeting each other. I try to think of what I know about her. She's Grant's mother. She's a newspaper reporter. She never married Grant's dad—or anyone else, for that matter. Clearly, more than anything, she loves Grant.

I can't tell if that lip-gloss-and-toothpaste smell still lingers in the air, but I'm just hoping she won't look at me and immediately know I was kissing her son in the middle of the hallway. My heart has literally never raced this fast.

"Hi," I finally say. It's the only signal I can make my brain send to my mouth. This is almost painful, but I had it coming: Grant has met my mom, and my dad, and Caroline, and Ethan. Now it's my turn to be presented to his family.

"You're home early, Mom," Grant says, rescuing the moment.

To my surprise, Nicole lets her poised veneer slip just long enough to roll her eyes. "I told them I'd finish my story here. I couldn't take another second."

"*Well*"—Grant walks past me, toward his mom, and hugs her—"go work on your story. We're making dinner."

Nicole's eyes light up like Grant has just bought her a new car. I've never seen anyone so excited about anything like this before.

He and I jump into action, plating swirled piles of pasta and tossing dishes into the sink. I know I'm being watched. I always know. I feel like I'm being assessed, like this is an assignment I'll be graded on. My hands start to shake, and I almost drip brown butter sauce all over the counter.

"So what's this story I won't believe?" Grant asks as we sit down.

Nicole laughs, a hint of embarrassment in her tone. "It's really not something for polite company."

It takes me a minute to realize she means me. "Oh, I'm not polite company."

We all laugh. I could've said that better, but at least it was effective.

"Okay." Nicole starts chuckling before she even starts the

story. "There was an incident at a construction site in Uptown. Not what you'd think, though. No one was hurt or anything."

"Why do you have to write about it if no one was hurt?" Grant asks. (That makes Nicole's job sound kind of soul-crushing.)

Nicole laughs in earnest, dropping her fork onto her plate and leaning her head back.

"It was *so* juvenile," she mutters before she makes a solid effort to calm herself down. "It was a prank war that got out of hand! Can you believe that? Grown adults, on a construction site. It's going to delay the whole building because they have to replace so many people."

"What kind of pranks?" Grants eyes are wide, like he's looking for ideas. That's terrifying.

"The most asinine things you could think of. I went over there today to talk to management, and I could barely keep a straight face. Tool belts in cement...*pants* in cement...convincing newbies you could sharpen chain saws on concrete curbs...putting olive oil in the gas tank of a van...They even rigged up some kind of harness to lift a guy up and swing him around on a crane!"

We laugh then, too. The mental image is unbelievable.

"They didn't even rat each other out—that's the funny part. But they're in the middle of Uptown, so someone in their office in a skyscraper looked down and saw a man being Tilt-a-Whirled around a crane at the speed of sound!"

All three of us laugh again. My stomach actually starts to hurt. If Grant's right—that he doesn't get time with her often—then

I'm glad he's getting some now. Nicole seems like too important a person not to spend time with.

"I just can't believe it. If you'd told me in college I'd be reporting on this kind of stuff nearly twenty years into my career, I would have dropped out."

"Is it always like that?" I ask. That's good, that's a meaningful addition to the conversation.

"No," Nicole says. "Usually it's worse."

That simmers in the air for a moment, all of us thinking about how much a reporter had to have seen in twenty years in this city.

"This was delicious." Nicole brightens up, putting most of her mom face back on. "I really can't thank you two enough for cooking. Especially you, Ivy."

I don't know how to take compliments, so I stand up. "I'll go get dessert."

Grant follows me. I thought he would, but it still makes me happy. I lift the cheesecake out of the fridge and admire the ribbons of chocolate I folded in myself.

"Hey," he says, rummaging around for something to serve it with. "Are you okay?"

I take a breath. I've been trying to avoid asking myself that question all through dinner. School, and then shopping, and then cooking—it was a lot, and I'm using up the last fumes of my energy.

"I don't just mean today, I mean in general." He looks really, really serious and really, really focused on me. "You don't just know me. I know you, too. I can tell a difference the last couple of weeks. Do you think your medicine is working?"

No. I don't.

In that moment, I realize he's the perfect person to talk about it with. He's standing right in front of me, my real-life human boyfriend. He's the only other person I've ever met with the same autoimmune antibodies running through his veins.

Grant tucks a flyaway strand of hair behind my ear. "Ivy?"

"I don't know," I whisper.

"Okay." He shrugs like it doesn't matter, like it's not a big deal that I'm criminally bad at talking to people and probably much worse at this whole *being sick* thing than he is. He shrugs as if my being a combination of disasters is nothing to bat an eye at.

We serve dessert, which Nicole loves. I try to listen, try to speak, but I space out, and they talk without me. All my joints are aching. They're always aching, but the volume has been turned up enough that I can't hear anything else. I can't feel anything but my own bone-tired weariness.

I hug Nicole goodbye. It's not as unpleasant as most hugs are. If I wasn't dead on my feet, it probably would've been nice.

Grant drives me home, and I have to force myself to stay awake. I hate this, this feeling. Being completely devoid of energy. I've turned off all human function that isn't necessary for survival.

He follows me to the porch. Turning around at the door, I weakly wrap him in what is probably the most pathetic hug I've ever given anyone. My head falls against his chest and his chin rests on my hair. If I could ever fall asleep standing up, I want to do it now.

"Good night," he whispers into the crown of my head.

"Good night," I breathe back, barely coherent.

"Thanks for helping me."

"Anytime," I say, except . . . maybe I can't make that promise. Maybe next time my energy will run out before dinner, not after. Maybe next time I won't be able to walk through the grocery store at all. Maybe next time I won't be able to get out of bed.

I'll help him anytime I can, though. Anytime I can feasibly do anything for him, I will.

Leaves rustle around our feet. A chill passes through me. I squeeze him tight, one last time. My head tilts up before I tell it to.

I don't know who moves first, but somehow, we end up kissing again, like nothing else matters.

CHAPTER TWENTY-EIGHT

———— • ————

SAT, OCT 24, 5:14 P.M.

Grant: I tried to make dinner for my mom again and I burnt it

Ivy: burnt what, exactly?

Grant: salad

"We need to talk, Ivy." Mom sneaks up behind me as I bring the last of the dinner dishes back into the kitchen.

I don't want to talk. There's no room in my skull for conversation these days.

"Oh God." It's never good if they're both here to talk to me. Dad's leaning against the fridge, and I know I'm in trouble.

I don't get in trouble, though, so I don't know what this could be about. I'd rather not find out. Maybe they learned about my falling-out with Rory, and now they're concerned I'm a friendless loser. They probably knew that would happen eventually.

"We'd like to talk about your birthday." Mom always sneaks that language in, as if it's really my choice where we actually have this talk or not.

"Can this wait? Like, another two months?" My birthday will be over by then. It's a feeble attempt at deflection, but it's all I can muster. I'd rather talk about Rory, honestly.

"No." Mom pulls me out of the kitchen and all the way to the living room—specifically, to the couch. This is unprecedented. Talks like this in our family happen in passing. Seated situations are for breaking terrible news. I can't handle terrible news.

"So…" Dad starts, not even bothering to attempt finishing the sentence.

"It's your eighteenth birthday," Mom says, grabbing both my hands.

They're good at this, ganging up on me. I hate it. Talking about myself like this, with both of them, is so intensely uncomfortable.

"I'm aware," I say, because I am.

"We have to do something." Mom sighs. "Think of what we did when Caroline turned eighteen. And when she turned sixteen. You didn't even want a party back then."

I try not to think about those parties. My ears rang for a full week after those horrors. They were probably the greatest days of Caroline's life, but that's not relevant.

"Or…we could just not do something." I shrug.

"Honey, you haven't had a birthday party since you were twelve."

So much comes up at once I think I might emotionally vomit. Everything's too much. We had my birthday party early that year, and my grandmother helped me make my own cake. It was magical, and it was also the last time I saw her. Now I associate birthday parties with crying headaches and funeral clothes.

"She was my favorite person in the world, Mom."

"I know. I promise, I know." Mom's eyes fill with tears. I don't know why this isn't horrible for her. "And you were hers."

"Still, you can't hate your birthday forever." Dad's trying to appeal to my rationality. It's too bad all my rationality is lost on this particular subject. *I can*, I want to say, *and I will*. They're asking me to celebrate my least favorite day of the year. There's just no way.

"I'm not talking about the kind of party we had for Caroline. I know that's not you," Mom says, tears already gone. I'll never know how she does that so easily. "I know socializing makes you anxious, but it would just be something small."

I know socializing makes you anxious. Yeah right. That's the understatement of the century. Like I'm not a social nightmare. Like I haven't actively sabotaged my own friendships, just because it's easier than dealing with the thorns in my own mind.

"Yeah, it doesn't have to be some kind of rager." Dad really thinks the word *rager* is still a part of society's lexicon. I roll my eyes.

"I was thinking we could have it at that botanical garden Grandma loved," Mom says gently. "It would just be your friends."

Friends. I think of Rory first. In this imaginary party scenario, I'd invite her. We'd have to talk about everything first, though, which would be intensely awful in a way I'm not ready for. "Hey, Rory, *it seems like you've totally changed, and I have, too, but it's because I'm really, really sick and afraid to tell anyone. Also, meet my boyfriend. You might remember us running from you on sight.*" I mean, I would have to figure it out; I don't think I could *not* invite her to my birthday party. I'd invite Grant, obviously, and everyone else in the support group. Then they'd meet her, and my worlds would collide again. My stomach knots up just thinking about it. I don't know if I can do that.

"You could even do all the food. Just like Saturday brunch, but with more people. You'll be home for your afternoon nap."

"How many people?" I ask. I don't mean to. I don't know who authorized the words to come out of my mouth, but there they were.

"However many you want." Mom leans in so close I can practically smell her breath.

"Let me think about it, okay?"

I'm still leaning toward no. There's more I want to say, but I can't really even think about it right now. Just the idea is scrambling my brain. It's scrambling everything.

"Think about it." Mom lets go of me.

CHAPTER TWENTY-NINE

— • —

MON, OCT 26, 6:14 A.M.

Grant: Only Top Chefs Can Identify 8 Out of These 13 Herbs

Grant: Take this and tell me how many you get.

Ivy: 13! How many did you get?

Grant: 1

Ivy: Which one?

Grant: Basil.

I've been obsessing over what Grant said at my first Deluca family dinner. He wasn't the first to say it, or even the first to notice—my mom did, and so did Caroline. But he actually got through my defenses. It seems like everyone but me knows that something needs to be done about my treatment.

Now it's all I can think about, despite the intensity of school lately. It's almost exam season, and everyone's freaking out. Then there's Rory, and how we're still avoiding each other. It's all painfully uncomfortable.

But I have bigger issues to freak out about.

More painful issues, specifically. Like waking up and being *unable to move my jaw.*

I go through my entire unthawing routine twice, without any luck. My knees and elbows are twice the size they should be. My hands are painfully stiff, and the joints in my feet feel like they're made out of crunchy gravel.

All of my alarm bells are ringing. This is bad.

No. It's bad until I walk to the bathroom sink and attempt to brush my teeth. Then it's catastrophic.

My mouth just. Won't. Open. If the joints in my feet are made of crunchy gravel, the hinges in my jaw are made of hardened cement. They're completely immobile. All I can do is look at my swollen red face in the mirror. I look like Caroline did when she got her wisdom teeth out. I wish I was as loopy now as she was then.

I stare into my own eyes. They seem almost sunken; my cheeks are so swollen. This is excruciating—a kind of excruciating I haven't felt before. This is the kind of flaring inflammation that is my body's warning it's being actively harmed, maybe even permanently damaged.

I always try not to think of that, how progressively disabling rheumatoid arthritis is. But I literally can't ignore it anymore. It's staring me right in the puffed-up, burning-red face.

There's usually a protocol for days like this. I've been sick long enough to know how to do the bare minimum to get through the day. No shower, comfortable clothes, not moving a muscle more than is necessary. This isn't a normal bad day, though. This is quite possibly the worst day.

I drop my toothbrush and leave the bathroom. Back in my room, I crawl under my deep purple comforter and try to position myself in a way that doesn't hurt anything. Curling up hurts my knees, lying flat hurts my hips. I'm in for a rough time.

"Are you not up yet? We have to leave in—" Caroline barges through the door, only shutting up when she sees my face. "I'm calling Mom." She pulls out her phone.

I groan. I don't try to talk—I don't think I can with a frozen jaw.

"Yeah, she's still in bed, and her face is, like, the size of a basketball."

I cover my eyes with the palm of my hand. Now this is going to be a whole thing.

It's entirely my fault, though. I should've listened to my mom when she said I need to be treated more aggressively. I hadn't liked that word: *aggressive*. Now, instead of my treatment being aggressive, my pain is. There's no telling how much harm I caused in the meantime.

Mom told me to find my baseline. This is definitely not my baseline.

"She wants to talk to you." She passes me the phone, but my hands are so locked up, I almost drop it on my face.

I make some noise in the back of my throat that sounds like a grunt.

"Is it your jaw?" Mom asks, no preface, no warning.

"Mm-hmm," I manage. My lips move, but my teeth stay pressed together.

"Put some heat on it, and I'm going to see how soon we can get you in with my doctor. I don't trust yours anymore."

I groan. I don't mean to do it out loud, it just slips out between my closed teeth.

"I know, honey. Everyone there is great, though. You'll be in good hands."

I understand that, deep down. It doesn't make it easier. Even knowing that my mom goes there, and so does Grant, I still feel this sense of trepidation.

"Do you need anything before I go?" Caroline asks when I pass her phone back.

I shake my head. Once Caroline leaves, all is quiet. Ethan left with Mom earlier, and Dad is still asleep. I plug in my heating pad and reach for my emergency meds.

With any luck, I'll sleep until the afternoon.

———◦———

When I wake up, harsh light streams in from between my blinds. I hear the natural commotion of everyone getting home, first Caroline, then Mom and Ethan. Dad is grumbling around, getting ready to leave for work. All is calm, as calm as a house with five people in it ever is.

The heat and muscle relaxers have helped some. I still don't have much range of motion in my jaw, but it will at least move. I can maybe, possibly consider speaking or eating solid food.

Footsteps get progressively louder then stop in front of my door. I brace myself, waiting for Mom's questions or Caroline's regaling of her day.

"Oh my God, your poor face." That's not my mom, or my dad, or Caroline.

"Hello to you, too," I say, shifting myself so my comforter is over my head. "What are you doing here?"

Even muffled by the comforter, my voice is stronger than it was. That's something. It's not much, but it's something.

"I called him," Caroline says from the doorway. "I didn't think you'd be up to going to support group tonight, so I thought I'd bring part of it to you."

"That's a good idea, actually," Grant says. "Disease-specific support delivered right to your door."

"You mean you're an emotional butler."

He laughs, and then I laugh. I laugh so hard it feels like my jaw is going to crack in two. That'll be fun to explain to the surgeon who has to piece my face back together.

Caroline leaves us alone.

I should be having more feelings about this, I think. This is the first time I've ever had a boy in my room, alone, with the door closed. I imagined this going much, much differently.

Grant pulls my desk chair over and sits in front of me with his feet up on my bed. He uses them to pull himself closer until

215

he's all but up in my face. With one finger, he brushes some of my nearly matted hair out of my eyes.

"Hi," he says. He's still looking at me like I'm more than the garbage dump I feel like.

"Hi," I say, making an effort to move my jaw the least amount I possibly can.

"This probably wasn't what you expected when you woke up today, huh?" Grant runs his hands over the sides of my face. I know he can feel the golf ball–sized joints in front of my ears.

"No, I definitely had other plans." They might not have been anything spectacular, but I had planned to get out of bed before the sun went down.

"Did you tell your doctor about this?"

I can barely understand his words. He's making distracting circles on the sides of my face.

"No...Well, not no. Mom's making an appointment with her doctor. She thinks it's time to make the..." I hesitate. "The switch."

"Ah, the switch. What a fun time to be alive." Of course he automatically understands what I'm talking about. "I forgot you're almost eighteen."

I try not to flinch. Any out-loud mention of my birthday is entirely unwelcome.

"I seriously don't want to go," I whisper.

"I don't blame you! It's hard."

It's so simple, the way he says it. As if it's just okay that life's hard, and nothing else has to be said.

"I've been putting it off for too long," I breathe. "It's my fault this happened."

"What? No. Of course it isn't." He leaps up from his chair and sits next to me on the bed.

"I mean, it is. Isn't it?" I try to think of a way to explain it. "Like, it's literally my fault. I knew I was getting worse—I just wouldn't admit it. And it's my own immune system, which is supposed to *protect me*, that's causing the problem in the first place. The call's coming from inside the house."

Every drop of blood coursing through my veins holds that autoimmunity. Every part of me is self-destructing.

Grant chuckles. "That's good. I'm going to use that one."

"I'm serious," I say, even though I crack a smile. "I should've listened to my mom, to you...to myself. All the signs were there that this was coming..."

My voice trails off as I think about it. I'd felt like a boat taking on water for months now. Everyone around me noticed, and yet, I'd actively decided not to listen. I decided to ignore the neon signs that read IVY, YOU NEED HELP.

"Yeah, maybe, but it's not like you could've fixed it with a Tylenol. It's not like you could've fixed it at all."

"It's just...the switch is such a silly thing to be afraid of." My voice is low and kind of pitiful.

"No, it's not." Grant shifts. "Changing doctors and medications is *scary*. It's a big deal, and something no one wants to do.
No one can fault you for not throwing yourself head over heels at
treatment."

"You think?" I ask.

Grant nods. "Being sick is no joke, Ivy. The way everyone
looks at you like you don't belong—like a cross between pity and
discomfort. You and I both know that can happen even in a doctor's office. Then, all the talking! Your old doctor knew everything, and now you have to repeat it all to some stranger who is
supposedly going to take care of your disease forever."

Exactly, I want to scream. *This is exactly what I'm afraid of.*

So, yeah, maybe I've been neglecting my treatment a little. It
just seemed easier than starting over completely. I'd just barely
begun to acclimate to my immunocompromised life, and now it
has to change?

"I don't like being like this," I whisper. My voice cracks on the
last syllable.

"What do you mean?" Grant asks. He's looking at me so
intently.

"Like this." I gesture to myself, to the generalized messiness
I've become. "I swear, I was almost excited when I got sick. Does
that make any sense? Mom and Caroline were already diagnosed,
and I went from helping take care of them to being one of them.
We were a sick family I was finally a part of. Now..." I let out a
soul-deep sigh. "I just feel worthless."

"Oh my God, Ivy." Grant reaches for me. I manage to sit up, and we hold each other.

There's nothing in the world like a bad pain day to make me feel discouraged: worthless, lifeless, as if my body and mind are completely out of my control.

"I know why you feel that way. I feel that way sometimes, too. Whether you can take care of anyone else, or take care of yourself, or walk, or talk, or anything, *you are worth something.*"

He takes a deep breath, like he's searching for better words, as if he isn't already verbally giving me galaxies worth of stars.

"I promise, Ivy. You are worth everything."

I kiss him, then, because I can't not. Even though I haven't changed out of my pajamas or brushed my teeth, I kiss him with a fervor that I hope speaks volumes. I hope it says that he's more than I could have ever dreamed of. I hope it says that he's more important to me than my favorite measuring spoons and safer than my own kitchen.

CHAPTER THIRTY

— ● —

TUES, NOV 3, 7:01 A.M.

Grant: I have an autoimmune disease because the only thing strong enough to kick my ass is me.

Ivy: Good morning to you, too.

Grant: Good luck today.

Ivy: Meh.

Ivy: Thanks.

Mom's rheumatologist has an appointment open Tuesday. Lucky, lucky me. I don't even get to leave school early to go, which would've been the only possible benefit in this scenario. It's not like anyone would've noticed, anyway. (Rory might've noticed, I guess, if I wasn't avoiding her. I really have to stop avoiding her.)

Things have improved only a little since my steel-caged jaw episode. I've eaten mostly gross, semi-solid foods, and I'm extremely tired of it. Ethan may think soggy cereal is fine dining, but I don't. Beyond that, my mobility has stayed stagnant. I've spent lots of hours on the couch and lots of hours in school wishing I were anywhere else.

As it gets closer, though, I find I'm almost looking forward to the appointment, just because it means something might change. It means I might be able to get back to whatever level of functioning is normal at this point.

Mom, on the other hand, is ecstatic. It's as if she's about to introduce me to an old friend from college, not the doctor she sees every three months.

I suppose I can understand that. I think fondly of my first rheumatologist. His office was a bright yellow and furnished like a daycare. They still used paper files, and I always had to have a new picture printed out for my chart because they kept falling out. There are probably tiny Ivys floating around all over their file cabinets. Going there was like stepping back in time, and some part of me is mourning the loss of that nostalgia. Another part of me is mourning the loss of the kid I was in all those photos. I almost wish I'd been diagnosed younger, like Grant had. Then I would have gotten to spend more time in that office, and not in the sort of imposing glass building that looms in front of me.

It's tall. It seems more like a Fortune 500 building than a doctor's office. I already feel out of place, and I haven't even gone in yet. I sigh under my breath.

"Ready to go?" Mom asks, tossing an arm over my shoulders.

No, I want to say. *I'll probably never be ready for this.* More than the panicked nervousness I expected to feel, I'm full of dread. It's heavy and dark, almost claustrophobic.

We walk through a glass door, and I realize the inside of the building doesn't match the modern, gleaming exterior. All the furniture is worn and dated. This is what a doctor's office looks like: all uncomfortable chairs and ugly wallpaper.

We check in and grab two seats in the middle of a long row. There aren't many other people around, a benefit of coming this late in the afternoon. Only three other people occupy the waiting room: a couple in the back corner, and an older woman on a faded gray loveseat near the reception desk.

I wait in silence, playing a puzzle game on my phone. It's something to do with my hands, at least. Mom flips through a magazine. I try not to think of what germs might be living all over it.

"You're so nice to come with your mom to her appointment."

It takes me several heartbeats to realize the woman across the room is talking to me. I had to do a process of elimination. As I appear to be the only one with a mom in the room, she has to be talking to me.

I look at her. The woman's smile is gentle, like she's looking at a toddler just learning to walk. That's what I am to her—a kid who doesn't belong here. There's not a way I can respond that's not rude.

"She's the sweetest," Mom says, patting me on the knee.

Part of me is grateful I don't have to speak. Part of me wants to tell her this is *my* appointment—to make her feel as terrible as I do now.

She really thinks she's complimenting me, making me feel good about myself. That casual assumption that I couldn't possibly be as sick as everyone else in the room cuts as deep as anything ever has.

"Ivy Harding?" someone says from the door beside the reception desk.

I stand up first, avoiding eye contact with anyone.

"I knew Harding sounded familiar. Is this your daughter, Becky?" The nurse holds the door open for us as she talks to my mom. Nurses are undeniably the best part of the medical field. I feel the slightest bit better, like I'm talking to one of my mom's many friends, rather than someone who is assessing me medically.

"My middle child, yes. Both my girls got the autoimmune genes."

I want to cringe. I don't like to be reminded I'm the middle child.

We enter an examination room. The nurse asks me to verify my birthdate, and I rattle it off with barely a wince. (Mom still notices, I can tell.) Then we go through the rest of the typical triage routine: vital signs, weight, questions about pain levels and medication changes.

That's what I'm afraid of. Medication changes.

Obviously, I know I can't be on the same immunosuppressant forever. *Logically*, I know I'll have to change medications every once in a while. Too long on the same medication builds up immunity, and the medicine stops working.

That immunity is the reason I've spent more time in bed than out lately. It's the reason I haven't been able to eat solid food. It's the reason everyone around me has been looking at me with this apprehensive gaze, like I'm about to drop any second.

"Hi, Ivy, Becky." Dr. Anthony steps in the open door.

I want her to leave and come back in twenty minutes—or never! However long it takes me to get the pieces of my brain back together. I mean, I just got myself comfortable on the paper-covered table. I haven't even had a chance to worry properly about what will happen. My foreboding feeling hadn't fully sunk in yet—it's just lodged in my throat, pressing on my vocal cords.

"So," she says, sitting on her rolling stool between Mom and me. "You've been diagnosed with RA for close to a year and a half, right?"

I nod reflexively. It doesn't seem possible that it's been that long. If I count back the months, it sounds right. I just don't know where all those days have gone.

"And you've been flaring more often lately?" Dr. Anthony stands and takes my hands. She runs her cold fingers over mine, pressing each joint from my knuckles down. I'm unbelievably grateful this isn't happening early in the morning, because it would hurt a lot more.

"Yes," I say quietly.

"You do have some significant swelling," she says once she reaches my elbows and shoulders. Then, she bends and presses on my knees and ankles.

I wince.

"I think that you've been at this long enough that you know the drill, right?"

I nod. I have to give it to her: I like these kinds of appointments, where the doctor assumes I'm competent enough to control my own care, where I don't really have to speak all that much.

"So, if you've been feeling worse lately, we need to make a change."

I nod again. Mentally, I hang my head. I *knew* this was coming, but it still feels like a gut punch. I'm back to square one; all the progress I made in over a year is just gone.

"Truthfully," Dr. Anthony starts, sitting, setting her laptop on her lap, and leaning forward as if this conversation needs to be more private than our already HIPAA violation–proof room, "we'd need to switch at this point anyway. We have to start thinking of you less as a child and more a woman of childbearing age."

Wait, no. What?

My mind reels so fast my train of thought goes completely off the rails. All I can think is *no* and *what?*

"What do you mean by that, exactly?" I hear Mom ask. She's leaned forward, too. I want to lean back so far I fall through the floor.

"Well, Becky, this is something we've never discussed in terms of your care, because you were done having children before you were diagnosed. Ivy is young, but not so young that we don't need to worry about future pregnancies."

My head snaps up. This time the gut punch is physical: I actually feel my stomach lurch up into my throat. This line of conversation has to be something my anxious mind just conjured up.

"Ivy, the medication I would like to start you on is something I only prescribe with two methods of contraception."

There are a few moments of dead space. In my head, they're filled with the humming buzz of bumblebees.

"I'm sure I don't have to tell you that immunosuppressing medication is very serious, and while this is what we usually start everyone on when they're first diagnosed, it is dangerous—disastrous, really—in the event of pregnancy. Pregnancies aren't always planned, especially at your age. So, really, it's best to eliminate that option entirely."

"So, if what she's on now isn't an option, what are you thinking of starting her on?" I hear my mom ask.

My ears zone out somehow. All my processing cells are replaying the last two minutes over and over again, wondering where that sharp turn in conversation came from. It just took me by surprise. It's emotional whiplash.

Somewhere in the back of my mind, I hear them talking about *biweekly injections* and *possible side effects*, something about a *specialty pharmacy*. I think I hear the name of the medication Grant takes. He'll get a kick out of that.

God, Grant. He's never going to have to have this conversation. We have the exact same diagnosis, we're even going to be on the same medication, but there's always going to be this extra step I have to take that he doesn't. This is all going to be on me, forever. This wouldn't have even been an issue a few months ago. For a split second, I want to blame this on him and avoid him forever. If I did, this wouldn't be a problem.

Then I remember his face and his hair and every word he's

ever said to me. Every wink, and every baseball game, and every unnecessary swear word.

So, okay, maybe I won't avoid him forever, but I can't talk about it with him, either. Talking about this kind of stuff is weird and awkward, and I'm just not going to do it.

"We're going to do your regular blood work. Sed rate, CRP, all of that. It's time for your TB test, too. You can get all of that done on your way out, and we'll see you again in a few months."

Dr. Anthony smiles and leaves the room, as if she hasn't just left me reeling. Mom waits until the tests are done and we're back in the car to bring up the elephant in the room.

"Did you like Dr. Anthony?" she asks casually, as if she was asking about my day or what I had for breakfast.

I scoff. I didn't mean to do it out loud.

"I know, I wasn't expecting that, either. I didn't realize the medicine would be so high-risk for pregnancies."

Someone should have told me this before now. Someone should've warned me that at eighteen, I go from a child to a potential carrier of one.

"It really isn't a big deal, I promise. A lot of girls your age use contraceptives."

I want to roll my eyes. When Mom turns her head to look out the driver's side mirror, I actually do. I mean, it's true. It's also true that a lot of girls my age are having sex. I'm not ready to do either of those things.

No one asked if I was, though.

"Caroline's on the pill, you know." Mom is really trying to make this easier for me, I know that. It just isn't working.

"That's because Caroline's having sex."

"Well, that's true," Mom says. She turns into our neighborhood. "Listen, it's perfectly okay if you don't feel ready. Just think about it as medicine, like anything else."

I nod. I've been doing a lot of that today, just nodding along as other people make big decisions that affect only me. Mom turns the car into our driveway.

Standing there, leaning against the hood of his car, is the only reason I've ever thought about any of this before today. Okay, so maybe this doesn't affect only me.

"So how did it go?" Grant asks before I even unbuckle my seat belt. He opened the door before the car was fully stopped.

"Great. It went great," Mom says before I can speak. "You kids going to head out?"

"Is Caroline coming to group?" I ask.

"She's working on a project with someone from class." Mom shakes her head. We both know that's code for doing something that's definitely not for school.

I walk to Grant's car without another word. I still can't wrap my head around the past hour of my life. There's never been a doctor's appointment more disastrous. No, that's not true. I've heard stories—of Lilah and Avery not being believed, of Parker being told he doesn't need his mobility aids, of times where they had to get an anesthesiologist with an ultrasound machine just to find a vein.

There have been worse doctor's appointments; they just haven't been mine.

"So what really happened?" Grant asks as he pulls out of the driveway. He backs out with one hand on the back of my seat, and I don't know why that's the single most attractive thing I've ever seen. It's probably because I can smell him. It's a sensory assault.

"It was fucking terrible."

"You sound like me." He laughs. It helps.

"On the bright side, I don't have to take pills every day anymore." Except...maybe I still might.

"Moving onto the big-boy stuff, huh?" He's looking at the road and not me. Somehow that makes this all easier.

"Yep. We're drug buddies now. I got the same prescription as you."

"We should get on the same schedule and have injection dates."

I laugh. Laughing feels something like relief, but it also feels wrong somehow, like I should still be allowed to be peeved about all of this.

"That's really weird! We're not doing that."

"Okay, fine. Your loss."

We both laugh again. He pulls into the gym and I feel that strange sense of calm settle over my tense shoulders. If I want to talk about this here, I can. There are people who can relate and empathize. I don't want to talk yet, though. I want to sulk and let myself feel whatever I'm feeling.

Still, this is as good a place as any to sulk.

CHAPTER THIRTY-ONE

—•—

TUES, NOV 3, 7:02 P.M.

> Mom: Already got an email about your prescription being sent over to the new pharmacy!

The group speaks around me as I think. Apparently, I have a decision to make. To do that, I think I need to talk about it. I don't normally have to talk about stuff like this, because I normally have a gut feeling to guide me. This time, my gut feeling is overshadowed by the sheer indecision swirling through me.

This is just not something I talk about in a big group like this. It's not something I want to go home and talk to my mom and sister about, either. They see things differently than I do. They feel things differently. I need to talk to someone who will think of this as a medical decision.

As the group breaks apart, I have an idea. I'm not the only one here who sees Dr. Anthony. Maybe I'm not the only one she's dropped an emotional bomb on, either.

"Wait for me just a minute, okay?" I ask Grant, stepping away from him and toward Avery's desk in the back of the room. I know Avery. I know her pretty well, enough to know how this gym came to be and how she would physically fight to the death to protect anyone in it. What I don't know is if I can just walk up to her and ask to talk about personal stuff.

"Hey, Avery?" I ask. "Can I talk to you?"

I'm not good at this; it's a known fact. I have to remind myself that Avery's just approachable enough that I almost feel safe talking to her. She's the reason I'm standing where I am, the reason this group is more than Grant, Parker, Manny, and Lilah in a church basement.

"Sure. What's up?" Avery smiles and sits back down in her seat in the circle.

I sit down, too, taking the seat that's usually Lilah's. Sitting in a seat that isn't mine feels weird.

"You see Dr. Anthony, right?"

Avery nods.

"I went to see her for the first time today. Apparently, I'm too old for a pediatric rheumatologist now. Anyway—"

"Wait, did someone go with you?" Avery asks, leaning forward like Dr. Anthony did. I smile, thinking of Grant making sure Avery hadn't gone into her appointment alone. That's my Grant, a good person, first and foremost.

"Yeah, my mom. She sees Dr. Anthony, too."

"Huh. Small world, I guess."

"Yeah…" My voice trails off. Now that I think about it, this isn't exactly a comfortable topic of conversation. Maybe I shouldn't have come over here at all.

"What's the matter? Did something happen?" Avery's eyes

soften into pools of protective concern, the way Caroline often looks at me.

"Sort of. I guess so." I sigh, sit up straighter. Something in me knows I have to talk about this with someone. I just have to commit to it. It's now or never. "I pretty much knew she was going to change my medication. I've been feeling worse. I knew I needed it. I didn't want to switch, but I knew I'd need to eventually."

"That makes sense. It's easy to get attached to treatment, especially when it's the first thing to work enough to give you any actual relief. If she was changing my treatment, I'd put up a fight, too."

I can see that, Avery putting up a fight.

"I..." My voice drifts off as I try to explain this. "I was nauseous all the time. Sick every other week. My hair changed. It got wavy. It fell out. And now I'm just supposed to give all that progress up and start all over again?"

Avery nods in understanding.

"It wasn't just that. She changed my medicine, but even if I hadn't been feeling bad, she was going to anyway."

"Why?" Avery's face crinkles up in confusion.

I take a deep breath.

"Apparently, my old medicine would be disastrous if I accidentally got pregnant. I think they're all kind of disastrous, even my new meds? I'm not sure. I sort of zoned out when she started talking about it, but I'm pretty sure I heard her say fetal demise."

"Oh my God," Avery says. She looks as taken aback as I feel.

"I know. I didn't know what to do. I still don't."

"Wow. I don't know what I was expecting you to say, but it wasn't that."

"She wants me to get on the pill anyway."

"What do you want to do?"

I want to sag in relief at just being asked that. Avery's the first person to actually consider my opinion in this scenario.

"I don't know. It feels like a big deal. I just wasn't ready to even think about it."

Avery nods. Her face is flooded with sympathy.

"Hold on a second. Let me get Lilah. She's an expert on this topic."

Before I can respond, Avery gets up and physically pulls Lilah out of a conversation with Parker and Grant.

"Ivy has a reproductive problem," Avery says once we're all seated again.

"It sounds bad when you put it that way." I look at Lilah. She's traded her box braids for her natural curls. "My doctor wants to put me on the pill because my meds would be bad for any hypothetical accidental pregnancies."

Lilah nods. "And you don't want to?" she asks.

"It's not that, it's just—" I sigh. "I wasn't even thinking about it, any of it. It wasn't on my radar, and now it has to be."

They both nod. I'm in a similar leaned-in circle as I had been with my mom and Dr. Anthony, but this time, I feel infinitely more understood.

"I know. I was on the pill at thirteen, because it's always the first step when you have 'bad periods.' I didn't really have a choice then, either," Lilah says. She puts air quotes around *bad periods*, and I get what she means, that some people think that's all endometriosis is.

I can't imagine having this conversation at thirteen. I barely even had a period at thirteen, let alone a bad one.

"Just take your time. No one can make you do anything you don't want to do, and that especially goes for medication."

"And sex," Avery says.

All three of us laugh, and I feel like I'm back in sex-ed class, only this one is less awkward by miles. Now, I sort of get what Caroline said so long ago about adopting more of me. Sitting here with Lilah and Avery, it's almost like I've adopted more Carolines.

"Speaking of, I would talk to him about this." Lilah shifts her eyes in Grant's direction. He's looking right at us.

"I would, too," Avery says. "For one thing, he's not squeamish about medical stuff, and the two of us have droned on and on about our periods with him before. He won't bat an eye."

"And another thing, he's your boyfriend. It's never a bad idea to talk about whether or not you're ready for sex. That way, there's no weirdness, and no one gets their feelings hurt."

I look at him. His eyes meet mine. I don't know if I can talk to him about this. I'm not comfortable talking about this with my own mother—there's almost no way I can bring it up with him.

At the same time, though, Avery and Lilah are right. They're too right. Scarily right. It's like they've lived this experience over and over and want it to go better for me than it did for them.

"You don't have to rush into anything. Just think about it." Lilah smiles. Something in her bright face is reassuring.

I'm intensely, infinitely grateful for the people sitting in front of me, for the people all around me, for the four walls that make up the gym we're all in.

"You'll make the right decision. Just trust your gut." Avery smiles, too.

Our tiny group disperses, and everyone goes their separate ways.

"You okay?" Grant asks. I can tell he has more questions. I don't know if I can answer them yet.

I shrug.

CHAPTER THIRTY-TWO

•———

Grant: Which Sluggers shirt are you wearing today?
I wanna match

Ivy: I only have the one?

Grant: Okay, well, wear it. But wear something under it, too. It's cold.

Grant: Only fake fans have just one shirt btw

Everyone spills out of the car and heads toward the field. I'm bringing up the rear. I haven't stopped my old medicine yet, but I might as well have. I took a full weekly dose two days ago, and my body is behaving as if I've never taken any of it at all. My dragging feet pick up speed when I notice the adorable boy waiting for me at the fence. I might feel gross, but that smile makes everything better. He's talking to someone, and he hasn't noticed me yet.

The late fall brings a chill to the early-evening air. It's entirely too cold for this. The day before my favorite unofficial holiday that no one but my family cares about (Thank-O-Ween!) is for prep cooking, not evening baseball. Nonetheless, I know this game is more important than the others. Ethan hasn't shut up about it for days. Something about his best friend being on the other team, and absolutely having to beat him, I don't know.

I don't care, honestly. What I care about is my favorite day of the year, which happens to be tomorrow.

When Grant spots me, he rounds the fence and waits, leaning against the open gate. We still haven't talked about my appointment, not really. I'm waiting for the right time, or the courage to actually speak up about it. Every time I look at him, all the courage I've built up bubbles away like draining water.

As soon as he's within arm's reach, I stand up on my tiptoes to kiss him. It's all too brief, and I'm pretty sure he caught me wincing as I lean back down onto my heels. He's space-heater warm, and I want to zip myself up in his jacket.

"I was about to say cold days like this really suck, but I can't remember why," Grant mumbles.

I smile wide enough my cheeks hurt. That doesn't take much, given the state of my jaw, but still. Even as long as I've been around him, I still have yet to get over the way he looks at me. No one's ever looked at me like this, as if I'm powerful enough to make cold nights warm.

"Ivy," Mom says, walking up to us in a frenzied hurry. "I just got off the phone with Dr. Anthony's office."

Mom looks at me with raised, slanted brows. She's asking for permission to keep talking with Grant here. I appreciate it, but I'll probably end up telling Grant whatever she says anyway. I nod, almost imperceptibly.

"Your blood work came back, and your inflammation markers are sky high."

"How high?" Grant asks before I can.

"CRP was twenty-two, and sed rate was forty-three." Mom expels the information on a sigh, like it's physically painful for her.

"Holy shit," Grant says. "That's higher than mine have ever been."

"Mine, too," Mom says. She doesn't even bat an eye at his choice of language.

"Okay, so what now?" I ask. Only, I know all too well what happens now. We all do. We all know what those higher-than-ever numbers mean. My brain is just ignoring that option because it's going to single-handedly ruin my favorite holiday that isn't a holiday.

Mom looks at me like she doesn't want to say it.

"Prednisone. Five-day step-down."

I groan. Five whole days of steroids, the dose getting smaller each day. Never have I ever wanted more to fling myself onto the floor and throw a juvenile tantrum. Damn steroids. Damn inflammation.

At least I slept well last night, because I won't be able to for the next five days.

"Well, that will be very cool, very nice," Grant says. If I couldn't tell he's being completely sarcastic, I'd lunge at him.

"Grant, you and your mom are still coming over tomorrow, right?" Mom asks. I'm grateful for the subject change.

"We'll be there. I told her she doesn't need to bring anything, but I'm sure she will anyway, even though Thank-O-Ween is kind of a thing y'all made up and definitely doesn't have a set of rules."

Mentally, I wince. Thank-O-Ween *does* have rules, thank you very much. When I was a kid, and my dad was working all the important holidays, we always ended up having them on different days. Then, one year, he got stuck working every Thursday in November, so we had Thanksgiving on Halloween, and a sacred tradition was born.

Whenever he has to work one of the holidays, we do both on the same day. This year, that means Halloween almost a week late and Thanksgiving a few Thursdays early. We buy discounted Halloween decorations instead of Thanksgiving ones, and I cook all of my grandmother's holiday recipes. One time, I used day-old Peeps instead of marshmallows on the sweet potatoes. It was an abomination. Someone will make a joke about it this year, I'm sure. They always do.

"We won't be offended, whatever she brings." Mom pats Grant on the shoulder and joins Dad and Caroline on the bleachers.

As soon as she's out of earshot, I turn to face Grant again.

"Please kill me."

He laughs, a spirited chuckle that makes me blush so deeply my ears burn red.

"And miss you roid-rage cooking a Thanksgiving dinner? Never."

"*Thank-O-Ween* dinner," I correct.

With a delicate kiss to my forehead, he jogs away to join the game. I take a seat on the frigid metal bleachers. They're absolutely unforgiving. We cheer until our voices break, but I'm a half second behind everyone else, because my mind is elsewhere. My vision stays unfocused, and everything on the field is hazy, even Grant. I'm thinking hard, deciding something.

The Sluggers win in a decisive victory, and Ethan got a triple and two RBIs, something I only know because Dad is keeping up with his statistics in a notebook, and he announces it every time he writes something down. In what seems like no time at all, the field empties and we're ready to leave.

On a whim, a puff of courage, and with a tense awareness that this could be a terrible idea, I stride over to Grant.

"Can we talk?" I ask. At some point, sitting on the cold torture-device bleachers, everything I'm holding in came bubbling to the surface, and now I can't ignore it anymore.

"Yeah, sure."

We walk to his car; I wave to my parents, and they nod. I can tell Grant wants to ask questions. As we each close our doors, my fierceness fades away to my all too commonly felt panic.

"So what's up?" Grant asks. He looks nervous. His hands won't stop running through his hair. I want to hold them.

I take a deep breath. *You can do this*, I tell myself. *You need to tell him.*

"I made donuts yesterday. I used this new recipe, and they came out pretty good—"

"This is what you wanted to talk about?" he asks, squinting. "Donuts?"

"No, I just thought donuts would make the talking part easier."

He smiles, just a tiny bit, but it's enough to break the tension in the air. I buckle my seat belt and he pulls out of the parking space. Gravel flies through the air, crunching under the tires, and I watch it like there are asteroids headed toward us, not small rocks.

The drive to my house is quiet. We get there first, and the house is also eerily quiet, actually.

I lead Grant to the kitchen. He sits on one of the barstools. I busy myself with putting donuts on plates and turning on the coffee maker. Once it starts to drip and the room smells like fresh brew, I calm down, just slightly. Grant is still silent, and I don't know if that's good or bad. I don't know if he's giving me space or mentally running away.

"I wasn't completely honest with you about my appointment."

There, that's something. That's a way to start this conversation.

"Okay…" Grant responds, his voice unsure.

"I wasn't just upset because of the medicine switch. I wasn't even upset because I was told I was nice for coming with my mom to her appointment."

"Seriously?" He's too attentive, too attuned to my every word.

I nod. If I stop talking, I'll never start again.

"I was expecting all of that. What I wasn't expecting was to be told I have to think of myself as a woman of childbearing age instead of a child." My tone is bitter, and I don't even try to hide it.

"What the fuck does that mean?"

He's immediately offended on my behalf, bless his heart. I lean back against the counter. The coffee smell is stronger back here, and it's centering.

"It means that if I got pregnant on my new medicine, it would be . . . bad. Apparently, I should get on the pill."

Grant is silent for the longest time. I don't know how to interpret that. His endless chattering, I can handle. His silence is almost painful.

"It's my choice, supposedly, but it doesn't really sound like it. It definitely doesn't feel like it."

"I have absolutely no clue what to say."

"I didn't, either."

Heavy silence presses into the room's atmosphere. I didn't really think this through, having this talk in the kitchen. If anyone walked in right now, they'd think we were fighting.

"How is it that we have the same disease, and you have to deal with shit that I don't?"

I smile a little. "I should've told you about it earlier, but talking about it is weird."

"Is that what you were talking to Avery and Lilah about?"

I nod. I don't want to explain that it's easier to talk about this with them than him. "They told me to talk to you about it, too."

"I'm glad they have faith in me." He smiles back, and it makes everything just the slightest bit better.

This isn't as awkward as I thought it would be. It's less painful than keeping something like this from him.

"Do you know what you're going to do?" He asks it quietly, carefully. I know the territory we're stepping into. It's the kind of space that's impossible to step back from.

Honestly, though. I invited him to Thank-O-Ween. Nothing is more sacred than that, not even sex.

"I didn't, at first." I sigh, fiddle with my fingers, do anything I can to keep from looking at him. "Can I be honest with you?"

I feel more than see him nod. This is the hardest part, the part I dreaded the most.

"If she had the same conversation with me a few months ago, I would've thought it was ridiculous. Like, absurd. It would've been beyond unnecessary."

A gust of wind blows by, and a few golden leaves dance across the window to my right. I can almost feel the gust on my skin.

"At the same time, a few months ago, the idea of me dating anyone was, like, inconceivable. I would've told her that I wasn't ready to date, and I definitely wasn't ready to do . . . anything else."

My eyes drift up, trying to see if he's understanding me. His eyes are glazed over, almost. I can't get a read on him.

"So what you're trying to say is . . ." I can't tell if he's processing or trying to get me to explain myself better.

"What I'm trying to say is: I didn't think I'd want to date anyone anytime soon. Then I met you. I don't think I need birth control right now, but I might in the future."

I let that settle into the air between us, hoping he'll understand what I mean. I don't want to explain any further. It's awkward enough for me as it is.

"Oh. You mean . . . oh."

I almost laugh.

"Maybe I wasn't ready to make a decision like that, but I have to, and I did. So . . . that's it."

I shrug, like it's not a big deal. In reality, it's probably the most adult decision I've ever made in my life.

I climb up onto the stool next to his. My movements are completely graceless, but I make it. In a split second, I lean over and press my too-warm fingers against his cheeks. I kiss him before he knows what hits him.

He pulls away, just enough to speak.

"Can we get back to how you maybe, eventually want to sleep with me?"

CHAPTER THIRTY-THREE

---•---

THU, NOV 5, 3:08 A.M.

Ivy: Are you awake?

Ivy: You're not. I'm sure you're not.

Ivy: You're asleep, because it's the middle of the night.

Ivy: And you're not on steroids, like I am.

Ivy: Anyway, you're cute and I'll see you tomorrow.

Ivy: Today?

Ivy: Whatever. You know what I mean.

Ivy: hApPy ThAnK-o-WeEn

THU, NOV 5, 9:13 A.M.

Grant: I know what you mean.

I'm going to crawl out of my skin. That's all there is to it. Day two of prednisone step-downs are always the worst. I took five steroid pills yesterday, and four this morning. With corticosteroids like this, I always feel them at once. Instead of a slow increase in energy and overall madness, it's the flip of a switch. It's a zero to sixty in 5.2 seconds.

"The green beans are in the slow cooker; the sweet potatoes are in the oven. Dressing needs to be made up next…"

I've actually started speaking out loud to sort out the deluge of thoughts overflowing my brain. There's not even anyone else in the room.

There's someone else's voice in my head, though, telling me to be careful not to overbake the sweet potatoes, or not to forget the extra pats of butter in the beans…

"Who are you talking to?" Caroline asks. Everyone else is steering clear of the kitchen because they know better than to get into the path of the steroid tornado I am right now. Caroline grabs a bottle of water from the fridge. Then she looks at me and grabs another one.

"Myself. I hate prednisone."

"I know. Are you sure you don't need any help?" Caroline passes me the bottle of water. She's a good sister. The best.

"I think I'm good. I should have everything done in record time. Have you checked on Mom and Dad, though?"

They're in the driveway trying to figure out the new deep fryer they bought for the turkey. I'm not sure they won't blow up the whole neighborhood. They probably look deranged out there, three weeks before Thanksgiving, deep-frying a turkey in the driveway. Such is the Thank-O-Ween experience, especially because Dad's already put his costume on.

"I'll go, but if they're yelling at each other, I'm leaving them alone."

I don't care if they're fighting as long as we have a turkey at the end of the day.

I check my list one more time. At least I had the presence of mind to make one yesterday, before the prednisone flood kicked in. I can't even stand still. I bounce from my heels to my toes and back again on the kitchen's laminate flooring as I read.

"Once I get the dressing going, I need to peel and boil the potatoes. I can do the mac and cheese last."

Rory came to Thank-O-Ween once. That thought just hits me as I pace the floor. She ate mashed potatoes and wore a witch's hat. Even though she couldn't come the next year because it was too close to actual Thanksgiving and she'd already left to visit her grandparents, she remembered. She texted me. She was getting on a plane to enjoy her holiday, and she texted me. I had made her a loaf of my rosemary and thyme bread, and she took it with her through airport security. I told her she could tell her family she made it because she wanted to impress them.

For the first time in what feels like hours, I stop moving. Maybe it's the prednisone talking, but I think I have to do something. I have to reach out. I could text, but that feels too impersonal. The idea of talking about this face-to-face feels overwhelming enough that I start pacing again. Thinking and pacing. Pacing and thinking.

I hear the front door swing open and click closed. Footsteps come closer to the kitchen. They're footsteps I don't immediately recognize. I know the exact decibel at which everyone in this family walks.

"It smells good in here!"

He's...very cute. It's almost like the first time I saw him, except now I know how lovely he is. I don't know if it's him or the prednisone, but something is turning my heart to mush.

Grant's dressed up, meaning he's wearing khakis instead of jeans. He has one of his vintage flannels buttoned up like an actual shirt, not something thrown over an '80s band tee. So he chose the Thank category of the Thank-O-Ween dress code. Interesting. I swore he'd come walking in here in a full baseball uniform. I kind of wish he'd come walking in here in a full baseball uniform. I've never actually seen him in one. I kind of want to. Wait, this is not what I'm supposed to be thinking about.

"What are you doing here? You're not supposed to be here for another few hours," I demand, almost breathless.

"I knew you'd be like this." He gestures to my fidgeting. "And you're gonna hurt yourself doing too much."

I want to pretend that I don't know what he's talking about, pretend I'm not doing exactly what he thinks I am. "I don't need a babysitter."

"I know you don't."

"That came out wrong. Steroids make me mean."

When I hug him, I finally let myself stop moving. My hands and feet already ache, and I know those aches will crawl up and down my limbs until they meet in the middle.

"Why are you better at this arthritis thing than me?" I ask, my cheek still pressed against the worn flannel of his shirt.

"I've just been doing it longer."

I kind of want to stay here forever, and I kind of want to go back to bed. The front door slams again, and Caroline appears at the kitchen counter.

"They're not fighting, but I still feel safer in here than out there."

"Me too," Grant says. "On the way in, your dad waved at me with a blowtorch in his hand, and with the clown costume, it's really unsettling..."

"Seriously? Why does he have a blowtorch?" I ask, pulling away from Grant to look at Caroline.

Caroline shrugs. "I'll be surprised if we still have parents by dinner." We really are safer in here.

I go back to working on the dressing, dicing all the vegetables into uniform pieces, but soon my fingers start to slip off the knife. My thoughts slow from a monsoon to a trickle, and I can barely piece words together to form sentences. I'm hitting a wall, hard.

"What do you still need to do?" Caroline asks.

"Just this and the potatoes. Can you guys peel them for me?"

Instead of answering, Caroline goes to get Ethan. Between

the three of them, it won't take long. They turn it into a competition, who can peel and chop their share of the potatoes the fastest. I can't even watch them.

"Be careful—no one lose a finger." That's officially the last of my good sense. That's all the wisdom I have left. It's a good thing I've already done the sweet potatoes, or I might end up putting Peeps on them again.

In the end, Caroline wins, and no one bleeds. She's always prided herself on efficiency, so I would've put my money on her, anyway. Exhaustion is dragging me down, and I know as soon as I sit, I'll be down for the count. That's the worst part of all this artificial energy—the crash. My adrenal glands might be flooded with cortisol, but it will only last so long. The final shreds of my energy go to delegating: Caroline finishes the potatoes, Ethan sets the table, Grant carries everything from the oven.

At some point, my parents come in with a turkey that actually looks done. The neighborhood is still intact, too. If there's such a thing as a Thank-O-Ween miracle, that's what this is.

Right on time, Nicole shows up wearing a perfectly Thanksgiving-appropriate wrap dress, and an accompanying blood-red cape, like a true Thank-O-Ween pioneer. She even uses the cape to stash the cake plate she's trying to hide.

"I couldn't come with nothing. I'm sorry." She reaches out for a hug, and I fight off a smile, and also tears, for some reason. They well up in my eyes before I can even think. I really need to get a grip.

If steroids make me mean, they also make me feel everything more deeply. I'm flooded with this sense of admiration. I look at Grant over Nicole's shoulder. Nicole, who raised this incredible person all on her own, who essentially created him from nothing.

"Grant told me about your appointment. I know it's a tough time, but it'll pass. He's hated every medicine switch, but he's really been better off for it." Nicole smiles. It's so soothing it makes me wonder how she was ever not someone's mother.

"Everyone sit down! Time to eat!" Mom declares, shifting dishes around in an attempt to make everything fit on the table.

I sit between Caroline and Grant. People are already reaching across me for one thing or another, and I don't think I can lift my arms. Fatigue presses on all my muscles, and everything I even think about doing requires energy I just don't have. My cells are completely depleted.

Taking scoops of food as it gets passed around, I feel chills of bone-tiredness wash over me. It doesn't matter, though. I made it! Dinner's on the table, and everyone's happy.

"You good?" Grant asks quietly.

"Just tired," I whisper back.

He huffs, and I feel the heat of his breath on the shell of my ear. "*Just tired* is chronically ill for *no*."

I giggle and try not to spit out the mashed potatoes in my mouth.

"Will you two stop verbally making out at the dinner table, please?" Caroline elbows me in the side. She's always doing that.

As soon as Grant's attention is diverted, Ethan steals it, yammering about baseball. Having him here is making this the most memorable Thank-O-Ween of Ethan's life. Across the table, our parents talk as if they've been friends forever.

Harmony. I haven't felt that in a long time. I didn't think I had the energy to feel anything anymore, but here it is, a prevailing sense of tranquility, like no matter how terrible I feel, or how badly some things suck, it might all be okay.

"Who made these green beans?" Nicole asks.

"I did," I say.

"They are delicious. Grant hates green beans, and even he's eating them."

Beside me, Grant blushes. I don't think I've ever seen his face so red, not even in the middle of the world's worst flare.

"I didn't know you hated green beans."

"I don't hate them." He stares at Nicole as if she's just shown the world his baby pictures. (As if she hasn't already.)

She looks back at him just as severely. "I once paid him five dollars to eat one."

"How come I don't get paid for eating vegetables? That's not fair," Ethan whines.

"You wouldn't eat them if we paid you. Look at your plate." Dad points to where Ethan sits at the opposite end of the table.

They go back and forth, the volume of the conversation rising as laughter takes over. I zone out, all my willpower going to just keeping my eyes open. Every blink, they threaten to close and not reopen.

"You're not even eating. You're crashing, aren't you?" Grant's back in my personal space again. I don't mind.

"Maybe. Probably."

"Definitely," Caroline says from over my shoulder. She presses her palm to my forehead. "You're running a flare-up fever. If any one of us looked like you do right now, you'd tell us to go to bed."

"She makes a good point," Grant says with his mouth full.

"I'll go to bed as soon as we're done eating."

The conversation across the table takes our attention as both moms roar in laughter.

"What do you think, girls?" Mom asks.

"Sorry, what?" Caroline replies.

"Grant and I always go to the movies on Thanksgiving night, to glimpse the Black Friday chaos but not actually be involved in it," Nicole says.

"Doesn't that sound fun? We could even go in our costumes! We'll just pretend the Black Friday crowds are there. What do you say? I want to see that movie where everyone has their shirt off. You know the one." Mom looks criminally excited. I've never seen her so thrilled about anything that interrupts her sleep.

"I know the one. We can let the kids watch something more appropriate, and we'll go off on our own. But Grant needs to nap first," Nicole says, pointing at him.

"So does Ivy," Caroline and Grant say at the same time.

"You can crash here if you'd like," Mom offers.

"That way you don't have to go home and drive back here," Dad says. He's always so practical, except for the fact that he has no qualms about the shirtless movie idea.

I have qualms about this whole idea, like the fact that there is nothing about moviegoing in the Thank-O-Ween rule book, but I can't say no to those excited faces. I might fall asleep, but I won't say no.

"But first, let me help you all clean up." Nicole's already started grabbing plates.

"And you kids can go on to sleep," Dad chimes in. It should be infantilizing, our parents insisting we nap so we don't get cranky, but I don't have the energy to argue.

"You guys have fun; I'm going to sleep through the night." Ethan leaves the table, not bothering to help clean up, or even offer.

"Same. I need my beauty sleep." Caroline picks up my plate of half-eaten food.

They start to talk over each other, discussing who should sleep where, and I don't even have the energy to listen.

"Just come sleep in my room so we can stop talking about it." I pull Grant away from the table by his shirt sleeve.

"It's just a nap. It's really not that serious," Caroline says on her way to the kitchen with a serving dish in each hand.

"Let the kids sleep. They're too tired to do anything else," Dad says with a smirk.

I can't even be embarrassed. I walk down the hallway on autopilot, and my hand almost misses the door handle when I go to open it.

"I didn't really pay attention to your room when I was in here before," Grant observes. "It's not what I expected."

I should probably have more feelings about this. There's a boy in my room, one that I kind-of sort-of might love. He's about to be in my bed. That's pretty monumental, and I barely care.

"What did you expect?" I mumble, my voice muffled by the pillow I've stuffed my face in.

"I don't know. More mess." Grant looks around the room.

I try to see it from his perspective, try to guess what my space says about me. It's not messy, but it's lived in. My white furniture is scuffed because I've had it for so long. The robin's egg–blue walls are faded from years of sunlight streaming through the blinds. Everything in here is bright and airy, the exact opposite of how I feel.

"I'm only messy in the kitchen." I pull my down comforter over my shoulders. At this point, I don't care if he sleeps on the floor of my closet. I don't have much oxygen left in the tank; I'm passing out soon, whether he's beside me or not.

He walks over to my bookshelf where some of my photos are displayed. It's not quite the museum he has in his house, but it's my version of a scrapbook.

"Who's this?" he asks.

I can't see what picture he's pointing to, and I don't want to expend the energy to lift my head. I can guess, though.

"You mean the strawberry-blond kid standing on a stool to reach the mixing bowl on the counter?"

"Well, yeah, I know that's you, but who's standing behind you? You were adorable before you grew into your front teeth, by the way."

I giggle. It's little more than a puff of air and a click of the tongue.

"My grandmother. She's the one who taught me how to cook. She died when I turned twelve."

"How old are you here?" He points at the picture again.

"That's Thanksgiving. She died just before Christmas."

"Right around your birthday, then." His voice is lower, closer.

"On my birthday," I whisper back.

That's the reason I don't like my birthday. I haven't since that day. My grandmother is the reason I live to cook, but also the reason the most food-centered holidays are the hardest. I heard her voice in my head all day as I cooked, even as scrambled as my brain was. Her spirit floats around me like my own personal atmosphere, influencing everything I do. I'm pretty sure her voice is the one in my head that looked at Grant one day and said *this one's for you.* Even if talking about her is hard, some part of me feels like she never really left.

"I'm sorry," he says softly. "That's terrible."

I don't know how to respond to that. It's been long enough that it feels like I've spent more time without her than with her . . . and accepting condolences still feels wrong.

Grant slips off his shoes and sits down on the bed next to me. He's so tentative, like he needs to be invited, as if I didn't physically pull him down the hall toward my room.

"She sort of named me," I say, now a sleepy kind of half delirious.

"Oh yeah?" Grant crawls in next to me, careful not to crowd me. I rest my head on his shoulder.

"My name's the only one out of the pattern. Dad and Mom are Andrew and Becky, then Caroline, then me, then Ethan."

"I've never noticed that." Grant's voice is practically a hum, I can feel it in the ear pressed against his shirt.

"Most people don't, because I screw it up. When my mom got pregnant with me, they were dead set on a name that keeps up with the pattern, but out of nowhere this wall of ivy started growing on my grandmother's house. It just took over. She insisted it was a sign, because she was, like, weirdly intuitive. So that had to be my name."

"What would they have done if you were a boy?"

"I don't know. I've asked; they didn't have a backup plan. The funny thing is her name was Daisy. She was one of three girls, all named after flowers, and she wanted to name me after a weed."

Grant runs his fingertips up and down my forearm. A shudder runs through me. Suddenly, I don't want to sleep anymore. I want to stay exactly where I am and keep talking, keep listening, keep feeling the way his chest rises and falls in time with his breath against the crown of my head.

"Daisy wouldn't have worked for you, anyway. It's too flashy, too much. You're quiet, and soft, and you creep up on people slowly, and then, suddenly, you're wrapped around everything."

I feel myself blush. I tilt my head up to kiss where his jaw meets his ear.

I fall asleep just then, with his arms wrapped around me like my namesake.

CHAPTER THIRTY-FOUR

———— • ————

THU, NOV 5, 9:34 P.M.

Ethan: take videos of all the fights you see

Ivy: you know it's not actually black Friday right

Ethan: where is your thank-o-ween spirit

I remember why I've never been to the movies this late before. As soon as we pull into the parking lot, we're thrust into a kind of chaos I've never seen. It's *crowded*. I'd assume it's like actual Black Friday, but I've never done that, either, so I wouldn't know.

Movies are hit or miss for me. On one hand, sitting in the dark with other people but not talking is theoretically my ideal social situation. In reality, though, I'm always worried my phone's going to go off, even though I put it on silent, or there's going to be a jump scare that'll make me spray popcorn all over myself and everyone else in a three-seat radius.

They're also very loud, and I'm way too easily overwhelmed.

"I love Black Friday," Grant says from the seat beside me. I squint for a second, until I realize he's actually pretending. His eyes are lit up with excitement, as if a Chipper Jones rookie card lies in that theater somewhere, and it's his pretend Black Friday quest to find it.

"We've been doing this for years," Nicole says. "It used to be that theaters didn't open on Thanksgiving night, but it's gotten so absurd now that people are camping out two days ahead for things, and they'll take shifts and go see movies as breaks. It looks so calm now, compared to what it usually is."

At least Nicole is staying rooted in reality. For now.

Mom finds a narrow parking spot someone has just pulled out of. Leaving seems to have been a smart move on their part. This is my nightmare. I don't know why I agreed to this.

"Does everyone have gloves? We don't need arthritic hands freezing off." Nicole turns around in her seat to face us. We both raise a gloved hand in salute.

"That sounds like something I'd say," Mom remarks, pulling her own gloves from the center console.

"Isn't it funny that they say like seven percent of the population has an autoimmune disease, but the percentage in this car is like ten times that?" Grant looks as if he's actually put a lot of thought into that statement.

"Birds of a feather flock together, I guess," Mom says.

I roll my eyes. All the other birds of a feather are asleep right now, as we should be. But we step out into the frigid air, and I feel the cold seep into my bones—more specifically, the space between them.

"Ouch," Grant says as he falls into step with me.

"I know." I take another step closer to him. I still want to bury myself in the sherpa lining of his coat, where it's warm and smells like him.

The moms walk ahead of us, as if some switch has flipped and they're practicing for *Supermarket Sweep*. They're practically sprinting. Grant calls out to them, but they're too far away to hear. We might as well not be here at all. My short legs don't have a prayer of keeping up. Normally, this Cineplex seems massive, but now it feels beyond cramped. I've never had so many strangers in my personal space at once.

"Oh God," I whisper. I see them as the crowd thins out. My worst nightmare is coming at us right now, a group of North Face coats and Starbucks cups. Three pairs of aughts-style UGG boots and one pair of Timberlands.

I want to dive behind the giant cardboard standup we're walking by. Maybe there's one of those giant lines around that I can hide in? Maybe they'll walk right by and pretend that they don't know me!

"Ivy? I didn't think you were capable of staying up this late." Rory's tone is light and airy, like she's happy to see me, but her words make me feel as cold as the air outside. I'd be able to see my own breath if I were actually breathing. "I thought you turned into a pumpkin at nine p.m."

Behind her, Sloane takes a sip of her drink. She looks like she wants to spit it at me. The other two girls are the rest of the group Rory was matching with at the school dance—that seems like an eternity ago now.

Grant tenses into this immovable wall of muscle, half beside and half in front of me. I didn't want him to see her again. I didn't want her to see him. They're two worlds that I'd hoped would never collide again.

I wrap my fingers around his bicep, silently asking him to let this all go, silently asking him to just move on, in more ways than one. If it were *actually* Black Friday, an impending fight like this might blend in to the eleven o'clock news, but on a random Thursday that's only important to me, we'd be the top story.

"Well, we have to catch up with our moms, so..." I sidestep around them. They don't know that our moms aren't expecting us for hours. Rory moves out of the way so we can pass by. She even smiles, in this partly resentful and partly genuine way.

Grant follows me, but he hasn't relaxed any. The tightness in my chest, however, loosens somewhat.

"Are you just going to let them talk to you like that?" Grant asks, his voice as tense as his shoulders.

Probably, I want to say. He won't understand. I don't have his uncanny ability to make friends. He wouldn't get how I've messed this all up.

"*Turn into a pumpkin*," Grant mumbles. His arms are crossed, and he's repeating the entire conversation out loud like he can't believe she'd dare say that to my face. "She actually said that, knowing that you—"

"She doesn't know," I say on a gasp of breath.

Grant stops dead in the middle of the aisle. He almost gets run over by a horde of people.

"She doesn't know? You haven't told her anything?"

I pull him into the nearest alcove that's not flooded with people. We're surrounded by discarded paper cups and the smell of burnt popcorn. It's probably not the best place for this conversation, but here we are.

"I haven't told her anything. Ever. I...I didn't think she'd understand."

"You've had a chronic illness for a year and a half. You had to have been gone from school for days at a time—gotten sick more than normal people..."

I understand what he means, and he's right. The first six months I was immunocompromised, I got sick every two weeks. She always checked in. She helped me catch up on work I missed. She just never asked for an explanation. Now, in hindsight, that feels like a gift.

"You know me, Grant. I didn't even talk about my illness at the first support group meeting. Literally everyone there was sick, and I _knew_ that, and I still couldn't. How do you expect me to explain this to someone healthy, when all she thinks about is where she's going to hike next or how she can shave another ten seconds off her mile run time?"

Grant is silent for a moment, and I suck in panicked breaths. This is why I don't like dealing with people. Conflict is as catastrophic as it is inevitable.

"She's not just someone healthy. She's your friend."

I know that. Deep down, I know that. I don't think Rory would hurt me, but it's happened before.

"There was . . . this girl," I start, knowing this isn't the time or the place for this conversation, but that if I don't say it now, I never will. "She was my friend. My best friend. Not Rory, a different girl. We went to school together, every year since kindergarten. She went to this STEM charter for high school, and it killed me to think of her not being there with me every day."

Grant nods, his eyes filling with sympathy, because I'm pretty sure he knows what's coming.

"We stayed friends freshman year, even though we were at different schools. We met up every weekend, we talked all the time. She was the first person I told when I got diagnosed, and then . . . nothing. It wasn't even like we drifted apart because I was sick, she just texted back *that sucks*, and . . . that was it. I can't have that happen again. Never again."

I don't have to explain anymore. The pain and the shame and the drama of it all wash over me like it's happening again for the first time, and it's shocking enough to take my breath away. Grant doesn't say anything. He wraps his arms around me, right there in the middle of the shadowed movie theater hallway. His chin rests on the top of my head and his fingers drift through the ends of my hair.

Eventually, his phone rings in his back pocket, and I remember that we're not here because of Rory or my secrets. He mumbles into the phone, and I see him roll his eyes.

"She wants to know if we're in our seats yet."

Now I roll my eyes. "That means somehow they know we're not at our movie."

"Exactly." He grabs my hand and pulls me through the chaos.

Chaos feels like an understatement, actually. It's so overwhelming that I actually forget that my friend is here, somewhere. I forget that she said things to me tonight that were kind of awful. I forget everything but Grant's hand in mine.

That is, until we go through the theater door. My eyes are flighty, my ears attuned to detail in the excessive noise. I don't know if Rory and her soccer girls are still here, but I don't want to see them again. I don't know what I'd do. Run, probably.

"Hey." Grant nudges me once we're seated, his elbow barely touching at my waist. "Don't think about it right now."

It sounds so easy when he says it, like it's actually possible.

I don't respond. My mind is so fixated on that conversation, it's like I'm watching it play back from someone else's perspective.

As the previews start, I come to a conclusion.

I want to tell Rory the truth. She deserves to know, and I deserve to tell her. Yeah, someone else hurt me, but Rory didn't. She never has.

It's important, and it's a fundamental part of me that I've been holding back from her. That's not fair to either of us. We need to talk.

CHAPTER THIRTY-FIVE

•

FRI, NOV 6, 2:13 P.M.

Dad: you just got a package that says "refrigerate immediately." is it food?

Ivy: nope. medical stuff.

Dad: okay well I put it in the fridge

Ivy: did you take it out of the box first?

Dad: no was I supposed to

So, listen. I don't want to do this. It's this big, scary thing that I've feared for ages, but apparently, it's happening now.

The switch.

I don't like the fact that thousands of dollars of medication just showed up on my doorstep unceremoniously. I don't like that I have to put the sharps container made of bright red plastic somewhere in my room. It's like a beacon, advertising that someone sick lives here. Grant must have one. I don't know where he keeps it. Probably, like, on display somewhere, next to his baseball cards. Mine goes on the bookshelf. There's no point in hiding it.

Then, Mom comes in, acting like this is a fun moment to be

celebrated. I'm not feeling it. Everyone seems awfully excited for this. Everyone except for me.

"So, first...," she starts, her tone positive and explanatory. This is her counselor voice. I don't like being on the receiving end of that voice.

There's a big difference between pills once a week plus vitamins every day and injections every other week. Plenty of people have to take pills every day, for plenty of reasons. Fewer people keep medication in their fridge and own sharps containers. It makes me feel like I leveled up somehow. Like this is senior-year sick, and I was just freshman-year sick before. Well, maybe it's just, like, junior-year sick. Maybe infusions are senior-year sick.

Grant called it the big-boy stuff. I don't think I want the big-boy stuff. I think I want the baby stuff.

"Ready?" Mom asks. She's explained the whole process, which is actually pretty simple. I've only been half listening, but I think I get the gist.

"Yeah." I nod. "I think I'm good." I nod again, just to convince her I'm not lying, even though I absolutely am.

I want her to leave me alone, but as soon as she does, something inside of me screams *why did you leave me alone?*

Now, it's just me and my reflection in my bathroom mirror. The weird, cylindrical pen feels heavy in my hand. It's futuristic looking, made of gray plastic with a burgundy cap on each end. They're numbered one and two, so it's easy to take them off in order. That's the first step. The needle is under one cap, and the spring-loaded plunger button is under the other. It's all very fancy.

Then, I use the alcohol swab to clean the patch of skin above my right hip. It's frigid, because I forgot to take it out of the fridge when I let the medicine acclimate to room temperature.

I hold the pen against my skin and press the button on the end.

There's a liquid rush I both hear and feel. Suddenly, my mouth tastes like I licked the bottom of a wishing well. I don't know why. Medicine is so weird. A tiny bit of pressure, a small bandage, and it's all over.

When I reemerge from the solitude of the bathroom, all of the plastic pieces get reassembled and tossed into the sharps container. There's a tug beneath my ribs that has nothing to do with my joints or the injection. I take a deep breath, try to identify it. It's shame, or regret, or wrongness.

I think I went about this all wrong.

I think I made this a sad, somber thing, when it didn't have to be.

This wasn't something I should've done by myself. I shouldn't have told Mom to go away. I shouldn't have told Grant his injection date idea was weird. I shouldn't have kept my illness a secret from Rory all this time.

Maybe it's just the medicine working its way through my skin into my system, but I feel an unexpected sense of power. It's like I really did just level up. Like I won a badge or something.

This is the beginning of the next phase of my treatment, and my life, and I shouldn't have excluded everyone I love from that.

Rheumatoid arthritis is a part of me—and I shouldn't exclude anyone from that.

For a second, I consider texting Grant, letting him celebrate this moment with me, but that doesn't feel like enough. Next time, I'll ask for his help. Next time, I'll make sure he's here with me.

My fingers run over the plastic of the sharps container, at eye level on my bookshelf, that beacon advertising that someone sick lives here. I think of what I could do to be more like Grant when it comes to stuff like this. Bolder. Braver.

Like telling Rory.

Grant would tell her. He would've told her already, because he wouldn't care if she reacted the wrong way. My mind drifts to him for a minute, to his easygoing smile and his heart-stopping eyes.

I can do this, because Grant could.

I can do this, because then Rory and I could be the kind of friends Avery and Lilah are.

I can do this, because then I won't be keeping secrets from anyone anymore.

I *have* to do this, because being sick is nothing to be ashamed of.

My feet take sure steps out of my room, out of the solitude. Mom is sitting right there in the kitchen, waiting for me.

"I did it," I say, unprompted, before she can ask how it went.

She smiles—proud, and gentle, and mom-like.

"Good for you, Iggy."

Yeah, that's it.

Good for me.

CHAPTER THIRTY-SIX

———— • ————

MON, NOV 9, 7:02 A.M.

Grant: You okay?

> Ivy: I think so. Maybe?

> Ivy: You should probably ask again in like ten minutes though.

"I have to tell you something I should've told you a long time ago," I say as soon as I sit down to lunch. I shouldn't have started like that, but it's too late now. "I've been keeping a secret from you, and I'm sorry."

Rory was sitting alone, and that felt like she was extending an olive branch, so I took it. I was planning on talking to her today about everything, but I thought I'd have to approach her at her locker or in the bathroom, someplace where other people might be paying attention. This is easier.

This is how I have to do big, scary things: with a planned impulsiveness, diving in headfirst until I'm in too deep to get out unscathed.

"Okay…" she mutters. I've caught her off guard. Of course I've caught her off guard, olive branch or not. We haven't talked in forever, and suddenly I walk up and blurt this out. This is practically an ambush.

There's a pause.

"Tell me what?" Rory prompts, leaning over her tray and staring like she's watching a celebrity gossip show. At least I think that's what it is at first. Maybe this is just what she looks like when she's paying attention to me. Maybe this is how she's always looked at me. I wasn't expecting that attention, not after all this time and all this distance.

I take a breath, one that's supposed to steady me, but it only reminds me of what I'm doing. It reminds me of the power I'm giving this situation over me.

"So right after freshman year... I got really sick and—"

"Oh my God. What does that mean?" She leans farther in. Her eyes get even wider. "Are you okay?"

"I'm fine," I say, even though that's debatable. It's the truth, though, compared to what she's thinking. She's thinking I'm dying or something, just because that's what most people think the word *sick* means. This is going badly. I should have known this would go badly, but I can still save this. I have to. "I have this thing called rheumatoid arthritis. It's—"

"Wait, arthritis? I thought that was a thing that happened to old people?" Her face is wrinkled up in confusion, like she's actually trying to figure this out. It's as if the word *arthritis* is brand-new to her—like it's something she needs to look up in a dictionary.

My fingers tense and I curl them into fists. *She isn't just someone healthy, she's your friend.* Grant's voice reverberates between my ears and behind my eyes, bouncing off my synapses like fireworks. *He* wouldn't be calm about this, but *I* need to be.

"Not really. It's an autoimmune disease where—"

"Whoa, autoimmune," she says, like the word feels strange in her mouth. "That sounds like it might be serious."

I stay silent for a moment, trying to compose myself. At first, I try to do the most basic emotional triage, figure out what I'm feeling and what I can do about it. No dice. There's too much coming up at once that I can't even begin to sort through. I try physical triage instead. My spine is pin straight, and my heart is racing. I try to relax my fists at my sides, but they're frozen in place. My teeth are ground together, and I can feel the pressure they're putting on the joints in my jaw.

"Is that why you were out all that time last year?" Rory asks. "I thought something might be wrong."

So she knew. Or she suspected, at least. She knew something was wrong. Of course she did. She helped me make up all the work I missed, and she called me every night I was gone from school to relay the minutiae of the day. That person was my friend. My best friend, and I just let her drift away.

Still, I dove headfirst into this, now I have to keep swimming until I'm out the other side. I take a deep breath and respond.

"Yeah. My meds lower my immune system, so I got sick a lot those first few months."

My lungs take in a deep breath, needing calm as much as oxygen. She's so intent on my every word that I could tell her that rheumatoid arthritis is caused by sucking the helium out of balloons, and it makes me shed my skin every so often, like a snake.

"Does this . . . confession have anything to do with what happened at the mall? Or at the movies?" She tents her hands and rests her chin on her fingers. Her particular brand of eye contact is so intense.

"It's complicated." I nod and sigh at the same time. "I didn't want you to know, because telling people is usually awful, and they treat me differently after. They look at me differently. After I was diagnosed, I just wanted some privacy at first. Just to figure it out on my own. But then it had been a long time and I hadn't told you or anyone else, really, besides my family, and it just felt easier to keep that up."

She nods, too, and I know that face she's making. This is the face she makes in class when she's staring at the board and tapping a pencil against her cheek. She's trying to understand. She's processing.

"So this . . . what's it called again?" Rory squints.

"Rheumatoid arthritis."

"Yeah. Right. That." She relaxes back in her seat, crossing her arms. "What does that mean? Like, I get that you're sick, but what's wrong?"

"It just means that my immune system attacks me instead of protecting me. My joints, specifically. They hurt all the time because they're slowly being destroyed."

"Wow," she whispers.

"Yeah…" My voice trails off because I can't think of anything else to say. This is why I don't talk about this. It makes loud people quiet.

"I appreciate you telling me." She's not looking at me, and that's even weirder. "I know we've gotten kind of off track. I mean, me and you. As friends."

"We have," I agree, sitting up straighter and actually making an effort to look at her, even if she's not meeting my eyes at the moment. "I don't know how we get back on track, but I'd like to."

"Me too." She nods. Smiles, just a little. Her posture shifts, too, going from leaning back in the chair to leaning in. "I thought you were kind of pushing me away, and now I know why. I thought it was just because you didn't like me anymore and you weren't mean enough to just say that to my face."

"No!" I scoff. I want to say that's ridiculous—but it's also almost exactly what I thought about her. "I mean… I understand. I worried about that, too, especially with your new soccer friends. I didn't know how to explain, but I should've tried. I shouldn't have pushed you away."

She looks down again. "I shouldn't have let you."

Silence settles between us for a moment, then another.

"That guy you were with—he's your boyfriend, isn't he?" Interest rolls off of her.

I don't know how to interpret the subject change. I don't know if this means that she really wants to know, or if she doesn't know how to talk about this stuff, or if this is her way of letting me out of this uncomfortable conversation.

"Yeah...he's my boyfriend. I met him at a chronic illness support group. That's...kind of why I didn't want you to meet him."

"I get that. He's cute, though. Are there more chronically ill boys at this support group I could meet?"

I laugh, a real laugh, and it feels like magic. I don't remember the last time I laughed with her. "There are. I don't know if they're single, though, if that's what you're asking? Actually, now that I think about it, the support group is kind of weirdly coupled-up."

"Interesting." She raises a brow, and I laugh again.

"I'm gonna go to my locker before class. We'll talk more later?"

"Definitely."

I stand up and walk out of the cafeteria with my head held high, but I take one last look over my shoulder. Rory's already gazing down at her phone. In profile, with her sharp haircut and her missing glasses, she looks like someone else. Beyond that, she feels like someone else. Actually, Rory *is* someone else now—but she's still someone who's my friend.

CHAPTER THIRTY-SEVEN

—— • ——

TUE, NOV 10, 6:27 P.M.

Caroline: Don't forget to tell Stella I'll call her later!!

Caroline: I don't want her to think I'm ditching her

Ivy: Fine, but I still think you're ditching ME

I walk into S&F Fitness alone.

The time before Thanksgiving and winter break is my least favorite of the whole school year. Everyone goofs off, teachers get irritable, I'm tired of my classes and everyone in them. Worst of all, though, Rory has gone on with her life as usual, acting like I didn't emotionally vomit all over her yesterday. We haven't talked again.

"Most people sit in chairs vertically, you know." I sneak up behind him, leaning over the back of my usual seat to run my fingers through Grant's hair. (I love his hair.) He's slumped over, his lower body on his chair, and his upper body on my seat.

He grumbles something unintelligible.

"You clearly feel terrible. Why didn't you stay home?" I haven't stopped moving my fingers through the waves of his hair. I don't want to.

"Wanted to see you," he mumbles.

I step into the circle and gently grab him by his shoulders. I sit down in my seat and lay his head in my lap. "You could've just called."

"Yeah, but you can't do this through the phone." He picks up my wrist and puts my hand back in his hair.

I smile. Such a remarkable human being, this boy. People are coming in and sitting in their spots, but no one gives us a second look.

"Is there a reason you feel so bad today?" I ask.

He nods, and his nose brushes my knee. "Tomorrow's injection day. I always feel bad the day before."

"I guess I have that to look forward to."

"It's not fun, but it's better than the alternative. Your hair might even stop falling out."

"That'd be nice. Maybe it'll go back to stick straight." I run my fingers through said hair, which currently feels as dry as red-tinted straw.

"Your hair used to be straight?" He tilts his head to meet my eyes.

"Yeah. Like Caroline's."

"Where is Caroline?" Grant asks, as if he just realized she's nowhere to be seen.

"At the movies."

"She ditched us for the *movies*?"

"She loves the movies. It's the only place she can eat what everyone else is eating."

Grant's eyes narrow. "Forget that. You seem distracted. What's up?"

My fingers are still at the nape of his neck. "I told Rory yesterday."

Grant sits up, and I wish he hadn't: Now I have to look him in the eye. Almost everyone else has trickled in, so we only have minutes before our conversation is a matter of public opinion.

"And?" he asks.

"It went... okay. I think. I mean, it didn't blow up in my face."

"So no ableist bullshit?"

I laugh, but the sound is almost pitiful.

"No. I mean, it was awkward, and she might be one of those people who think only old people get arthritis, but it wasn't the end of the world. I don't know why I put it off for so long."

"Abled people don't know how to talk about this stuff. Most of the time they get it wrong somehow. That doesn't make them bad people, but it does kind of hurt. It's okay to protect yourself from that."

I nod. There's a sudden lump in my throat the size of a baseball. I don't think I could speak around it if I tried.

"There are plenty of people who get it, though. Try talking to them. I promise it won't hurt." Grant tilts his head to one side, subtly gesturing to the circle of chairs we're sitting in. I remain silent until Lilah starts the meeting.

"Anyone want to start?" Lilah asks.

"I do," I spit out before I can stop myself. Planned impulsiveness—it's the best way to operate.

Lilah nods with a supportive smile. Everyone's looking at me. I feel panic creeping in under my skin. Things might be crawling all over me, and I might be about to cry. They'll listen, though. They'll understand.

"I, um…" My voice trails off, too many thoughts bouncing around in my brain. None of them want to float down to my vocal cords. "My best friend at school didn't know I had RA until yesterday."

That's a sentence.

Maybe it's not the most descriptive, or even effective. It's still a whole sentence, and it even gets most of my point across. The words *best friend* taste bitter in my mouth, like burnt coffee. I don't know if that's still what Rory is, even though I think that's what I want her to be.

"But you've been diagnosed for a while, right?" Avery asks gently. She seems so fierce most of the time, but she's always had this docile tone with me. I appreciate it more than I can say.

"Yeah." I nod. I look at my shoes again, just to make this easier. "Almost two years. It's something I had to say early on, and I just… didn't. It never felt like the right time."

"And then it had been years and you'd never spoken up," Lilah finishes for me.

There's this immediate relief, as strong as my muscle relaxers. They understand. They're not going to laugh or brush me off or act like my feelings don't matter.

"It happens. It's hard to explain," Manny offers, always positive.

"He's right. I usually don't explain it to new people until I get hurt in front of them." Parker smiles.

"It's not always safe," Stella says. She rarely speaks in group, but I'm glad she's speaking up now. "You never know how people are going to react."

"She reacted...okay." I don't know how else to describe it. I tilt my head back up to look at the circle again. Their faces are tight with sympathy. Some are tensed in a muted kind of anger, probably reliving similar experiences.

"I mean...she didn't suspect anything was wrong? Haven't you missed class and stuff?" Holden asks. He's tentative, like he's asking something inappropriate.

I nod.

"She noticed. She helped, even. She just didn't ask if there was something more going on...and when I told her everything yesterday, she sort of got quiet. She didn't react much. It was like I told her my socks don't match."

Little bursts of laughter fill the room, and I can't help but smile.

"I know it's hard, but it gets easier with time. Now she knows, and now you can move on." Avery's plain-spoken advice hits me like a brick.

Yes. I can move on. I can decide to accept whatever the outcome will be.

"Thank you," I say, making eye contact with everyone in this precious circle one by one. "This really helps."

CHAPTER THIRTY-EIGHT

— • —

WED, NOV 11, 6:06 A.M.

Grant: have a good day

Ivy: thanks 🖤

It's finally almost Thanksgiving. The first bell rings, and Caroline squeezes my shoulder before tromping off to her morning class. My locker door springs open, and I have just enough time to grab the books, notebooks, and other miscellaneous junk I need for the day before I turn around...

...and they're all looking at me.

Everyone is looking at me.

No, they're not. They're looking over my shoulder or above my head or something. They're not all looking *at* me. There's no reason for them to be looking *at* me.

Unless...unless Rory told people about me.

No. That would be my worst fear. I'm overthinking this. I'm exaggerating. I have to be.

They can't *all* be staring at me.

Right?

I try to think of what Grant would do in this situation.

Probably act like it's not bothering him. I think of the text he sent me this morning, and I imagine having a good day. If I imagine hard enough, it'll actually happen. Manifesting, despite the bullshit.

That's it! I think. That was sort of an angry thought. Imagining what Grant would do isn't enough, because he's not angry enough. He's sweet and funny and sort of my favorite person in the world. So I put my Caroline face on. I put my Avery face on. I pretend I'm some shorter yet no less fierce version of the two of them. It's totally fake, but I need it to work. I need to feel like I can breathe fire if I have to.

With only slightly shaking hands, I slam my locker shut and walk to my first period class.

Just a few more days. I let it echo through my brain like a mantra, then I start counting the hours, and later, the minutes.

The hallway is quiet, but classes are quieter. For the first time ever, my lab partner carries the microscope for me.

I keep my head down but my chin up, and I don't let anyone see me sweat.

CHAPTER THIRTY-NINE

—— • ——

THURS, NOV 12, 4:03 P.M.

> Ivy: you know I like you more than like 99% of other people, right?

> Grant: omg are you flirting with me???

This is it. The last recipe.

I saved it for last for a reason. It means the most. It hurts the most. I had half planned to keep it in the in-progress box forever, collecting dust by itself while the other recipes live on in the completed box.

In a way, I'm surprised I still have it. So many times I've thought about letting it slip through my fingers.

When Mom brought up my birthday, she made some valid points. She made me feel like I should at least *consider* a party or a dinner or something. She made me feel like I could take this recipe out and let it see the light of day. Just for a second, she made me think I could celebrate my birthday.

The index card this recipe is written on isn't worn. It's practically pristine, except for the purple ink that's faded with time. The corners aren't even bent.

The last time I made this cake, my grandmother died. It was the last thing we ever made together. It was the last thing she ever made, period.

Ivy's Inside-Out Birthday Cake

I run my fingers over the slanted scrawl. It makes me smile. It's just marble cake, really. My seven-year-old brain couldn't comprehend that, though—I thought it was inside-out chocolate cake. (Besides, she let me do the swirling, so it wasn't so much marble as it was a rocky-looking mottle of chocolate clumps baked into the vanilla cake.)

On the one hand, it would be almost too easy to adapt this recipe. All I have to do is reach into the completed recipe box for my gluten-free vanilla and chocolate cake cards. I probably don't even have to do that. I know those by heart.

I could build a few layers up...vanilla icing on the bottom... chocolate icing in the middle...another layer of vanilla on top. Maybe get some blue flowers to decorate with. Real ones. (Except I don't really know anything about flowers—Lilah does, though. She'll save us from eating poison.)

But no. No.

I can't do this. There's no way I can do this. This is painful. Baking isn't supposed to be painful. It's supposed to be calming and healing and—

"What are you thinking so hard about?" Mom asks. Somehow

she's right next to me. I must really have been thinking too hard. She takes the card from my hand. "Oh," she mumbles.

I want to take it back. I want to tell her I'm just thinking. I haven't decided anything yet.

"Come with me." She takes my hand and puts the recipe card back in its lonely, otherwise empty box. "I want to show you something."

I follow. My sock feet shuffle down the hallway to my parents' room. On the bed is an off-white square box I've never seen before.

"What's this?" I ask, brushing a dust bunny off the box's lid.

"Open it."

We sit cross-legged on the bed and I pull the box onto my lap. More dust kicks up as I move it, which makes the breath in my nose feel fuzzy. There's a baby blue satin ribbon tied around it like a present, and I pull the bow apart. Crumbling tissue paper lines the inside, wrapping up something I don't recognize. It seems so delicate that I don't even want to touch it. It might turn to nothing if I breathe the wrong way.

"I know you've seen it in pictures, but it's different in person." Mom gently pulls the contents of the box out. It's a short dress made of delicate, embroidered cotton. It's the lightest powder blue, so light it probably looks white from far away.

It's always looked white in pictures, anyway. Maybe that's just something I assumed, given that it's a wedding dress.

"She wore blue to her wedding?"

"And wanted me to wear blue to mine, too." Mom holds the

dress up to her neckline. "Short dresses were the thing back in her day, but she was tiny like you are. It was above the knee on her—on me, it was nearly indecent."

I giggle. The mental image is hilarious, my tall mother walking around in a too-short cotton dress at her wedding, rather than the poufy-sleeved gown I've seen in so many pictures.

"Why are you showing me this?" I run my fingers over the embroidery threaded through the fabric.

"I found it yesterday. I was pulling a box of winter clothes down from the top shelf, and it fell down at my feet. Like she threw it at me. At you."

I feel my brows scrunch together. "I still have no idea where you're going with this."

"Listen, Ivy. She would skin me alive if she knew I'd let you go this long without a birthday party. I wish I knew how to explain this, how she felt about you."

"I know," I whisper, my voice cracking between the words.

"She would want you to have this. She would want you to celebrate yourself. She was my mother, and I knew her for almost forty years. There was nothing that made her happier than you did. You are her heart walking around and cooking her recipes. No one ever has enough birthdays, Ivy... Please don't feel guilty celebrating yours."

Hot tears roll down my cheeks. They're the same tears I've cried countless times. It's not guilt that keeps me from celebrating my birthday—not really. Besides the residual trauma of waking up one birthday minus my grandmother, there's this innate fear, fear that comes with a progressively disabling disease. There's fear that even at seventeen, I'm running out of time, and that my mother's timer is leaking sand even faster than my own.

Getting older means progressing through life, and I find that hard to celebrate, not when what most consider to be the prime of my life is filled with pain, and I know that pain will only get worse.

But maybe birthdays should be about celebrating what we have *now*. *Today*.

"You don't have to decide anything now. Would you just try it on once? Just for me?"

I wipe my eyes and stand up. I don't tell her that I've sort of already decided to have this ridiculous party. My mom holds the dress up and undoes the pearl buttons down the back of the bodice.

"I don't remember her ever telling me much about her wedding." I disappear behind the bathroom door to change. I'm convinced the dress won't fit. It'll be awkwardly long, or too baggy at the top, or hang off my hips in an unpleasant way. The party is one thing, the dress is another.

"Well." Mom's voice sounds close, like she's leaning against the bathroom door. "That's because she wasn't exactly proud of it. It was a courthouse wedding, not the dramatic affair I had."

"I can't reach the buttons." If I reach back any farther, my shoulder is going to pop out of place. According to Parker, that's not pleasant. The door creaks open.

"She was pregnant with me then, but no one knew."

"What?" I spin my upper body around so fast my hair whips the side of Mom's face. Oops. It's her fault, though. She can't drop a bomb on me like that and not expect retaliation.

Mom nods.

"She never talked about it because she didn't want anyone to do the math. When I say no one, I mean *no one*. Not even me, technically. It's just that when you count backward from my birthday to their wedding, there aren't enough months there."

"Whoa," I breathe out. Somehow, it feels like there was a whole other person my grandmother had been that I never knew. "Does that bother you, Mom?"

"Not really. I wish she would've told me, that's all. The idea that my parents weren't married when I was conceived is really nothing, but that she was so ashamed of it that she never told me is sort of sad."

"Yeah, I guess it is," I whisper. "Is that why you're so open with me and Caroline?"

"Yes, it's exactly that. In my family, everything about sex was so secretive. Growing up, I was never comfortable asking questions or talking about it. I know you probably weren't ready for that conversation at the doctor, and it wasn't easy, but I'd like to think that we have an environment here that makes anything safe to discuss."

"You're right. I needed to have that conversation with myself at some point, anyway."

"That's one thing about being sick, isn't it? It's always showing us what we are and aren't ready for."

I nod. At the bottom of my waist, I feel Mom tugging the last button into place. As if by magic, the fabric seems to fall around me in just the right way.

In the mirror, I see structured sleeves that fall a few inches above my elbow, and a wide, swooping neckline that graces my collarbones. I run my fingers over the stiff embroidered flowers dancing across the bodice. Below the cinched waist, structure flows into whimsy as the skirt drapes.

It's beautiful, and the delicate blue sets off the orange tones in my auburn hair. I'll have to leave it down, I think.

I realize that I want to keep this dress on forever. And that's when I know, without a doubt, that I want to make that cake.

"Me, you, and her. All wrapped up in one dress," Mom whispers reverently, as if she's speaking in church. "What do you think?"

"I'll need shoes."

Mom cocks an eyebrow in my direction.

"Flats this time, right?"

CHAPTER FORTY

—— • ——

SUN, NOV 15, 9:33 A.M.

Grant: I'd like a refund on my body. It's defective and really expensive to fix.

Ivy: At this point, you're just typing out chronic illness memes so you can take credit for coming up with them

Grant: Damn. I was hoping you wouldn't notice.

Ivy: I noticed, but I appreciate it anyway.

"It was so close. They played six games and five of them were only won by one run. All the Hall of Famers on that team, it was incredible."

Grant rambles on behind me, sitting on the counter while I bake. I don't know what I'm baking yet; I've just gathered a grocery store's worth of random things from the cabinets. I'm finally done with Grandma's recipes, so I think it's time to make something of my own. Something new.

This week has been very strange. I sat with Rory at lunch a few times, and that went okay, but eyes seemed to follow me everywhere I went. It feels like I'm the new kid at a school I've spent three years in. Everyone stares, but no one talks.

"What are we talking about again?" I ask, turning around to face him.

"The '95 World Series. They didn't win another one until 2021, remember?"

"Oh yeah. Right. Sorry. Keep going."

"There were so many Hall of Fame guys on that team. Bobby Cox. No manager has ever gotten ejected from more games than him. That's the record I'd like to break."

I laugh. I can picture that. That's my boy, Hall of Fame rule breaker.

"Tom Glavine. Chipper Jones. Greg Maddux. John Smoltz. I swear, when he retired, I cried."

"You cried?"

"I was a kid." He shrugs.

I turn back to my ingredients, using a knife to even out the cup of sugar I'm measuring.

"Kimbrel came up after Smoltz retired. He was one hell of a closer. Him and McCann were the best battery."

"Hey, Grant?" I ask, dumping measured flour into my mixing bowl. Whatever this ends up being, it's going to be a hot mess. I can already tell. I don't care.

"Do you want me to shut up and leave you alone?"

"What? No." My hands drop the measuring cup of their own accord. "Why would you ask me that?"

Grant scratches the back of his neck. "I don't know. I talk a lot and you don't say much."

I walk over to where he sits on the counter and stand directly in front of him. "Maybe I don't say much, but that doesn't mean I'm not listening." I rise up on my tiptoes to kiss him, just the quickest brush of my lips against his.

"You know," Grant starts as I turn back to my monstrosity in progress, "I think words are different for me than they are for you."

"What do you mean?" I ask.

"Words are like vanilla extract to me. Not the good Mexican vanilla, either. The cheap, watery kind that only changes the flavor of anything if you add, like, way too much."

I stop working, completely confused as to where he could be going with this.

"To you, though, words are like real vanilla beans. The expensive kind that come in glass jars. You only use them when you really want to change something. You might say less, but you always mean more."

My ears burn like I've been in the sun all day.

"So how's Rory?" he asks. It's a one-eighty, but, somehow, not a completely unwelcome subject change. He knows I get all weird when I'm complimented.

"It's really odd," I admit, working the dough with the heels of my hands. "Something about the whole thing doesn't feel right." I laugh, and a puff of flour dust flies through the air.

He jumps off the counter, and within a breath, he's right beside me. I have butter wrappers and a half-open bag of flour lying around. Grant starts to clean up behind me.

"Doesn't feel right how?" Grant reappears on my other side, leaning one elbow onto the counter. He's so effortlessly graceful. It's not fair.

"The way they're acting, it just doesn't add up. Rory acting like nothing is wrong is one thing, but everyone else has been avoiding me, too. Like, people I say hi to in the hallways won't even look at me. My lab partner was acting weird. He said he should put the microscope away because it's heavy, but I do it all the time."

"Fuck." Grant's brows pinch together. "This started right after you told her, didn't it?"

I feel his words like a kick in the ribs. All the air whooshes out of me at once. All the pieces dance around in the air until they fall together into the most devastatingly heartbreaking puzzle I can imagine.

She couldn't have. There's no way. She couldn't have willingly shared the information I trusted her with. That would be callous and vindictive and spiteful. To weaponize something like this against me—that would be downright malicious. It's a level I can't imagine anyone would stoop to, especially not her.

"I'm so sorry, Ivy. I shouldn't have pushed you to tell them. People did this to me, too. I should've known they would—"

"You should've known?" My voice goes quiet, dangerously so. He's right. He should've known. He told me to tell her. "Why did I tell her?" I whisper-scream. "This is going to ruin everything. She ruined everything. We ruined everything. I—I . . ."

Grant leans closer, and I push him away. I can't.

"Ivy," he pleads.

"Leave me alone."

I take a step back. I have to. I can't breathe.

So does he. I look at the dough in front of me. My mind hadn't known what I'd been making, but my hands were forming my usual bread recipe. Except I used almond flour instead of my homemade GF flour mixture. The whole batch is grainy like its made of sand. I make this recipe every week. I can do it in my sleep.

I ruined it.

I pick up the failed batch of dough and throw it into the garbage. It lands at the bottom with a resounding *thud*, and I think I actually feel it in my chest. I have to make it again. My hands repeat the familiar process, but my mind is laser focused. I'm not going to mess this up again. I'm not going to ruin this again.

I work at a frenetic pace, butter and flour and yeast forming dough in record time. My hands pound the dough until it feels like my fists must be bruised. Everything is moving so fast, I can't keep up. I don't know if I'm angry or hurt or devastated or some combination of all three. All I know is that my fists are flying, and dough forms before I'm ready for it to. I don't know if it takes minutes or hours or days. I set the dough aside to rest.

The kitchen is a mess again. I close the jar of baking soda, because it's not even supposed to be out in the first fucking place, and wait. Grant. He's not cleaning up after me anymore because I told him to leave me alone. I pushed him away. A spell breaks or panic fades or the vapor of whatever poison has come over me drifts out the window.

"Wait, Grant, no," I whisper again. "I'm sorry, I shouldn't have—" My voice breaks as I step forward. I have to stop him. He can't leave. "You, of all people, should not be the one apologizing for this, and I should not be the one blaming you. Not in a million years."

The words just keep coming as I make my way through the kitchen and past the living room and into the foyer.

The realization I just came to is earth-shattering, and I almost let it ruin everything. I almost let it ruin Grant.

I don't know how I'll ever look at Rory again, how I'll ever trust anyone with that information again.

"I can't believe this," I whisper again, to no one.

I throw open the front door. The driveway is empty.

Grant's gone.

He left.

I pushed him away, and he left.

The door closes with a fraction of the energy I opened it with. I walk back to the kitchen in a haze. It still smells like the cinnamon I had open on the counter. I don't even know why I had cinnamon open on the counter.

How did this even happen? How did I fuck this all up so badly?

Crying over this seems so foolish, but God, it hurts. She was my best friend. I'd spent every day of my high school career with Rory, and it all went away with the blink of an eye. Every laugh, every video call, every lunch period. Gone. All those memories tainted, forever.

This is what the rest of my life is going to be like, I think, mediocre friendships and an illness I have to hide. As my illness gets more degenerative, maybe the rest of my life will deteriorate, too. Maybe I'll keep pushing people away, even if they're the best thing that's ever happened to me.

CHAPTER FORTY-ONE

— • —

TUE, NOV 17, 4:41 P.M.

> Ivy: can you meet me at the park before group?
> I want to talk about everything.

Grant: ok

We're at the park where we watched the movie on our first date. I don't think I've been back here since then, actually. It's much more charming in the daylight, as children finish burning off after-school energy and small groups carry on afternoon strolls.

Also, there's this taco truck I've heard so much about. It's a legend among the original support group, and it's basically their only tradition. They got tacos after meetings, always. Maybe they still do, without the rest of us.

I don't care about any of that, though. All I care about is getting Grant back. The past few days have been a special kind of misery without him, and I need to apologize. I need us to be okay again.

The park bench beneath me is cold. Caroline is waiting in the car, staring at me. I told her she could leave, but she wouldn't. She didn't need to come in the first place, but she said I was too shaky to drive. I guess if this all blows up in my face, she gets to bear witness. I let my face fall forward into my palms. This is all my fault. All the confusion and all the dramatics and all the messiness. It's all on me.

Then I hear footsteps, ones I recognize.

I look up at Grant from between my fingers.

God, I missed him. It's only been a few days. I didn't think that was even long enough to miss someone. There's an ache in my chest that lessens at the sight of him, and I feel like I can finally breathe.

I look up at Grant again. Grant's looking down at me. He's wearing a beanie, and his hair is peeking out of the front, and I've never seen it like that before. It's way too much for me right now. I stop looking at him, to save my delicate heart.

Wordlessly, I stand up and leave the cold bench behind. Grant follows. His presence next to me makes me feel like I've won something. Like I've won everything.

I haven't though, not yet. We're still not okay. I still have to make sure that we're okay. Somehow, we end up on the playground, sitting at the base of the monkey bars. This is weird, but that's okay, because we're weird.

He sits down next to me. I look up at him.

"I'm sorry," we both say at the same time.

I giggle. He chuckles. He tries to speak again, at the exact same time I do.

"Let me," I say, because I really need to apologize, and I need him to hear this. "I'm so sorry I pushed you away. I shouldn't have. I knew it the moment I did it. I was just...overwhelmed and scared and sort of heartbroken, but, like, in an angry way, and—"

"It's okay. I promise, it's okay."

At the sound of those words, my heart relaxes.

"I shouldn't have left, but you said to leave you alone, and I wasn't sure you meant it, but leave means leave, so..."

"I won't push you away again, okay?"

He nods. It's exactly what I needed him to say, and he didn't say anything at all.

"It was kind of a mess, huh?" I whisper into the air.

"Yeah. But we're good now. Right?" He leans into my space, resting his weight on the arm that's extended out behind my back.

"Right."

"I really wanna kiss you right now, but I think Caroline's spying on us from the car."

My hand splays out across his shoulder, just to move him out of the way. I peek past him to where Caroline is, of course, still staring. I glare at her, and she glares right back. Okay, fine. So she's not planning on moving.

I lean back, but stay in Grant's space, breathing his air and his grass and clean soap scent.

"She is, but that doesn't mean you can't do it."

He smiles, just before he leans in, and it knocks the wind from my chest. The kiss is soft, and gentle, cold, and barely there, but it is the epitome of peace. It's the physical representation of my heart putting itself back together.

"Grant?"

"Yeah?"

"Please don't ever leave me alone."

CHAPTER FORTY-TWO

— • —

TUE, NOV 17, 5:54 P.M.

Ivy: I'm talking tonight.

Caroline: Like, talking, talking? About...everything?

Ivy: Yep.

Caroline: I'm so proud of you.

I have something to say. I've been practicing my speech all afternoon. Apologizing to Grant was first on the list of difficult things I need to do today, and this is second.

I'm determined, and just angry enough to stomp holes into the gym floor and leave with my boots covered in rubble. Since the realization that my illness has become both (A) public knowledge, and (B) an excuse for people to either shun or stare at me, I've been gliding through the five stages of grief.

"You look mad," Grant says as soon as we walk into the gym. He's so blunt sometimes, this boy who's the center of my world. He hasn't let go of my hand since we left the park.

"She is mad. She stress-baked for hours yesterday. If you'd like a muffin, scone, or brownie, you know where to find them." Caroline walks past us to where Stella sits.

"That's what you do when you're mad? Bake?"

"I guess." I shrug. "I don't usually get mad. It's not like I have a protocol."

Grant rolls his eyes. "Okay, but do you want to talk about it?"

"I think I'm going to." I tip my chin in the direction of the circle of chairs.

"Good. I want a muffin, though."

This time, I roll my eyes. I don't tell him that I made the raspberry cheesecake ones he likes. He'll figure it out later. They're Grandma's recipe, of course.

As I take my spot in the circle, my stomach starts to roll. It's a reflex, I tell myself. It's because I don't like public speaking. It's because Rory hurt me. I repeat Grant's words in my mind: *They won't all be like that.*

"You can do this," I whisper under my breath over and over again, until I start to believe it. These are my real friends. I know that now.

"Anyone want to go first?" I hear Lilah ask.

"I do." My hand shoots up before I tell it to. Lilah nods in my direction, and my mouth takes off running. I think speaking last week made me bolder. "So, settle in, because this is a rough one. To recap from last week, I have exactly one friend at school, and she didn't know I had RA. I told her, and only her."

I sigh, because I don't know how to say this next bit. "I don't know for *sure* that it was her, but..."

"I'm sure," Grant whispers under his breath. He's all growly, even though his thumb is still stroking circles over the back of my palm.

"I think she told other people," I continue, buoyed. "I don't know who she told and who she didn't, because now everyone is avoiding me anyway. Or gawking at me like I have three heads." There's a collective groan throughout the room. Someone even boos. Parker, maybe? Grant joins in. That's a bit excessive, but I'll allow it.

"Do people really think chronic illnesses are contagious or something? It's not like we all have the plague." Manny gets animated when he speaks sometimes.

"I don't know why it hurts so much," I admit. "I don't really even like any of them. It's not like my life's been any worse just because some people are looking at me like an alien."

"It still sucks!" Grant says, loudly enough for everyone to hear.

"Exactly," Avery speaks up. She gets passionate about things like this, things people should be angry about. "It sucks, and you really have to just let yourself feel your way through that. What you don't have to do is bend to anyone else."

Beside her, Lilah nods over and over again.

"And it hurts because your privacy was violated. She used you and your disease as grist for the rumor mill. To me, that's unforgivable."

"If there is one thing that having a chronic illness will show you, it's who your friends are." Parker looks at me with a deeper meaning in his eyes. I get it.

"That's true." I heave a breath out through my nose. "I know who my friends are, and apparently she's not one of them."

As if they sense that I need time alone in my head to process what was just said, the conversation progresses away from me. As they speak around me, I grieve. I grieve for every high school memory tainted, for every diverted stare I'll have to endure, for the whole person I was seen as before.

"You good?" Grant whispers in my ear. On my other side, Caroline squeezes my hand. It's possible I've never considered the true value this group of people has in my life. This is more than support—it's understanding. It's being seen and heard and felt, all for the first time.

"I'm good," I whisper back.

CHAPTER FORTY-THREE

•

TUE, NOV 24, 7:03 A.M.

Grant: HAPPY LAST DAY OF SCHOOL

Ivy: One. more. day.

Ivy: Couldn't have made it without you

Grant: do you make stuff for regular people thanksgiving?

Grant: bc I kinda really want several forms of potatoes

Ivy: I can probably handle several forms of potatoes.

There's a feral vibe in the air. One of just barely contained chaos. Everyone's goofing off; half the seniors aren't even here. (I would've skipped, too, but chronically ill people like me can't waste our limited number of absences on a day like this.)

I feel a little chaotic, too. I think I might even invite a few people to the party. Some kids have just finally started talking to me again, and I hope some of them might like to come.

"Hey, Addie," I say, like always. Addie is one of my *say hi in the hallway* friends. I think she counts as a friend, anyway. Recently, I've realized the definition of the word *friend* isn't as concrete as I'd like it to be.

"Hi," she says back, like always. She smiles, but keeps walking.

"I'm, uh, having a party. A party for my birthday. A birthday party. If you want to come."

Well, that was potentially the least smooth party invite ever, but Addie doesn't seem to mind.

She smiles again and nods. "Yeah, sure."

"I'll, uh, get you the details later," I say, because I'm too nervous for the details to come out smoothly.

I do this several more times throughout the day...with my lab partner, with my final project group in History class. It gets smoother each time. By the end of the day, I'm not even stumbling over words anymore. I'm inviting people to the party with such conviction that I actually believe that I want them to come. Maybe I do want them to come.

This actually might work. This actually might be okay.

"I would assume my invite got lost in the mail if you weren't giving them out by hand," Rory says from behind me.

I'm cleaning out a semester's worth of scrap paper from my locker before I leave for the day. I almost made it. Five more minutes, and I would've been out of here.

This might not work. This might not be okay.

I turn around and face her, because I have to at some point. I don't remember the last time I saw Rory, exactly; I just know it was before I realized she had apparently told absolutely everyone she could that I have rheumatoid arthritis like it was hot gossip, not a crucial piece of my life.

That hurt may still be fresh, but I set it aside. As I look at her, I don't think about myself. I think about her. I try to understand why she could've ever shared that information with anyone. I try to rewind through years of memories, to picture what I could've done to her that cut deeply enough to require this level of vengeance.

There's nothing.

"I'm not actually handing out physical save the dates." I can't tell how my voice sounds. I'm going for even and calm, but I could be giving off either terrified or infuriated, I can't be sure. My fingers tighten around the books I'm holding, because they feel like a shield in front of my rib cage. I don't know why I feel the need to protect myself from her, but I do.

"You *were* going to invite me, though, right?" She cocks a hip to one side. "I think this is the first birthday party you've had since I've known you! Is it because this year's eighteen?"

Honestly, this is ridiculous. This has all gone on for too long. There's nothing I want more in the world than to have this behind me.

I *could* invite her—let her come to the party where my boyfriend, sister, and friends might do her emotional or even physical harm. That's sort of tempting, just for a second, because some part of me does want to lash out at her for hurting me.

But that's not me.

"Why did you tell everyone?" It's the only thing I have the courage to ask.

Her face tenses up in confusion, then freezes entirely. She must know what I mean.

"You have no idea what it feels like," I say quietly. "I hope you never do, honestly. I hope you never know what it feels like for someone to take something you told them in confidence and basically paint the walls with it. I hope you never know how bad it feels to watch someone take your friendship and blast it into space."

I don't think I'm capable of actually fighting. What I just said to her feels about as aggressive as I can get. That monologue took everything I had.

"I didn't..." she starts to whisper. "Oh my God." All the breath whooshes out of her at once. She looks horrified. Mortified. Just the slightest bit angry. "Ivy, I am so, so sorry."

For a second, I just blink. That's all I can do.

"You're talking about your illness, aren't you? I...I was with Brooke and Sloane, and I just mentioned it to them in passing. I never expected they would..." Her voice trails off.

"Yeah, well. They did." I shrug, not because it's not a big deal, but because I don't know what else to do. "I told *you*. Not them. And I explained what it's like once people know, how they look at me differently. And now it's going to be the first thing that pops into anyone's head when they pass me in the hallway. Whatever they knew about me before doesn't even matter."

The anger is draining out of me. The only thing left is hurt.

"Oh my God. I can't believe this." She sort of falls against the locker next to mine, like she can't hold herself up anymore. You know what, I don't blame her. I'd let my muscles go slack and slide down to the floor if I knew for sure I could get back up.

"I can." I laugh bitterly. "This is exactly why I keep RA to myself."

Rory picks up her head and lets it fall back against the locker over and over again. The repetitive banging is more than I can handle.

"I'm—so—sorry," she says again. "I shouldn't have said anything, and they *definitely* shouldn't have repeated it. I just felt like you were pulling away from me, and I've talked to them about it, *a lot*, and they always said you were a bad friend, and I thought they'd *get it* if they knew. I thought I was...defending you."

Her words hit like a baseball to the chest.

"I was a bad friend. I *am* a bad friend." My lungs heave in a deep, ragged breath. "I *have* been pushing you away, and there's really no excuse for that. I've just been so tired, almost too tired to be a friend, and I'm just so...scared. In case you haven't noticed, I have a ridiculous level of social anxiety, and it makes me pretty bad at communicating. But you're not bad at it. You have other friends. Not that you shouldn't have other friends...I just felt... left behind. Like you didn't need me anymore if you had them. Which only made me want to keep my secret more. And it was just easier to keep saying no to you than to push myself to say yes. Especially because you didn't know. No one knew."

Rory nods.

"I get it." She smiles sadly. "I don't blame you, Ivy. Now I understand, but before, it hurt. I kept reaching out and you kind of ignored me. I thought it was my fault! And when I had this explanation for why you'd been distant, I thought everything finally made sense. *That's* why I told them. But I didn't even consider the impact it could have on you if they blabbed. I didn't even consider the possibility that they *could* blab about it."

The bell rings, and I look around us. We're the only two people left in the hallway. We're supposed to leave, but I don't think I have the energy to walk out to the lot right now. I might just hide in the bathroom for a bit.

"I don't blame you, either," I whisper. Because it's not exactly her fault, is it? All she did was trust someone, the same way I did.

"I'll talk to them about this, okay? They shouldn't have said anything. It's disrespectful, and it's none of anyone's business."

"Thank you." I nod, immediately feeling better. "And I'm sorry. For everything."

"I'm sorry, too." She rings her hands. "I don't really know where we go from here, though. I mean, I'm sorry, you're sorry, but... what do we do?"

"I don't know, either," I admit, even though that feels like failure. "Maybe we just take it one day at a time."

CHAPTER FORTY-FOUR

——— • ———

FRI, DEC 4, 11:28 A.M.

> Grant: If I screw up your party food, are you going to dump me?

> Ivy: No.

> Ivy: But please try not to screw up my party food.

I flip the last layer out of the cooling pan. It lands smoothly on the center of the cake board. My lungs heave out a sigh of relief. Gluten is pretty much the thing that holds stuff together when it comes to baking, so keeping gluten-free cake intact is actually pretty hard. Now, I have six serviceable marbled layers from which to build a tower of cake. I set them aside to finish cooling and start assembling my icing. Powdered sugar clouds the air, and butter greases up my hands.

There's a knock at the door just as I start to flip the hand mixer on to whip the icing. Everyone's gathered in the kitchen, prepping food for the party tomorrow: Mom, Dad, Caroline, Ethan, me. When I decided to go through with it, I made it a priority. It's actually fun, the idea that all my friends and family could be in one place, just for me. It's still marginally terrifying when I think about all the attention, but fun.

"That should be Grant—" I start to say.

"I'll get it!" Ethan jumps off the stool behind the counter. I hear the front door creak open, and then their casual conversation approaching the kitchen.

"Brought you this. The mail guy dropped it off just as I pulled in." Sometimes I love how Grant launches into conversation without preamble.

I know what's in that box. It's nondescript and made of Styrofoam, only one sticker on it next to the label, something about refrigerating immediately. I forgot it was time for another medication delivery already.

There are seven more appetizers to make, and a variety of desserts. I've made lists and done all the prep. Everyone has a comprehensive set of instructions to follow. This is going to go smoothly, because I've planned every last detail.

"Let's get started." I put my medicine in the fridge and move everything else to where I can't see it. Out of sight, temporarily out of mind.

"You're giving me the easiest thing to do, right? Like putting cheese and crackers on a plate or something?" Grant steals some of the bacon I crumbled for the quiches.

"No." I smack his hand away. "Ethan has the easiest job, and even it's not that easy."

I dole out directions and answer questions. I get Ethan a new spatula when he drops his. I compliment everyone on their technique. Even if taking a chance on this party ends up being a terrible idea, I'll always have this: time spent in the kitchen with everyone I love. It's special. Cooking has always held this magic for me, but today it's more intense. It's as if the kitchen itself is enchanted, coming alive to wish me a happy birthday. It's as if the person we're missing lives in the air we breathe, floating in between the specks of dust only visible in the streaks of sunbeams.

Puff pastry rises in the oven; spices and butter scent the air. Everything is slowly coming together. All my senses are at peace. We spread wire racks over all the counter space, letting everything cool as it comes out of the oven.

It's quite a scene: a beautiful display of food, nearly all of my own creation.

We all start packing away food, arranging everything so it'll survive the trip across town to the botanical garden. I can already picture tomorrow: the green array of the garden; my family, my friends; my grandmother's wedding dress. It'll be quiet and calm and serene.

Even as my limbs operate as normal, shuffling food from place to place and tossing dishes in the sink, my mind drifts elsewhere. There's something I have to do.

"Hey, Grant?" I tug on his shirt sleeve, whispering. He looks at me, so close he doesn't even need to respond with words. "I need to do my injection. Will you help? Last time I did it, it didn't feel right. Maybe you have tips."

He smiles and winks. "In other words, you're asking me on an injection date?"

I try to glare at him, but I can't. He's just so...special. I can't help the rush of tenderness I feel. Every time I look at him, the only thing I'm capable of thinking is *that boy is mine.*

"If that's what you want to call it, sure." I smile back.

We move to clean up the kitchen and Grant takes the medication and a bottle of water out of the fridge.

"Did you let it warm up for a while before you did it? Because injecting cold liquid into warm skin hurts like a bitch." Grant doesn't even bat an eye at swearing in front of my mother. Ethan's right, Grant is undeniably cool. "And don't forget to take the alcohol swab out, too. Cold alcohol swabs are gross."

I laugh at the grimace on his face. Sometimes I forget Grant and I are the same kind of sick, and then sometimes he does things like this, showing me he knows infinitely more about my medication than I do.

"Make sure you're, like, really hydrated." He hands me the water bottle. I drink half of it in one go.

When the timer on my phone goes off, the kitchen is clean. The food is packed up, and I want to make more. If I had a molecule more of energy, I really would. I don't want this to be over.

"You ready?" Grant asks.

Rather than responding verbally, I gather up all my scattered supplies and carry them into my room. My arms form a disheveled bundle, like I just robbed a pharmacy. Behind my closed door, I lay everything out.

"Are you afraid of needles?" Grant asks as he takes the pen out of its plastic packaging.

"Not really. I get blood work done every three months. I don't really have a chance to be afraid of needles. They're not my favorite, but who likes needles, anyway?"

"I don't know. People with a lot of tattoos? Acupuncturists?"

"Grant," I whine, shoving at his shoulders.

"You're right," he says, his face no more serious than it was. "This is no time to dick around."

I wish it were. Grant passes the pen to me and I feel the weight of it on my knuckles.

"Okay, so you have to decide if you're a stomach person or a leg person. Technically, you can have someone else inject it into your arm like a flu shot, but that's not usually a good idea."

I know all this, but I let him keep talking. This already feels better than it did before, with his warm voice chattering in my ear.

"I'd go with the leg, but that's just me. You probably have more fat there, anyway."

"Excuse me?" I huff.

"What? I didn't say it was a bad thing."

I glare at him and he smiles back.

Grant passes me the alcohol swab, and I pull the waistband of my leggings down a few inches, until one side rests above my hip bone. This feels strikingly intimate. I've never shown anyone else this part of myself before. Maybe it's only a patch of skin, but it's more than anyone else has ever seen—and it's dangerously close to territory I can't come back from, and don't want to regret going to.

I wait for the rush of apprehension, the wave of wrongness. I expect my body to run and hide behind the nearest closed door of its own volition. Instead, I meet Grant's eyes with my own. He's always had this intensity about him, even in the softest parts of who he is.

"You good?" he asks. I love it when he asks me that. It's different from the way others ask the same question. It means more, like he already knows exactly how I'm feeling, but wants the confirmation anyway.

I nod.

"Alcohol wipe first. I'm sure you know how to use one of those."

I do. He keeps on.

I just enjoy listening to the sound of his voice, so low and so close. He's captivating and compassionate and dependable. I love him. I love him kind of a lot, actually. So much. I'm listening, but only halfway. I'm more interested in feeling.

I go through with the injection, Grant hovering. He was close before, but now he's all but pressed against me.

I smack my tongue against the back of my teeth a couple of times. The metallic taste is still weird.

Before I can react, Grant's pressing a Band-Aid against my

skin. At my semi-shocked face, he meets my eyes. "What? I know where you keep the bandages."

The fluttering skin of my stomach still feels warm from the slightest brush of his thumbs.

"You're really good at this," I whisper. I'm not exactly sure what I mean. He's good at being sick. He's good at being with me. He's good at being sick with me.

Without my permission, my body goes lax, my muscles relaxing out of a suddenly overwhelming sense of exhaustion. My arms decide to fall around him of their own volition, and my cheek ends up resting at that place I love, where his neck meets his shoulder.

"It makes some people sleepy," he whispers into my hair.

"I was already sleepy."

There's more to do, more last-minute party details to figure out. There's more I want to say to him, too. I want to tell him that I've named each of the three shades of brown in the one curl falling over his forehead. I want to tell him that I hope I get to live here forever, with my chin resting against him. I want to tell him that I love him so, so much.

I can't say any of that, though. All my connective tissue feels pliable, like everything holding me together is about to dissolve. I'm a few minutes away from melting into a puddle like the Wicked Witch of the West.

"Go to sleep," Grant whispers as his hands shift to my shoulders. "I'll see you tomorrow."

I'm not technically in pajamas, but I'm not in clothes I can't sleep in, either. My feet shuffle across the floor to the head of my bed. At the last second, I stretch up to my tiptoes for a kiss so lazy I almost miss his lips entirely.

Grant waits until I organize myself as comfortably as I can under my warm covers, then he walks to the door. I wish he hadn't.

"Ivy," he asks from the doorway. The light flips on.

"Hm?" I hum back. My eyes aren't even open.

"Happy birthday."

That's a ridiculous thing to say. My birthday isn't until tomorrow. At least several hours away. He probably just wants to be the first one to say it, because he's the best.

Grant won't hear what I whisper back, but I say it anyway.

"I love you."

CHAPTER FORTY-FIVE

●

SAT, DEC 5, 12:01 A.M.

Grant: It's midnight. Happy birthday, Ivy Grace.

Ivy: You already said that yesterday. Remember? Like three hours ago?

Ivy: Thanks, though.

Grant: Some things are worth repeating.

Grant: Also, go back to sleep.

"Happy birthday!" Lilah hugs me with an excitement I'm not expecting.

"It's the flowers. This is what heaven looks like to her," Grant says from the other side of the table. He and Parker do one of those weird handshake-back-smacking-hug things that guys do, and Parker and Lilah drift over to where everyone else from support group is sitting. My parents rented a room in the botanical garden's indoor exhibit hall, and we're surrounded by orchids and dogwoods.

To my friends, this may seem like a strange place to have an eighteenth birthday party. To me, it's perfect. I can feel my grandmother in every floral-scented breath I take.

"All the food we made, and you're eating the stuff I put out for decoration?" I rearrange one section of the table to fill the gap Grant made.

"They may be decoration, but they're still food." Grant pops another grape into his mouth. "What do you keep looking around for?" he asks, grape juice spurting out of his mouth. That's sort of disgusting.

"I don't know," I admit. "I just feel nervous. I'm jumpy."

"That's because you're at a party." He knows me too well.

"Yeah, I know, but it's more than that, I think. I don't know if anyone from school is going to show up."

"If they do, then great. If they don't, then all of your real friends are here."

"You're right," I whisper, still not able to deny the sense of discomfort crawling up my spine vertebra by vertebra.

"I don't mean to bother you kids." Dad hovers over us. "But there's a young man over there who's folding his hands behind his back like he's praying, and that seems like something I should be concerned about."

I roll my eyes. I know people with hypermobility call their displays of extra flexibility party tricks, but I wasn't aware that they actually used them at parties.

"Parker, stop. You're scaring the ableds." Grant's voice carries across the room. There's a roar of raucous laughter from the few tables that hold basically our entire support group.

I feel the slightest tap on my shoulder. Briefly, before I turn around, I think it might have been a ghost.

"Hi," Addie says quietly. She's always been timid. Deep down, she was one person from school besides Rory I was hoping would show up. I wasn't expecting anyone, but I'm grateful I got her.

"Hi," I reply, reaching out to hug her. I'm genuinely surprised I still have the ability to hug anyone after the revolving door of hugs I've already been through.

"Happy birthday." Addie's nervous, I can tell. This is uncomfortable for her. She won't stop moving; her fingers fiddle with the handle of the blue gift bag she holds.

"Thanks. I'm glad you came." I really am.

"I think we can let people start eating, honey," Mom says from across the table. Conversation swirls around the room, making it feel much fuller than it actually is.

"Okay," I say, and step back. I run my eyes over the food display one more time. It's perfect. It's beautiful. The cake is stunning. In fact, it's basically the best thing I've ever created—the three tiers are perfectly straight, and it made the trip across town in one piece. Lilah even managed to find some blue daisies that I arranged on the top and between the tiers. I have one in my hair, too, and Grant's has one in the pocket of his jacket.

I take a mental picture, then another, as Mom gets everyone lined up to eat. They're going to destroy these pastries, because that's what happens to food when it's good, but I'm going to remember the spread like this forever: untouched.

Lilah asks who made the cream cheese danishes, even though she knows I made the cream cheese danishes. Parker eats three of them, including the one Lilah put on her plate. Manny and Holden fight over the sugar-free jam, even though I made enough for both of them. I hand Grant a raspberry muffin, and he smiles at me like he's a plant and I'm the sunshine he needs to live.

Addie compliments my baking and my dress and my pitiful attempt at makeup and I thank her profusely while Ethan stands behind her, eating a donut in one bite in an attempt to make me laugh. Thankfully, Caroline comes by and smacks him on the back hard enough that he doesn't choke.

Everyone is in their seats, eating and enjoying my work. I'm about to make a second plate for myself, when, out of the corner of my eye, I see her. Short, choppy dark hair. No glasses. A light pink dress.

Rory.

She came. She meant what she said the other day. Suddenly, I realize I did, too.

"Sorry I'm late," she says when she reaches me, all out of breath. "There was traffic, and then I got lost, and—"

"It's okay," I reply, pulling her into a hug. I don't even remember the last time I hugged her.

"Really?" Rory asks, her arms wrapping around me and her head all but resting on my shoulder.

"Really." I pull back some, actually look her in the eyes for what feels like the first time in forever. "It's okay."

Then music starts playing from somewhere and Caroline is pulling on one of my hands and Avery is pulling on the other.

We're dancing? Oh God. We're dancing.

My grandmother's wedding dress might have been made for dancing, but my body was not. It's not even the arthritis, it's just me. Everyone moves around me in smooth, elegant motions, and I feel like a literal fish out of water.

Across the floor, Lilah and Parker are slow dancing to a song that must be playing telepathically, because they're not listening to the same one that we are. It's way too fast for this. Caroline and Avery are spinning each other under their arms like they're tipsy, and it's kind of hilarious.

My eyes flit around the room, trying to make sure I know where everyone is. Addie looks like she's doing okay. She's not much of a dancer, so she's holding up the wall near the door. Rory walks over and they start laughing together, taking pictures in front of the floor-to-ceiling windows. Manny, Holden, and Ethan are hanging out, and they look like they're scheming, sitting cross-legged on the floor in the corner of the room. They're either talking about video games or plotting our doom. Maybe both.

Mom and Dad are sitting at a table, watching us. Dad has the entire quiche tray sitting in front of him. What's left of it, anyway. They look happy. Maybe it's just because of the quiches. Mom winks at me. I smile back.

I try to fight it, but I can't. Caroline spins me first, then somehow, I'm spinning into Avery's orbit, then Grant's. It's dizzying and rambunctious and chaotic, and everything I thought I didn't want in a party, but in reality, I'm having the time of my life.

At some point, I'm going to need a break, though.

My feet start to throb just the slightest bit, and I can't catch my breath, because there are too many people too close to me. Okay, so, maybe I need a break now. Avery and Lilah are dancing with Caroline now, and they've moved a half step away. Maybe I can slip past them.

I do.

Parker and Grant are talking at the punch bowl. I think I can slip past them, too. Then, I'll be outside, just for a minute. Just long enough to catch my breath.

I walk on my tiptoes, making the smallest, most subtle movements I can. Parker doesn't even notice. I chance a look over my shoulder. Mom and Dad didn't notice, either.

I'm almost there. My hands tense around the metal handle as I push it open, the botanical garden in full view behind the glass door.

"Hey, where are you going?" Rory asks. She was sitting at a table with Addie last time I saw her. She's sneaky, though. I should've known she'd be the one to find me.

"I...um. Need a second." I should've said I was going to the bathroom or something, but the honest answer was the only one I could think of.

"Okay." Rory nods. "We should do something, though. For your birthday. Just me and you. And maybe Addie, if that's okay."

I nod back. I still don't know where we go from here, but this feels like a nice first step. Rory lets me go, and I move out into the expanse of the garden. It's obviously freezing. I wish my grand-mother's wedding dress had longer sleeves. Still, as I rub the chill off of my arms and feel the occasional stab in my wrists and elbows, I can't say I hate it here.

There's not a designated path back this way, and no one else is brazen enough to walk through the garden in near freezing temperatures. I'm not sure the outside of the garden is even open. As I make a turn at a wall of green leaves, I hear footsteps behind me. It isn't that I recognize them; they're frenzied and out of their normal pace. I just feel a tug on the invisible attachment we've always had.

"Jesus, you walk fast." Grant catches up to me and nearly sags forward into my arms.

I huff out a laugh, and I can see it spilling out in front of me in the cold air.

"You all right?" He stands up straighter after he catches his breath, putting his hands on his hips.

"I'm okay." I cross my arms, too. It's way too cold out here, and my joints are staging a revolution against me.

"Really, though. Are you okay?" He takes a step closer.

"I'm fine, really. I'm good. I just needed a second to breathe. There's only so much partying I can take..."

"That's my Ivy-profen." He leans forward and kisses my forehead. Half a step back and he's taking off his denim jacket. He slips it around my shoulders. I hadn't realized how cold I actu-ally am.

"I should get back—" I start to say. Grant stops me, slipping one hand around my waist underneath his coat. I can feel the warmth of his fingertips on the buttons down the back of my dress.

"Dance with me," Grant whispers into the practically non-existent air between us. I don't respond. His other hand comes around my hip until his fingers intertwine in the middle of my back.

My ears hadn't registered the fact that music is playing, drifting out of speakers tucked into greenery somewhere around us. It's not dancing music, not really. It's just something they play to drown out the quiet conversation that usually happens back here. It's just something to keep the peace.

We aren't so much dancing as swaying to music. My feet rest between his, my arms around his neck. The hair on the back of his neck is the thickest, and I can't help but run my fingers through it.

"What are we doing?" I murmur. A cold breeze drifts by and rustles the leaves surrounding us. Through the music, I hear more footsteps, louder ones than I heard before. This is like a clock striking midnight—the real world creeping into our enchanting cocoon of safety.

"Staying away from everyone else together," Grant replies. His voice is like a hum, something I can feel behind my own ribs.

I thread my fingers through his hair one last time, run my chilled fingertips over the planes of his face, my thumbs over the apples of his flushed cheeks. The footsteps get ever closer. There are more of them than I thought, my mom for sure, and probably Caroline, too.

Stepping away breaks the embrace, but not the spell between us. At the glass door I burst through only minutes ago, I can see my parents headed my way. Close behind are Caroline and Ethan, behind them, nearly everyone else who is supposed to be enjoying my party. They've all left it behind to make sure I'm okay.

I take the deepest breath I can, until the cold air filling my lungs actually hurts. Then, I open the door with one hand. The other, I wordlessly extend in Grant's direction.

He takes slow, methodical steps toward me. I watch his lips move. The words don't carry on the breeze long enough for me to hear, but they weave their way into my bones, into the space between them. The words add another stitch into the thread that connects us.

Only when his fingertips touch mine does my mind catch up. I know what he said. *I love you.*

It's the same thing I said yesterday, my words half asleep, and his, wide awake.